NO SIGN OF ANY STRUGGLE

She turned on the bathroom light. Unused towels, wrapped glasses, cosmetics on the countertop and a toothbrush, dry. Shower curtain pulled across the tub.

She jerked it aside, then let out a breath. The tub was empty, clean and dry. No dead body sprawled on the white porcelain.

The closet had one small suitcase and a few items of clothing on hangers.

Her eye caught a quick glint of something small and shiny beneath the bed. She went to the bed, leaned down to lift back the spread and stared into a blue, mottled face.

Blood roared in her ears, air got trapped in her lungs, an acid taste filled her mouth.

There was a loud pounding on the door.

"Police! Open up!"

———————————— ★ ————————————

25¢

THE WINTER WIDOW

CHARLENE WEIR

W⊕RLDWIDE®

TORONTO • NEW YORK • LONDON
AMSTERDAM • PARIS • SYDNEY • HAMBURG
STOCKHOLM • ATHENS • TOKYO • MILAN
MADRID • WARSAW • BUDAPEST • AUCKLAND

To Chris and Leslie and Bruce

THE WINTER WIDOW

A Worldwide Mystery/September 1993

First published by St. Martin's Press, Incorporated.

ISBN 0-373-26128-4

With thanks to Ruth Cavin, Nancy Sephton,
and all my writer friends who helped.

ONE

DEFINITE DISADVANTAGES to being chief of police, Dan Wren thought as he headed the pickup along the graveled, hilly road past tree-dotted fields with barbed wire fences. When prominent citizens beckoned, you came on the run, even if it meant leaving your brand-new wife and warm, soft bed.

Hell, maybe he was getting too old to be slipping into a warm bed at four o'clock in the afternoon. It was all this smitten-with-love stuff. Hard to believe.

Spotting the wood-slat fence, he pulled over, jounced to a stop, and slid from the truck. Thin clouds, the color of dirty cotton, stretched over the winter sky. The cold air seemed heavy with silence. He crunched to the gate, went through and closed it behind him, then stood, gloved hands on his hips, looking across the empty pasture. All right, Guthman, I'm here, where are you? Wind brushed his face with two or three needles of sleet. Dead grasses rustled under his boot heels as he set off for the far end.

A sharp crack tore through the stillness.

He dropped instinctively and rolled toward a ravine. The second shot gouged a chunk from the rim as he tumbled in. Goddamn idiot! Why didn't the asshole look where he was shooting? "Hey!" Dan shouted and waved his cap.

The next shot splintered echoes in his ears.

He stared at the cap—nice neat hole right at the crown—and poked a gloved finger through it. Jesus. Good his head hadn't been there. A sniper with a rifle, hidden in the brush on the rise two hundred yards to the north, was trying to pick him off like a crow on a fencepost.

Guthman? What the hell?

Didn't matter if he couldn't figure it, he'd better figure on how to get out of here. Rising slowly, he slid the .38 from the holster. Not much use against a rifle and he was a lousy shot with a handgun anyway, but it was all he had. His own rifle was back in the pickup a half-mile south; lot of good that did. He'd never get there.

A few poplar trees, bare limbs against the gray sky, grew on the gentle slope to the east. He'd stand out like rabbit tracks in the snow if he tried zigzagging across winter-dead grass in his dark jacket. Nothing else but empty pasture with shallow dips and rises that offered no cover. If he stayed put, the sniper had to come out in the open and down the slope to finish him. Standoff, he thought sourly. Not good enough.

Keeping his attention on the brush, he moved toward the narrow end of the ravine. Autumn rains had caused heavy erosion, and now in mid-January the steep, corrugated sides were frost-hard.

Fading light and steady concentration played tricks with his eyes. Fancied movement brought up the gun, but he stopped himself from firing. He couldn't afford to waste a shell.

Muscles cramped. His feet got numb. At least the sniper was as cold as he was. Easing the fingers of his left hand from the glove, he curled them against his palm. They were stiff and unresponsive; much longer and he wouldn't be able to fire. Better think of something.

One thing in his favor: If he no longer saw sharply, neither did the sniper. He had an idea and considered making his try now, while he was reasonably sure of cooperation from stiffening muscles.

Stupid. Wait for more darkness.

Wait.

He thought of Susan, snug and warm in the house, waiting for him to come home. Susan, nearly eleven years younger, his wife of six weeks, snatched from San Francisco and set down in the northeast corner of Kansas.

A convention for law-enforcement officers, for God's sake. He hadn't even wanted to go and there she was, breathtakingly beautiful, in the shadows of the hotel bar. A glass-enclosed candle threw highlights across a smooth clean line of cheek and jaw, dark hair fell softly around an oval face, blue eyes held a glint of amusement. A lady cop. Jesus, San Francisco must have some recruiting program. She was expensively dressed, tall and slender with the uncompromising carriage of a big cat and the go-to-hell look of city-bred women. Love grabbed him by the throat and he'd boggled at her in stupefied silence.

Sleet stung his face as though someone had thrown a handful of sand and he shivered, glanced at the darkening sky, then put the gun back in the holster. If he were to have any chance, he'd better move now before he was completely frozen. With luck, the sniper would be watching the other end of the ravine, the one closest to the road.

All right, you son of a bitch, I'm not going to let you kill me. He took off his gloves and rubbed his hands, then stuck them under his shirt and rubbed them against his chest to work some feeling into them. Wedging his back into the frozen dirt, he planted his boots on the opposite wall with his knees slightly bent. He inched up the side.

It was slow going; sweat broke out in his armpits and, rapidly chilling, across his forehead. Several times, he slid back hard-won inches, rested, cursing silently, and started again. Bracing both elbows behind him, he eased one foot up the side, then the other. He put one elbow farther up, moved the other elbow, and then levered up his body. He repeated each maneuver over and over, slow and careful.

At the top, he eased one foot over the rim, turned, grabbed at dead grass, and hauled himself out. He jack-knifed, rolled to his feet, and ran in a fast, random half-circle around the base of the rise toward the poplars fifty yards away. He skidded behind a tree, stumbled on a twisted root, and fell. His breath came hard and rasping; cold air clawed at his lungs.

No shot.

Had he gotten out unseen?

He stayed only long enough to get his breathing under control, then worked numb fingers back into his gloves and took his revolver from the holster. Keeping low, aware of the danger of being outlined against the deepening slate sky, he scuttled to the first patch of brush.

He crouched, waited.

No sound from the top of the rise.

He moved on, quickly, quietly, to the next patch. Again, he waited.

A spot high up between his shoulder blades itched and tingled. Instincts pricked and nagged that he was being lured into the exact position the sniper wanted.

He raised his head like an animal testing the air. It smelled of coming snow and long dead grass and his own fear. He searched for movement, listened for sounds. In the distance, he heard the raucous cry of a crow and, farther away, the musical baying of a hound.

Tense, senses jangling, he ran at an angle across the slope, pausing in what cover the brush afforded, working his way to the top.

Once there, he snaked silently forward until he could see down the far side. The sniper, back turned, sat on a boulder twenty feet below, rifle across knees.

Dan rose, gun ready. "Drop it," he said with harsh anger.

The sniper whirled and raised the rifle.

Oh Christ, he thought when he realized who it was. Why? "Move a muscle and you're dead," he said.

The sniper hesitated.

"I can't miss at this range."

The rifle slowly lowered to the ground.

Dan motioned with the gun and the sniper stepped a pace away.

"What the hell were you doing?" Roughly grabbing a shoulder, he shoved the sniper belly-down over the boulder and caught both wrists in the handcuffs.

He holstered his gun and picked up the rifle. A smattering of sleet pelted his face as he prodded his prisoner down the rise and across the pasture to the road. Anger, mingled with relief, made him breathe heavily.

At the gate he was careful, opening it, jerking the prisoner through and closing it again. When they reached the pickup, he drew his first easy breath and the muscles in his shoulders relaxed.

He was tired and hungry and felt a small satisfaction that he wasn't even going to be very late for supper—dinner, to Susan. She was probably swearing under her breath and banging pans. Susan and things domestic didn't pull together.

He shoved his prisoner against the side of the truck and reached for the door handle.

A giant sledgehammer smashed into his back at the instant he heard the ringing bark of a rifle. He saw a sick look come into his prisoner's eyes.

The prisoner saw Dan's eyes go blank, saw him slammed into the truck with a wet bullet hole punched high in his spine, through the leather jacket and blue shirt, dead center, between the shoulder blades.

Dan's body bounced and went down in a curiously ugly and boneless drop. He lay totally soft and flattened on the gravel road, his blank eyes open to the black sky. No twitch, no sound.

The sleet came down in earnest with a stealthy sinister hiss, driving into the slack exposed face, icing the road and coating each dead blade of grass in its own frozen sheath.

TWO

SUSAN STIRRED the stroganoff, scooped out a spoonful and tasted it, then gave the spoon a suspicious look, raised her eyebrows and tasted again. Heavenly days, it was actually good. Her forays into cooking often brought forth, at best, mixed reviews. She swirled the spoon through the pot, banged it against the side and put back the lid.

Sleet chattered against the window and collected on the ledge outside. She shivered. Sleet, snow and frigid temperatures the whole ten days she'd been here.

Truth to tell, she couldn't quite figure it out. There she was, one of San Francisco's finest, going about upholding and protecting, a semi-hard-bitten cynic, unattached and with a hefty caution about the male-female stuff. She'd come close to marriage twice before; once she'd backed out, the other time the guy backed out. After that she decided to give the whole thing up. Not for her this whither-thou-goest shit.

What happened? Daniel happened. Six foot three and lean as a greyhound, with his sweet smile and soft voice. She had liked the look of him, the easy sure way he moved, the laugh lines around his eyes.

What the hell, he was only in San Francisco for a few days; spend a little time with him. What did she have to lose? Only her mind. Nothing important.

The jokes running around when she turned in her badge ranged from the merely crude to the truly inane. She'd danced off with Daniel to marriage and a month in Mexico. And here she was in Kansas.

The radio on the counter told her she had just heard Beethoven, Symphony no. 6 in F major, played by the Columbia Symphony Orchestra, Bruno Walter conducting, and the time was six-twenty-six. The clock on the very same radio showed six-twenty-eight.

Daniel was late.

Meant nothing. Cops' hours.

Hampstead wasn't a big city where you took your life in your hands when you hit the streets. No crazies here with knives, or addicts looking to score, or eleven-year-old kids who shoot cops. Crime in Hampstead ran along the lines of candy bars lifted at the market or car doors slammed after midnight. The most dangerous thing that had occurred since she'd arrived was Otto Guthman's prize bull getting loose.

The radio said seven fifteen.

The weather's bad, the roads slick.

Automatically, her hand reached toward the drawer for a pack of cigarettes before she remembered she'd quit smoking.

He's fine.

She tossed kindling in the fireplace and set a match to it, put Vivaldi on the cassette player, sipped coffee and leafed through the *Hampstead Herald.* Her eyes kept sneaking glances at the clock. Seven-thirty. Seven-forty. Seven-forty-eight. *Sleet, cars sliding, smashed metal.*

At eight she phoned the station and got young O. C. Pickett, who gulped and stammered. Osey always gulped and stammered when he talked to her. He said he didn't know anything, he'd find out, he'd call her back.

Three minutes before ten, the doorbell chimed and she yanked open the door. Ben Parkhurst, a compact man of average height with smooth black hair and olive skin, stood on the porch.

No. Involuntarily, she took a step back and folded her arms tightly across her chest. He came in, closed the door behind him and stared at her. His face was set, dark eyes flat and guarded.

No. She knew that look, that was the look a cop got when he came to say— No.

A muscle rippled at the corner of his jaw. He pulled at the fingers of his black leather gloves, slid them off and shoved them in the pocket of his fur-lined gray jacket. A black scarf hung loose around his neck.

"I think you better sit down."

"No."

"Please sit down."

"Tell me."

He hesitated; his black eyes seemed to glitter. "Dan's been shot."

"No!"

Parkhurst took two strides, caught her shoulders and walked her backward until her legs hit the chair, unlocking her knees, and he forced her down. He left and returned a moment later with a glass. "Scotch. Drink it."

She took the glass, sipped Scotch and stared at the fireplace, seeing each individual stone: the shape, the rough uneven texture, the pale creamy color. She heard the sound of Parkhurst's voice telling her where Daniel's body had been found, but the moment the words were spoken, they were gone. She couldn't hold onto them, couldn't realize anything but the varied irregular shapes of the fireplace stones. Creamy white. Limestone, Daniel said.

Parkhurst, seated on the hearth, was saying sharp, hard words like shiny bright diamonds that immediately wavered and flattened and melted to ooze together and slip away like raindrops down a windowpane.

She swirled the amber liquid in the glass and heard the ice cubes rattle. She took a sip. "Where is he?"

"The body's been brought in. The medical examiner is—"

"I want to see him."

Parkhurst looked at her. She felt his anger and his impatience to be away from here and back to the investigation, and beyond that, she thought, worry about her. She'd barely reacted, barely spoken.

"Is there someone I can call to stay with you?" he asked.

"I don't know anyone here. Take me to Daniel."

"You shouldn't be alone. If I can use your phone, I'll call Hazel."

Hazel? Oh, yes, the dispatcher at the station.

"You listen to me." Susan put emphasis on each word. "You will take me to Daniel. Now." She tossed off the Scotch, slammed down the glass so hard ice cubes bounced out on the carpet, and stood up. "If you don't, I'll go myself."

She strode to the door, turned, crossed her arms and stared at him.

The muscle rippled in his jaw. He leaned forward to pick up the ice cubes and dropped them in the glass with a little clink, clink. "You'll need a coat," he said quietly.

THE DIM HALLWAY seemed endless, and she experienced the nightmare illusion of forever moving woodenly along its length and never getting nearer a destination. My husband is dead and I've been married not yet six weeks.

Parkhurst put a hand on her elbow, opened a door and herded her through. Bright overhead light sent slivers of pain through her head and pungent odors filled her nostrils.

A large white-haired man with heavy dark eyebrows, wearing a green surgical gown, scowled at them. "What is it? I haven't even begun. Who is this?"

"This is Mrs. Wren," Parkhurst said.

The large man closed his mouth, exhaled a long breath of shocked reproach and spoke earnestly. "Mrs. Wren, I'm Dr. Fisher. I extend my deepest sympathies. My dear, you shouldn't be here."

Daniel— Daniel— On his back on the stainless-steel table.

A rush of sound surged over her. She couldn't breathe. Clenching her hands in the pockets of her down jacket, she felt nails biting into her palms and heard her flat-heeled boots clomp against the tiled floor. I can't think—I can't realize—

Blood on the leather jacket and blue shirt. Large ragged wound. Exit wound?

"Turn him, please."

"What?" Dr. Fisher stared at her, startled.

"Turn him, please, so I can see his back."

"Dear lady, this is too much for you. Let Ben take you home. Come." He took her arm to draw her away.

She raised her glance. "Turn him," she repeated.

Dr. Fisher, face flushed with outrage, looked at Parkhurst. Parkhurst shrugged.

Reeking of disapproval, Dr. Fisher eased the body onto its side, gently and carefully.

She stared at the blood, more blood on his back, stared at the bullet hole high in the spine. Entrance wound. Daniel had been shot in the back.

She nodded at Dr. Fisher and he replaced the body in its original position with the same care and gentleness. Only then did she allow herself to look at Daniel's face. It was unmarked, but gray and slack, mouth slightly open, eyelids slitted over crescents of white.

Her throat closed; a pulse pounded in her ears. She touched his cheek with the back of one hand. Cold and unyielding.

The pounding in her ears grew louder. I've got to get out of here. With shallow panicky breathing, she turned her back on Daniel.

Parkhurst opened the door for her, his dark eyes expressionless and watchful. Any sympathy he might feel was buried deep inside the man, and the police officer observed her, ready to exploit her confusion and grief if it would further his investigation.

In the dim hallway, a young woman called out, "Ben!" and hurried toward them with a tweed coat swirling around high-heeled boots.

To hold herself together, to block out images of Daniel dead on an autopsy table, Susan concentrated hard on the young woman: plaid skirt, white sweater, black belt slung low around her hips.

When she got nearer, Susan recognized Lucille Guthman, a reporter for the local paper. Lucille had been at the house this afternoon looking for Daniel. Danny, she had called him, and eyed Susan with surprising hostility until Susan realized Lucille hadn't come so much to see Daniel as to get a look at his wife.

"I've been looking everywhere for you," Lucille said to Parkhurst, then darted a glance at Susan. "Oh. I didn't—"

"Mrs. Wren," Parkhurst said.

"Yes, I know." Lucille's blue eyes got teary. She raked a hand through the ash-blond curls spilling around her gamine face. "I'm sorry, so very sorry," she said awkwardly, hesitated, and then turned back to Parkhurst. "What have you found out?"

"We're proceeding with the investigation."

"But, Ben, why was Danny killed? Who had a reason to kill him?"

She looks frightened, Susan thought. I wonder what I look like.

"Questions that need to be answered," Parkhurst said.

"What can you tell me? Have you got any leads?"

"I'll let you know when we have anything definite."

"I have a right to know."

Parkhurst raised an eyebrow.

"For the paper," Lucille insisted. "As a reporter I need to write the news."

Susan's mind was detached, observing from a distance, as though none of this had anything to do with her.

"What did you find at the scene of the crime?" Lucille stuck a hand in her coat pocket, then yanked it out again as though her fingers had been stung.

"I have nothing to give you yet." Parkhurst took a step and reached for Susan's elbow.

"Wait, Ben, what—"

"It's too soon." Parkhurst looked angry.

Something scary about him, Susan thought, some aura of suppressed violence. The pressure of his hand tightened and she allowed herself to be guided down the hallway. She felt Lucille's eyes staring at her back and wondered why Lucille had been looking for Daniel that afternoon, and if she'd found him.

At home, Susan refused to let Parkhurst walk her to the door, refused to let him call anyone to stay with her, told him to leave. I want to be alone, she thought, and choked on a swell of manic laughter at that tired old line.

From a kitchen drawer, she took a pack of cigarettes, held it in her hand and stared at it, ran a thumb across the smooth cellophane. She'd quit because she and Daniel were flirting with the idea of a baby. There wasn't going to be any baby. She opened the pack and lit a cigarette.

HOURS STACKED UP like unclaimed packages.

On Friday people came: Daniel's sister; Sophie the cat lady; the Reverend Mullet; the cops of Daniel's force; neighbors. They brought food and spoke gently, sadly, quietly in shocked voices.

She turned a cold face and stony eyes on all of them and left Daniel's sister, Helen, to cope with casseroles and expressions of sympathy.

Her mind was filled with distances, mists and wraiths. Her parents arrived from San Francisco; Patrick Donovan brusque and grim, Anna pale and anxious. Susan felt the expensive softness of her father's cashmere jacket against her cheek as he held her too tightly. With the exactness of a camera recording, she noted his look of helpless anguish.

Through the next two days, she moved with heavy effort and made decisions about her husband's funeral. Emmanuel Lutheran Church, every pew filled, people standing in the rear, pulsed with strains of Bach. She sat in the front row and heard the Reverend Mullet speak about Daniel. All these people had known him longer than she had.

The day after the funeral, her father told her the plane reservations were confirmed and she wasn't to worry about anything; he would send someone out to deal with all the legal matters, pack up the household and sell the house.

For the first time in four days, she felt a crack in her icy numbness, felt a flicker of relief just behind her breastbone.

In the bedroom, she sat on the end of the bed she had shared with Daniel, smoked cigarette after cigarette and stared blankly at the deep blue carpet under her feet. A suitcase lay open beside her; her mother neatly and efficiently folded garments and placed them inside.

"Susan?"

She focused her eyes on her petite, fair-haired mother.

"Darling, do you want to take this coat? It seems suitable for Siberia. Probably entirely too warm to wear at home."

Home. Susan looked around the bedroom, at the solid oak chest and dresser, the white walls and blue drapes. This was Daniel's home, for ten days hers and Daniel's. She gazed at the small silly painting Daniel had bought at a street fair in San Francisco, a wolfhound with an expression of apprehension, apology and half-concealed alarm. A haughty, elegant Siamese cat crouched between his outstretched paws.

"That's us," Daniel had said with glee. "The one with the dopey-ass look is me."

They had been drunk that day, on love and crystal sunshine and heady discoveries of each other. They were funny and clever and their games were inexhaustible. Laughter affected them like wine. Every color was sharpened, every odor pungent and every sense overreceptive.

With incomparable clarity, she saw him standing on the balcony of her apartment. She had a sharp-colored image of his profile with the strong line of chin and jaw. Bluegreen water dazzled in the marina below. Tearing off chunks of French bread, he threw them to the gulls in flight. She came out through the open sliding door with two glasses of red wine and joined him at the railing.

Cupping her face with his capable, long-fingered hands, he smiled. "This sure doesn't look like Kansas, Toto," he had said and kissed her.

"Susan?" her mother said.

She blinked. For God's sake, where is my brain? She thought back over the last few days and looked at the packed suitcase, angry and appalled with herself. She felt fragile and light-headed as though she were just awakening from a long illness.

At least my mind is working again.

I can't go home.

THREE

THE CHILD LIVES ON in the adult body, she thought as she paused in the kitchen doorway, ridiculously nervous about telling her father she was staying here.

Patrick Donovan sat at the kitchen table, suit coat draped over the back of the chair, white shirtsleeves rolled up, reading the *Hampstead Herald*. In appearance, she was definitely her father's daughter. She had his height and dark hair and blue eyes; her facial features had been planed down to a feminine version of his. She had none of her mother's gentle blondness, as though even Anna Donovan's genes had given way to those of her overpowering husband.

Patrick looked up and shoved the paper aside. "Daring to beard the lion in his den?"

As she sat down across the table from him, she felt a cottony rush of nostalgia. He still had the provoking ability to read her mind. She loved her father and knew how much he loved her, but they had always fought. As a child, she'd been defiant. So many fights took place in the kitchen, her mother had started calling it the lion's den.

"I'm glad you came, Dad. This one was—" She waved a hand, searching for words to explain her confusion and paralysis. "An inextricable problem."

"I'm always here for you, baby," he said with a soft smile and reached for her hand to stop its movement. "But 'inextricable' doesn't quite fit with 'problem.'"

Always critical. She slid her hand from his. He understood she was saying thanks, but had to correct her way of saying it. Damn it, I'm not a child anymore. I no longer need your approval. I'm not that little girl striving for little drops of praise. Even when he said something nice, he'd immediately followed it with criticism. He picked up the glass of orange juice and took a sip.

"You're not drinking coffee," she said in surprise. He habitually drank endless cups of a lethal brew she used to call roofing tar.

"I've cut down."

With a little clutch of fear, she looked at him closely and wondered if he was all right. She saw a little more gray in his dark curls and a few more lines in his face, but he was still a very handsome man.

"I have to stay, Dad."

"What do you mean?"

"I'm staying. In Hampstead."

"Of course you're not. You're coming home."

"No."

"Susan, this is a bad time, a hard time. You're not thinking clearly. Staying is a mistake. Finish up your packing so we can get out of here."

She'd hoped he would understand and give his support. She should have known he'd just point out the reasons why she was wrong.

"Susan," he said persuasively, "you can't stay."

"I'm thirty-four years old. 'Can't'?"

She felt her mother's anxious presence in the doorway behind her. It was ever her mother's place to act as a buffer between them. If her mother had stepped aside years ago and let them claw at each other, would they have torn down some walls? Or would they have ended up hating each other?

They were trapped behind their own defenses. Even the death of her husband hadn't changed anything between them. They just got into the same old games and, always, always, he managed to make her feel that nothing she did was ever quite good enough.

"If only—" he began.

She stiffened. If only what? I hadn't married Daniel? *He's too old for you. He's been married. His background's too different.* Come to this godforsaken place? *Kansas? Good God, there's nothing in Kansas but wheat fields. What do you think you'll do there?* Or was it even worse than that? If only I had obediently followed your blueprint for my life and joined your firm after I graduated from law school.

The doorbell rang and her mother murmured, "I'll get it."

Patrick shook his head. "Amazing Grace, you always were the most stubborn kid I ever knew."

Tears prickled against her eyelids. He hadn't called her that in a long time. Grace was her middle name, and whenever he had been angry or exasperated or disappointed, she was Amazing Grace. It had as many inflections and interpretations as any Chinese ideogram.

Some kind of weird guilt stuck to her like fingerprints on sticky varnish. She wasn't so addled she felt responsible for Daniel's death, but she'd frolicked into marriage, singing "There's a bright golden haze on the meadow," without giving a thought to life ever after. Deep down in some yeasty corner of her subconscious, doubts had fermented, doubts that no matter how much she loved Daniel, she wouldn't hack it as a housewife. It was those doubts, as though they were some kind of disloyalty to Daniel and he had deserved better, that created the guilt.

How could she explain something to her father she couldn't even explain to herself? He'd never understand, certainly never give his approval. Screw it.

"Susan," her mother said. "Honey, the mayor is here. He'd like to see you."

Patrick rose. "I'll take care of it." He rolled down his sleeves and reached for his suit coat.

Susan scooted back her chair and jumped up. "I want to talk with him," she said, and heard an echo of the defiant child.

"Susan—" Her mother placed a hand on her arm as she scurried after her father.

In the living room, Martin Bakover, seated in the blue chair by the fireplace, cane leaning against his knee, stood up to shake hands with her father.

"Such a very sad occasion," the mayor said, looking at Susan. He was a man in his late forties with the beginnings of excess weight, dressed in a black suit and white shirt. He had sandy-gray hair and a fleshy face with a tendency to ruddiness. "Before you leave us, I felt I must again express my deep-felt sympathies." He rested both hands on the silver handle of the carved ash cane he always carried—mostly for effect, she thought.

"Very kind of you," Patrick said.

"Dan was a good man," Bakover said. "A good man. We all feel his loss keenly. He won't be easy to replace. Please—" He gave each of them in turn a solemn look of his deep-felt sympathy. "Please, let me say how very sorry I am—we all are." He stopped at Susan. "Is there anything I can do for you, anything at all?"

"Thank you," Patrick said, "but there's nothing—"

"Yes," Susan said.

Three pairs of eyes regarded her inquiringly, her father's narrowed in wariness.

"Anything," the mayor repeated.

"I want Daniel's job."

A startled silence followed her clipped words; then Patrick said, "Susan—"

"Why don't we all sit down," Anna said. "Mr. Bakover, please have a seat." She gently nudged him to the chair behind him, turned to Patrick with a warning look, then took Susan's arm and chivvied her to the couch, sat beside her and picked up her hand. Patrick settled in the chair on the opposite side of the fireplace.

"Oh, my dear young lady," Bakover said as though there had been no interruption, "I know how you must feel."

The hell you do, Susan thought.

"But you are not to worry. Rest assured this murderer will be caught." He smiled, a small condescending smile from adult to child-who-doesn't-understand-the-ways-of-the-world. "Dan's job." He shook his head. "That's simply not possible."

"Why not?"

"Susan," Patrick said, "this had been a dreadful blow. You're not thinking clearly." He turned toward the mayor. "She's still in shock."

Don't talk about me as though I'm not here.

"Of course she is. Understandable. Entirely understandable."

"Why not?" Susan repeated with an insistent edge.

"Well, my dear, a murder investigation, you must understand, requires someone . . . trained, trained and uh . . . tough, you understand, tough enough to handle the enormity of the job." He paused and then added reasonably, "You can see how you'd be unable to handle it."

"I'm a cop, Mr. Bakover, a good cop. I had nine years with the San Francisco police force."

"Nine years?" Bakover said in surprise.

Yes indeed. Nine years of proving I was tough enough, handling the enormity of the job, you pompous ass, and being the butt of jokes that were thinly disguised insults and listening to crude remarks about how I got my promotions.

"Well," Bakover said. "I didn't know that. Well, well. And I'm sure a very fine policewoman you were too."

"Damn fine policewoman," Patrick said. "You couldn't get a better investigator. Her work is noted for its excellence. She has two commendations for valor, and nearly gave her life in the performance of duty."

"Very impressive. Yes. But this isn't San Francisco. This is a small town."

"You feel," Patrick said, "an officer trained by one of the finest police departments in the country is unsuited to cope with small-town crime?"

"Dad—"

"Not at all," Bakover said. "But I'm not sure this town is ready for a woman in the position of police chief."

Patrick put his elbows on the chair arms and placed his fingertips together across his flat stomach. "What did you say?" he asked in a voice like silk, adversarial gleam in his blue eyes.

"Dad—" Susan said, a harder edge to her voice.

The mayor smiled a politician's smile; he recognized a litigator when he saw one. "Perhaps you misunderstood me."

Patrick smiled.

"I simply meant to suggest that Miz Wren"—Bakover nodded at Susan—"is an outsider here. She doesn't know the town or the people. That could be a handicap."

Patrick gently tapped his fingertips together. "Let me see if I have this clear. You stated—"

Goddammit, let me fight my own battles. She opened her mouth, but before the words came out her mother said, "Would anyone like some coffee?" She was ignored.

"You need someone right now," Susan said.

The major nodded. "There are good people in my police department. George Halpern has been an officer here for more than forty years."

Susan didn't know about the good part, but she did know from talking with Daniel that George Halpern, the logical choice, had never wanted to be chief and was now close to retirement. Osey Pickett was still so young he'd barely recovered from the acne of adolescence, and he didn't seem overly bright. That left only Ben Parkhurst, another outsider, and the antipathy between him and Bakover raised hackles on both sides. The mayor would be wary of putting power in Parkhurst's hands.

"Appoint me acting chief. That'll give you time to find somebody."

Bakover gazed at her long and thoughtfully.

"Mr. Mayor—" Patrick began.

Susan glared at her father.

"Temporary basis?" Bakover asked.

"Yes."

"Maybe," he said after a long pause, "maybe it could be worked out."

She took a breath.

"Temporarily," Bakover added.

She nodded with a small twinge of uneasiness as a shrewd, calculating look appeared briefly in the mayor's eyes. Was he judging her capability, or did he have his own reasons for giving her the job?

THE SUN, sliding low behind the shallow hills, cast a long shadow as she stood on the road where Daniel had been shot. Emptiness surrounded her. The wind blew. The dead grass shivered. The gravel was black with Daniel's blood.

I promise, Daniel, I promise you I'll get the bastard.

FOUR

TUESDAY MORNING. This is it, lady. Knock 'em dead. Oh boy. She stood a long time in the shower, trying to sluice away doubts and feelings of inadequacy under the gush of hot water. It was important to keep moving. Action impeded reflection. Action would keep her from visualizing the lift of the rifle, the tightening of a finger on the trigger.

She slipped on a gray wool skirt and white cashmere sweater and tied a blue-and-gray scarf around her throat. As she shrugged on a navy jacket, she caught a glimpse of herself in the mirror. Oh my God. Dress for success. All I need is a briefcase.

Spurning her little brown Fiat, she clambered into Daniel's pickup and pointed it toward the police station. Felt like driving a truck. Ha ha. Little nervous, are we? The sun shone in a cloudless blue sky and the temperature was much warmer today. She had to admit Hampstead was a pretty little town: wide clean streets with large trees that arched overhead, mixture of houses, old and new, brick and wood frame, all settled cozily into gentle hills. And space between the houses. This must be what's meant by wide open spaces.

Stop it, compose yourself.

At the police department, a square red-brick building next to city hall, she trundled into the parking lot. She'd been sworn in yesterday and met the officers, most of whose names she couldn't remember.

Okay, *Chief,* you can do it. So what if you have no idea what a police chief does. How hard can it be? Just smile at everybody. Even as a kid she'd been able to hide uncertainties beneath a cape of confident control. In her rookie days, she'd perfected the skill, snugging the cape up tighter in defense against sneers from superiors and ridicule from peers.

She was going to need it now.

The entry was framed in a strip of cement with octagonal lantern-type light fixtures on either side; two cement steps led up to the recessed door. She braced herself and went in, then felt as if she'd shoved a wall that turned out to be a curtain.

Different. Of course, different. None of the dirt and noise, clutter and chaotic activity she was used to. Neat, quiet and clean. Even the pale-green walls were clean. It didn't smell the same either; no essence of stale cigarette smoke, disinfectant, hopelessness and unwashed humanity that permeated big-city police departments. It smelled of Hazel's flowery perfume.

Hazel was the dispatcher, a stocky woman in her late forties with short auburn hair. She beamed with a welcoming smile, tinged with a little maternal worry. According to Daniel, she looked out for everybody with concerned clucks and fusses. Her desk sheltered under a thicket of spider plants, the offshoots of which she treated like puppies, agonizing over finding good homes.

Susan said good morning and asked that Parkhurst be told she wanted to see him. With a firm tread and an expression of what she hoped was steely-eyed command, she got through the area clustered with desks, nodding to two uniformed officers, and opened the door to Daniel's office.

She closed it behind her, briskly slipped off her jacket and threw it over the coatrack, and sat in Daniel's chair, at Daniel's desk, and picked up Daniel's pen. So far, so good. While waiting for Parkhurst, she glanced through the stack of reports she'd spent a good part of yesterday reading.

On Thursday Daniel had been in his office catching up on paperwork and laboring over the budget, a chore he hated and groused about. Nothing unusual happened; Hampstead appeared to be crime-free until two o'clock when a man named Harve Green filed a complaint against Sophie Niemen for stealing his cat. Daniel went out to see her.

Sophie the cat lady, nutty about cats, collected strays and kidnapped pets she felt were mistreated. ("Damn Sophie and her damn cats. I spend half my life chasing around for irate pet owners.") At three, he returned, fuming because he'd been unable to find Sophie. He told Hazel he was going home for a time and would be in later.

Susan was painting the kitchen ceiling when he arrived about three-ten, straight from the department. There wasn't time for him to have gone anywhere else.

He was home for less than an hour, and during that time he'd received three phone calls: one from his sister, Helen; one brief call from someone as yet unidentified; and one from Hazel. Hazel reported that a man identifying himself as Otto Guthman claimed to have evidence of cattle rustling. Daniel was wanted immediately.

A few minutes before four, Daniel left for Guthman's. Susan had just gotten back to the kitchen when Lucille Guthman came by looking for Daniel. An hour or so after Lucille left, Daniel was killed in her father's pasture.

Since the murder occurred outside the city limits, the county sheriff's department held jurisdiction, and technically Sheriff Holmes was handling the investigation. She wondered about him, whether he was a good man. Hector Holmes. Okay. At least he was acting in conjunction with the Hampstead police—something to be thankful for.

In theory, all law enforcement agencies working the same case were supposed to cooperate with each other. In her experience, it didn't always work that way. Competition, personality conflicts, even petty jealousies often kept pertinent information from being released. According to George Halpern, Daniel's senior officer, that wasn't a problem here. The sheriff had a large county, a manpower shortage, too much to handle, and was glad to have Hampstead PD investigating.

Parkhurst didn't exactly snap to and hustle in. She was reaching for the phone when the door opened. He stood there, face expressionless, dark eyes hard, hands loose at his sides, feet planted wide apart, like Marshal Dillon come to check out the saloon.

Oh shit. He was going to give her trouble. She should have expected it. She'd known some like him—arrogant pricks who resented working with women, who stubbornly believed she got her job through affirmative action and her advancements through sleeping with the right people.

She gestured, palm up, toward the chair at the side of the desk. He pulled it out a few feet and sat, a maneuver that forced her to change the angle of her own chair to see him comfortably.

Parkhurst, my friend, this isn't a debate. The decision, management level, is already in and you're stuck with me. She rose, moved to the end of the desk, rested her rear against it and looked down at him. His sharp gaze touched her with amused acknowledgment. Well. A sense of humor? Maybe there was more here than met the eye.

Daniel had liked him, described him as extremely intelligent and self-contained, and a good cop. Parkhurst had originally been with the Kansas City force. Several years ago, his younger sister, apparently the one person in all the world whom he loved, had been killed two days before her seventeenth birthday. She'd attended an evening class and on her way back to her car was abducted by adolescents, raped and strangled. Daniel never said whether Parkhurst had been asked to leave Kansas City because of a tendency to cuff suspects around, especially teenage suspects, or whether he'd resigned to avoid being asked.

"Tell me everything you've got," she said.

Parkhurst regarded her coldly. "You shouldn't be here."

"Any particular reason?"

"You ought to know, big-city cop. You're too close to it. Emotions have a way of wiping out judgment."

She could almost hear him thinking: And besides, you're stupid, you don't know what you're doing and you'll be in the way.

She nodded, not in agreement, but in acceptance of his right to an opinion. He could believe whatever he damn well pleased, as long as he gave her what she wanted.

"It's all in there." He nodded at the reports on the desk. "Unless you left out something that happened when Dan was home."

She felt her face grow warm. He wanted to make love to his wife, but if you think I'm going to tell you about it, you're crazy. Anyway, it never happened: The phone kept interrupting. Who made that second call?

Parkhurst smiled maliciously at her discomfort.

"It's all in here," she said dryly, tapping the reports.

He raised an eyebrow and she felt her poise start to slip. "New leads?"

"So far, zip."

She didn't believe him. She didn't exactly know why, but a bell had gone off in her mind. She'd learned to pay attention when her cop's instincts were roused.

"What did you find at the crime scene?" She shifted and crossed her feet at the ankles.

"Dan on his back in a pool of blood."

She saw it, just as Parkhurst intended, a vivid picture of Daniel— She jerked her thoughts up short and managed to keep her face impassive, the weeping woman buried deep inside.

"Bullet came from a northwesterly direction. Severed the spinal column. Death was instantaneous."

She lit a cigarette, gratified to note her hands were steady.

"Indications the body had been moved around some after death. Reasons unknown—go through his pockets, maybe. Gun was in the holster, no shots fired."

Pushing herself away from the desk, she moved around it to sit in the chair. "Guthman denied making that phone call." She'd tried to see Guthman early yesterday evening after she'd examined the site where Daniel was shot, but he was in Kansas City and not expected back until late today. "You believe him?"

"I haven't found anything that suggests otherwise."

She was aware that he hadn't answered her question. "Who made that call? Why? Was it simply a ruse to get Daniel out there? Did it have anything to do with cattle rustling?"

"There have been some reports, but Otto claims no losses, no indications attempts were made."

"Motives? Who had a motive? If cattle theft wasn't involved, why was he killed?"

Parkhurst sat like a sphinx.

"You know something you're not telling me," she said. "I want to hear it."

"Pardon?"

"Which part didn't you understand?"

He stared at her, apparently finding it hard to open his mouth; his teeth seemed locked together.

"Prejudices have a way of wiping out judgments," she said sweetly.

His look sent a chill through her. A muscle ticced in his jaw. "Before Dan went home, he said he needed to talk to me when he got back."

"About what?"

"He said it could wait. Just something a little puzzling, might be nothing."

"Well?" she said. "Thoughts. Guesses. Hunches."

Parkhurst was silent so long, she thought he wasn't going to respond. "I don't know. He saw something, heard something, something happened. I don't know. The only thing I do know, there was no report of any crime in that hour he was out looking for Sophie. Nothing even unusual or peculiar."

Hazel stuck her head through the doorway hesitantly, as though testing the climate and prepared to duck if conditions were unfavorable. She gave Susan a soft look of encouragement and said to Parkhurst, "Sorry to interrupt, but we got a call from the mayor. He'd like you to fill him in on any new developments."

Parkhurst nodded curtly and rose, then looked at Susan. "Unless you'd rather?"

She shook her head, doubting Bakover wanted filling in; more likely, he wanted to underline his authority and rub in a little salt. She hoped the mayor knew what he was doing; Parkhurst was probably a dangerous man to cross. He inclined his head in a brief little bit of servile mockery and left.

She crushed out the cigarette. When Daniel returned from his unsuccessful trip to find Sophie, something was troubling or puzzling him. What? What the hell could it be? Could he have seen something on the way to Sophie's? At her place? Whatever it was, it hadn't been urgent. He told Parkhurst it could wait.

Sophie Nieman.

That second phone call. They had been in bed when it came and Daniel was short. "He did, did he?...No more...No...Better be the last." Then his voice had gotten soft with threat. "I won't put up with it any more."

Better be the last. The last cat kidnaped? Was it Sophie who made that second call?

Susan pawed through the reports stacked in her in basket. Vehicle damaged by rocks thrown from an open field. Obscene phone call on an answering machine. Flower bed vandalized. Petty theft. Green, Harve Green. Here it was. The cat had been returned or had found its way home on its own.

She was reaching for her jacket to go find Sophie when the phone rang.

"They're waiting for you at the hardware store," Hazel said.

"Hardware store."

"They're taking down the old sign."

"Old sign."

"Didn't Ben tell you?"

"No, he didn't. Why are they waiting for me?"

"Well, it's kind of special. It's the oldest sign in town and they're taking it down to put up a new one. Arrangements were all set up for—uh, Dan to be there."

"I see. Would you get George and tell him to take care of it."

"Well . . . uh, you might want to go. Public relations, starting out on the right foot, you know? The photographer will be there and Lucille Guthman to write it up for the *Herald*. She wants to interview you."

Susan replaced the receiver. God help us, a new sign at the hardware store. The mayor was right: Small towns were different. She slipped on her jacket, thinking she had some interviewing of her own she wanted to do with Lucille.

A SQUAD CAR blocked each end of the street, and a large crowd was gathered around Perley's Hardware. After the cold weather, the temperature seemed almost balmy at forty degrees, and the winter sun felt warm. People laughed and chatted with each other and called out joking remarks to the slight gray-haired man—Mr. Perley, she assumed—standing in the middle of the street, holding a small gong in one hand and a hammer in the other. The work crew lounged against the front of the store, waiting for him to strike gong with hammer as the signal to begin. He was waiting for the reporter.

Susan stood across the street in front of the bank and collected curious glances, as if she were some exotic animal in a zoo. Several people spoke to her, most with an affable "Good morning," but some conveyed disapproval. "Never had a lady police chief before." "Surely do look young." "Big responsibility. Sure you know what you're doing?"

She smiled: polite, confident. Public relations. The photographer, a rangy kid with brown shaggy hair, swiveled through the crowd, snapping pictures.

"Where's Lucille?" she asked him.

"Haven't seen her." He snapped Susan's picture and slid away.

Restlessness drifted over the crowd and the jokes to Mr. Perley got louder.

A short man with an air of self-importance came out of the bank and strode purposefully over to her. "Morning," he said.

She nodded. She'd met him at Daniel's funeral and remembered he was the bank president, but couldn't remember his name.

"We're all right sorry about Dan," he said sympathetically. "And we know just how hard it is for you."

He paused and she nodded again. Up yours, pal.

"But we're all just a mite surprised at Martin for appointing you chief."

Who's "we"? Everybody, no doubt. For the first time, she appreciated what it might cost the mayor to have given her the job. She gave Mr. Important Bank President the brave smile of the newly bereaved. "There's no need to apologize. I'm only too glad to step in and help you out. Daniel would have wanted it."

She smiled sweetly and left him frowning after her, uncertain whether he had been insulted or misunderstood.

Public relations. Ho boy. She wasn't going to worm information from these people if she made it so clear she didn't like any of them.

"Perley!" someone shouted. "You gonna wait all day?"

"The sign's gonna be old before you ever get it up there."

"What are you waitin' for?"

"Can't start till the reporter gets here," Perley shouted back.

Where the hell was she?

"Hey, Floyd," a man behind her said. "Lucille was asking about you the other day. Got her locked up at your place, do you? One way to keep a woman." He chuckled at his own wit.

Susan turned around.

"Naw." The large man in a red-plaid shirt grinned. "Wouldn't want to keep her. Always sticking her nose in." When he noticed Susan looking at him the grin disappeared. He was a solid square man, about thirty, with bushy red hair and muttonchop whiskers around a weak chin, brawny shoulders and heavily muscled arms.

"Floyd?" she asked.

An instant of assessment flickered behind his reddish-brown eyes and then he grinned again. "Yep."

"What's your last name?"

"Kimmell."

Beneath all that muscle, she thought, lurks the soul of a bully. "You know Lucille?"

"Everybody knows her." He cracked his knuckles.

"Where is she?"

"That's what everybody's wonderin'. Me, I don't mind. As long as the boss is out there"—he nodded at Mr. Perley in the middle of the street—"no work needs doin'."

"Floyd," one of the work crew called. "Get on the phone and see what's holding her up."

"Sure thing," Floyd called back. "Excuse me, ma'am," he said to Susan and tromped to the hardware store. Before he'd turned away, she'd caught the expression on his face, a smirk familiar to any cop: the look of a man who thinks he's getting away with something.

A loud crash and the screeching crunch of metal suddenly silenced the crowd. Then a babble of shouting rose.

The crowd surged into the street and as a solid mass swept toward the corner.

She pushed into the throng of shrieking, yelling people and seized the arm of a kid running past. "What happened?"

"Pigs!" he screamed.

Well, you little creep. She elbowed her way through to the front of the crowd, then stopped dead.

Holy shit.

Pigs. Eight large white pigs trotted in a group along the center of the street, making anticipatory little grunts like a group of tourists. They were huge, mean and ugly, and looked able to demolish anything in their path. Hooves clacking, they milled around as though deciding where to go first.

At the corner, an old truck with stake sides and steam rising from the hood sat half on the curb, straddling a bent stop sigh. One uniformed cop was talking with the driver; another was scratching his head.

In sloppy formation the pigs headed for the barbershop. The leader put its front feet on the brick facing and peered in the window into the face of the barber, who shook his fist. The pig gave a startled squeal, infecting the rest with panic, and all eight shot off down the street at incredible speed, scattering spectators in their charge.

Several able-bodied men set off in pursuit, shouting instructions at each other. The uniformed officers loped into the fray. The people, regathered along both sides of the street and clustered in shop doorways, hooted and whistled.

"Hadn't you ought to do something?" a man said to her. "They're getting away."

At a loss for what else to do, she joined the chase.

Cheers and boos came from the sidelines.

They were all—pigs, men and Susan—pelting more or less straight down Main Street when a small brown dog with a shrill yapping bark streaked into the action.

The pigs broke and galloped off in all directions.

The dog harried one, which backed up against the shoe store with murder in its eye. Susan made a grab for the dog and he danced out of reach. She grabbed again and caught one leg. The dog shrieked and sank his teeth into her sleeve. She shook him by the scruff of the neck. He gave her a sheepish look and went limp.

She handed him to a spectator. "Hold on to him."

"Yes, ma'am. Mighty fierce way you got with little dogs." He grinned and tucked the dog under one arm. "Why don't you grab that by the leg?" He nodded at the pig, who grunted and rolled toward her like a tank.

She backpedaled slowly.

"Wa-hoo!" A man chased a pig down the middle of the street, whacking it with his hat.

Bunch of cowboys, she thought grimly. Think. Another truck. Herd all the pigs—

"Look out!"

She spun. Two pigs sped toward her from the other direction. She backed, dodged and fell over the pig behind. Squeals and grunts.

She covered her head. Cloven hooves clattered around her.

"Hey, lady," someone said. "How do you expect to catch a killer, if you can't even catch a Chester White?"

FIVE

IT WAS PAST NOON when Susan stomped, grimy and tattered, into the police station, stalked past Hazel, ignoring her startled look, and flopped into Daniel's chair.

Hazel warily came to the doorway. "Did you round up all the pigs?"

"Seven of them," Susan said grimly. "The eighth was last seen heading for Topeka at a good clip."

"That's most of them," Hazel said with a motherly kind of encouragement.

Susan stared at her.

"Well, at least nobody got hurt." Hazel folded her arms across her ample bosom and leaned a shoulder against the door frame. "They can be dangerous sometimes, pigs."

"Tell me about it." Susan picked at the small rips in her jacket. "Hazel, Lucille Guthman never showed up. Is that like her?"

"She didn't? Oh my heavens, no. That's not like her at all. She tries to be Lois Lane so everybody won't think she only got the job because her father is Otto Guthman. What could have happened?"

She peered at Susan. "Are you all right? You seem a little upset."

Upset? That hardly covered it. "Just great. I made a terrific impression this morning with my first official act. Fell on my ass in front of the whole town." At this very moment the mayor was probably reaching for the telephone. *You see? Not competent. I'm yanking the job and giving it to Parkhurst.*

"Don't fret," Hazel said soothingly. "Things happen."

"Fret? Ha!" The morning's events would no doubt be rehashed with hilarity for years to come. Defeated by pigs. Now that was humiliating.

"No, really, it'll be all right. You'll be great."

Susan snorted.

Hazel nodded. "I've started a whisper campaign. Pretty soon everybody will know how great you are and won't any of them even know how they know."

Susan smiled wryly, thinking it would take more than a good word from Hazel. "Why would you do that, Hazel?"

Hazel shrugged. "This is my town. I grew up here, raised my children here. It's a good town. I love this place, and Ben— Well, Ben puts people's backs up." Hazel smiled, exposing one slightly crooked front tooth. "Besides, you lend a little class to the place."

There's nothing like undeserved credit to make you feel shabby. She didn't give a damn about the town, or the job. She wanted Daniel's killer. Then she'd be gone.

The phone rang, saving her from the need for further comment, and Hazel bustled out to answer it. Sailing under false colors was shitty, but so was losing your only supporter. Shrugging off her blue jacket, she tossed it at the coatrack and it caught on a hook. Ha, first thing that went right today.

In the bathroom, she washed her hands and face, dabbed at the mud on her gray skirt and yanked a comb through her hair. Riots she knew how to handle; livestock hadn't been in the training manuals.

She plodded back to her desk and made several phone calls trying to track down Lucille, with no success. Nobody had seen her, nobody knew where she was. Leaning back in the chair, Susan shook out a cigarette and lit it, then inhaled deeply, placed it in the ashtray and, carrying the lighter, headed out for coffee.

Osey, sprawled in his chair with an elbow hooked over the back, was speaking on the phone. His sharp features, all crowded together in the middle of his face, showed perplexity, and he raked a hand through his yellow hair. She walked up behind him.

His head swiveled, ingenuous blue eyes spotted her, and he slammed down the phone and shot to his feet, knocking the lighter from her hand. He jumped back to pick it up and his size thirteen boot crunched down on her toes.

She yelped and limped around in a small circle muttering, "Oh dear God."

He gulped and stammered apologetic sounds, his Adam's apple jerking convulsively.

He retrieved the lighter, rubbed it against his brownchecked shirt and offered it to her on the palm of his hand. She took it with murmured thanks. He gulped and fled.

"Here." Hazel handed her a steaming cup of coffee. "That's one way of getting his attention."

"Are there less hazardous ways?" Osey had an outstanding characteristic that had endeared him to Daniel: a photographic memory. She didn't find him endearing, she found him a disaster.

"Osey's a good kid. He just needs a little sanding on the rough edges."

Susan refrained from comment and sipped coffee.

"Uh, Susan—"

"Don't tell me there's something else?"

Hazel grinned. "Mrs. Willington called. She said there's a pig in her backyard."

Susan closed her eyes and took another sip of coffee. "Roberts and White are supposed to be on the trail. Call them and let them know where the *swine* is." She handed the cup back. "I'm going out to find Sophie."

On Railroad Street, she headed Daniel's pickup southwest and, at the edge of town, passed the park with the bandshell used for concerts during the summer. On the evening after their arrival in town, she and Daniel had wandered through the park with snowflakes swirling around them, and then sheltered in the bandshell, snuggling close in the dark to watch the snow fall.

Three miles beyond the park, she came to a big rural mailbox and turned left onto a graveled road. On one side was a pasture with a large pond; a dozen white-faced cattle gazed curiously at the pickup and ambled toward the barbed-wire fence. Across the road was an empty field and beyond it an area of woods.

If there were a patron saint of cats, it would be Sophie Niemen. In her dedication to needy cats, she roamed around at all hours and poked her nose into everything. And she knew, according to Daniel, everything about everybody. Sophie's husband had been one of the most prosperous farmers in the area; after his death, she had sold off the stock and most of the land, keeping only the house and two acres surrounding it.

She was vituperative about the practice of destroying unwanted kittens and, with an acid tongue, lashed and bullied people into having their pets neutered. If they refused or ignored her, she simply kidnaped the cats, had them taken care of herself and then returned them. She was forced to go further and further afield because the nearby vets knew her and were leery of getting embroiled with irate cat owners. Any cat she thought was abused simply disappeared and she denied any knowledge of it, but somewhere an unsuspecting farmer or spinsterish crony would be harboring a stolen animal.

The old farmhouse was a large three-story gray shingle, almost Victorian in architecture, with bow windows. Some distance behind it was a barn. Susan parked at the rear of the house and stepped carefully around small puddles collected in shallow spots on the driveway.

A horse neighed. From around the corner of the house, it clopped toward her in an ungainly trot, a sway-backed white mare with the gaunt frame of age and splayed feet the size of dinner plates.

Bloody hell, more livestock.

Ears laid back, the old mare snaked out her neck and clacked long yellow teeth. Susan backed toward the truck. The mare shambled faster. Susan backed faster. The mare stretched out her head and snapped those evil teeth.

Sophie came out the kitchen door. "Buttermilk!" she yelled. "Hold. Hold."

Susan scrambled into the pickup and slammed the door. The mare waggled her bony head at the window. Susan rolled it down an inch. "Mrs. Niemen? I'd like to talk with you."

"What for?" Sophie was a tiny woman with spikes of short gray hair sticking up all over her head. She wore faded patched blue jeans, a red plaid work shirt neatly tucked into a wide leather belt with a silver buckle, and hiking boots.

"It won't take long."

"I'm busy."

"Just a few minutes."

"Wasting a body's time," Sophie grumbled. "Stay right there. I need to tell this fool mare here everything's all right." Sophie stomped out to the mare and rubbed her fondly behind the ears. "Buttermilk, okay. You hear, you old nag? Okay."

She pulled a carrot from her back pocket. "Get on now. I don't have time to mess with the likes of you. Get."

Buttermilk peeled back rubbery lips and daintily took the carrot, then lumbered slowly off, huffing and snorting. Susan got out of the truck.

"All by myself out here," Sophie said. "It's a comfort to have the old nag let me know when somebody's around." Her pale-blue eyes squinted in the sunshine and her expression said, No time for the likes of you, either. She had a puckered little face that reminded Susan of an apple doll her grandmother Donovan owned. "What is it you want?"

"To ask a few questions."

"Come on in if you have to," she said grudgingly.

All that irritability was pretense, Susan thought. Behind Sophie's eyes was a ferment of avid curiosity.

The kitchen was a large, rectangular room originally designed to handle meals for numerous farmworkers and probably not changed any over the years. The orange-patterned linoleum was faded and spotlessly clean; crisp orange curtains hung at the window, and the winter sun shone through with a warm orange glow. In the corner was a monster of an iron wood-burning stove.

"Sit yourself." Sophie nodded toward the large wooden table, a soft gold color from years of scrubbing.

The odor of perked coffee and the sweet spicy smell of cinnamon filled the air. An old rocker with orange-flowered cushions sat in one corner, and on the floor near the stove was a wicker basket with three black cats tangled in comfort. One opened green eyes and blinked with the benign satisfaction of having a warm spot to sleep. The place looked like a stage setting for some nitty-gritty play by Tennessee Williams.

Sophie poured coffee into two thick mugs from a blue enamel pot on the stove and plunked them down. Grabbing a towel, she slid a pan of cinnamon rolls from the oven, put them on a plate and joined Susan at the table.

"Mrs. Niemen—"

"Might as well call me Sophie, everybody does."

Her faded eyes raked over Susan from head to toe, and Susan found her spine automatically stiffening as she thought of her aunt Frances van Dorn. Frannyvan had a look like that. She was the person Susan went to for solace when life treated her ill, for advice when she was confused, for consolation after fights with her father.

When Frannyvan looked at her with a certain look, she knew smoke screens were futile. Frannyvan knew she wasn't telling the whole story, wasn't facing the real issue, had failed to examine her motives. Frannyvan could see through every layer of self-protection, clear to the inner soul, and expose every pathetic unworthiness there.

Sophie was calmly gazing at her with that same look, probing, purposeful and seeing all the doubts and uncertainties and inadequacies. Frannyvan had been a woman of steel, who went her own way regardless of consequences and tried to teach Susan to do the same. Sophie would be another one who went her own way.

"Never seen you close to before," Sophie said. "Haven't done any grieving yet, have you? You're still just mad." She broke a steaming roll and popped a piece in her mouth. "Can't tell what you're made of. Maybe you have it, deep down there someplace, but you won't get to it until some grieving's been done."

Little feathers of irritation stirred around in Susan's mind. "Have what?"

"Grit."

Grit. Right. I'm losing my grit. Comes of fending off attack horses. "Daniel came out to see you the day he was killed."

Sophie picked up her coffee. "You lost him before you got to know him."

Sharp old witch.

Sophie shook her head slowly. "Can't tell if you're worth keeping. Were you wanting a baby?"

Susan sucked in a breath with a little hiss.

"I been a widow for more years than I can remember," Sophie said. "Had three babies. All boys, all three of them. They all died. I always wonder if I'd had a girl, would she'da been stronger. The first one I kept almost a week. That was the longest. The second one lived a day. The third one just a few hours." Sophie crossed her arms as though cradling a baby and rocked them back and forth.

Susan's throat tightened; the threat of tears stung her eyes.

"After the last one, my Ed didn't seem to be there any more. Oh, he worked, even made something, but it was like he had no reason and worked just to get through the day. He never could grieve. He was the kindest, gentlest soul with young ones. Why, he hand-raised old Buttermilk out there. Killed her mother, that one did, comin' out. And Ed, hours he spent taking care of that little orphan. But the heart just seemed to go out of him."

Sophie's blue eyes pinned Susan in a steady gaze. "You got to grieve, child."

A brassy taste flooded Susan's mouth. I'll grieve in my own time, damn you. She swallowed. This interview hadn't started out under her control and the situation was rapidly deteriorating. Now she was letting little old ladies intimidate her. You better pull up your socks, Amazing Grace. "Daniel came out last Thursday to talk with you." Her voice was tight, but level.

"I don't hold much with talking. Waste of time and I got no time, myself, for wasting." Sophie wrapped both hands around the mug and lifted it to her mouth. "Nephew's coming. I haven't seen him for ten years or more. Got to air blankets. Tidy up a room."

"Daniel got a complaint you had stolen a cat."

"Bah. What would I want with another cat? Got three of my own. Worthless creatures. Drink your coffee. Not good if it's cold."

Susan took a sip and scalded her tongue. "Harve Green was quite sure you had stolen it."

"Don't you worry none about Harve's cat." Sophie pushed the plate of cinnamon rolls closer. "Have one. You don't look like you've been eating much."

Susan picked up a roll. "Is that what you told Daniel?"

"Didn't talk to him. I wasn't to home."

"Where were you?"

"Can't remember. Memory's not what it was."

Memory probably as sharp as the knives hanging over the drain board. "Maybe I can nudge it a little. You phoned Daniel shortly before four o'clock."

"Who says I did?"

"I do."

Clamping her mouth in a grim line, Sophie waited for Susan to continue.

"Why did you call him?"

Sophie grinned. "Tell him Harve's cat came home all on his own."

One question answered. Sophie had made that second call. "He was not pleased, Sophie. He warned you, no more stealing cats." Was that the troubling thing he mentioned? Wanting to put a stop to the whole silly nonsense, he decided to talk with Parkhurst about arresting her?

Something sly flickered through Sophie's sharp eyes. Was she nutty enough to kill Daniel if she felt he would prevent her from carrying out her mission in life?

Susan decided to try another tack. "What can you tell me about Lucille Guthman?"

"Oh now, Lucille. You've met her, have you? Goes about things the wrong way lots of times, brings sorrow on herself."

"Sorrow?"

"Lucille's not quite grown-up. Part of her's stuck back there in childhood. Happens to a lot of young girls, growing up trying to get attention and a good word from a busy father."

She squinted at Susan over the rim of her mug. "Might be a little of that in you."

There it was again, that look of Frannyvan's that saw through any camouflage. Susan had counted on Frannyvan for support when she decided to be a cop. Frannyvan, exasperated, had said, "Susan Grace, when are you going to learn to examine your motives?" It wasn't until recently that Susan understood. She became a cop instead of practicing law because she was afraid she couldn't live up to her father's standards.

"She tries hard, Lucille. Had a mind to have Dan—" Sophie set her mug down with a clunk. "Here, you aren't thinking she killed your man."

The possibility had crossed Susan's mind.

"Oh my dear Lord," Sophie said slowly.

Susan couldn't tell if that meant Sophie flatly rejected the possibility or if it hadn't occurred to her before and she was thinking it over.

"Well, there now." Sophie shook her head. "I can't make sense of this killing. I'll just have to find out." She shook her head again. "I just wonder."

"Wonder what?"

Another shake of Sophie's head.

Susan had had enough of Sophie. If she knew something, she wasn't going to spill it; if she'd killed Daniel, she wasn't going to admit it. Susan needed to know more before she tackled Sophie again. "Do you own a rifle?"

"Oh, yes. It belonged to Ed."

"Where is it?"

"Hump." Sophie put her hands flat on the table and pushed herself up.

Susan followed her to a hallway off the kitchen.

"In here." Sophie yanked open a closet door and stood peering in. "Should be, anyway." She rummaged through clothing and boxes and old boots. "Ah." She emerged carrying the rifle and held it out.

Susan thought of fingerprints. "Set it down, please."

Sophie's blue eyes held a gleam of malice as she placed it butt down with the barrel resting against the door frame.

Susan crouched on her heels and clamped down hard on her back teeth. Blood pounded in her ears. Images flashed through her mind: of hands raising the rifle, stock pressed against a shoulder, sighting down the barrel, zeroing in on Daniel's spine. Finger curling around the trigger, tightening—

"Hasn't been used in a dozen years or more," Sophie said. The telephone rang and she clomped off to the kitchen.

Susan sucked in a breath and clenched her hands, concentrating on pushing down the roar of sound in her head. She stared objectively at the rifle. It might not have been fired recently, but it had certainly been cleaned. It smelled strongly of oil, the stock was polished, and the inside of the barrel was free of dust or spiderwebs.

"For you," Sophie said.

Susan looked up.

"Phone."

She went to the kitchen and picked up the receiver lying on the counter.

"Ben Parkhurst."

She lowered her voice. "Sophie has a rifle."

Silence. "Everybody has a rifle."

"Well, have you fired any and made comparison tests?"

Another pause. "Can you show cause? Even here people have rights. When you can tear yourself away from Sophie, you might want to come out to Guthman's."

SIX

AFTER GETTING directions from Sophie, Susan headed the pickup north under a vast blue sky. Summoned, by God. And with a great deal of that damn patronizing arrogance. She took a breath. Watch yourself. The point here is not one-upmanship but getting cooperation toward a common goal. Guthman's had been her next scheduled stop, anyway. Maybe, maybe Parkhurst had something.

The sky seemed huge and endless, stretching forever above the small hills. An eerie feeling of unreality stole over her, a frightening sense of having slipped through some doorway into another world.

God damn you, Daniel Wren, why did you do this to me?

Her life with him seemed long ago, a dream she groped to recapture, managing only niggling irritation because she couldn't quite remember. Angrily, she tried to grasp a moment, any moment, when they were together, but her mind found only shadowy images and she saw two strangers. Even the female figure didn't have any connection to herself. In a panic, she realized she couldn't remember what Daniel looked like.

She lit a cigarette and became aware of abdominal pains and the furry tickle of nausea. Lack of food, too much coffee, too many cigarettes. And all these wide-open spaces. If I'm not careful, I might fall off the end of the world.

Eleven miles from Sophie's, she rattled the pickup over the cattle guard onto Guthman's land. Five days ago, Daniel had driven out in response to a phone call. Last Thursday had been bitterly cold with wind and sleet; today the sun shone, but she was here in response to a phone call. From Parkhurst. Who had made the call to Daniel?

It was over a mile of curving road with open land and sparse trees on both sides before she reached the sprawling complex of main house, barns, bunkhouses and outbuildings. Otto's fiefdom, as Daniel had called it, spread out before her, the tangible evidence of Guthman's power and influence. One building looked like an Old West-type jail, a squat gray rectangle with bars on the windows. Uh-huh. A law unto himself, Mr. Guthman?

The place had a working flavor of purpose and movement with men going to and from the outbuildings, shouldering large sacks or trundling wheelbarrows. Dogs trotted around intent on their own business. Two riders on horseback clattered toward her and one touched his hat as they went by. She waved and drove up to the front of the main house, a large red brick two-story building, imposing and ugly, with a porch across the entire front.

As she got out of the pickup, Parkhurst came down the wide steps to meet her. If he said anything about pigs, she was going to kick him in the shins.

"What's going on?" she asked.

"Lucille's missing."

"Missing seems rather vague. Care to expand a little?"

"Probably nothing to it. She hasn't been seen since last night, bed not slept in, car gone. Mrs. Guthman's worried."

"Mrs.?"

"See what you can get from her."

"You don't have time to see what you can get from her?"

"I lack your finesse."

"While I'm exercising finesse, what will you be doing?"

"Otto found a fence cut. I came out with the sheriff to check into it."

Ah, Parkhurst was throwing her a bone, giving her something to do, showing how cooperative he was. He probably thought she couldn't do any harm talking with Mrs. Guthman. "Have cattle actually been stolen?"

"I intend to find out."

I see, she thought, and wondered if he knew Lucille hadn't showed up for the sign ceremony. She didn't feel inclined to tell him.

Inside the house, she followed him along a hallway and into a room obviously belonging to the master of the house. A large wooden desk sat at one end; at the other was a stone fireplace with two burgundy leather chairs in front of it. Pictures of cows covered the walls.

A man with close-cut gray hair and a lined face stood unobtrusively in a corner beside a file cabinet. Sheriff Holmes, she assumed, since the arm patch on his dark jacket said FREDERICK COUNTY SHERIFF. He looked at her with polite interest.

Ella Guthman, a plump woman with round cheeks and fading blond hair, wearing a pink flowered dress, was perched on one of the chairs by the fireplace, eyes fixed on her husband.

Otto Guthman stood with his back to the fireplace, glaring at his wife. About sixty, big-shouldered, broad-chested and bow-legged, he wore finely crafted boots, denim pants and a denim shirt open at the throat.

"You've got to do something," Ella was saying agitatedly. Her feet in sturdy brown shoes were pressed flat against the floor, as though to keep her from leaping up, and she twisted a handkerchief through short thick fingers.

"I told you, Lucille is fine. No need for all this fuss. She's gone off someplace to cause worry."

His voice was odd. The words came out equally spaced with equal emphasis on each, as though it hurt his throat to speak. An easy voice to imitate, Susan thought.

"You've got to find her," Ella said.

"She'll call. Stop fussing." His thick black hair was mottled with gray, his nose bulbous over a wide, narrow-lipped mouth; his powerful arms were long and anthropoid. He was the male beast and this was his turf. He should have been the head of a large dynasty with successive wives and scores of children. Instead he had only one wife and two children. Susan wondered if that was why he'd gone into breeding cattle.

Parkhurst introduced her. Guthman lowered his chin to his chest and examined her from under shaggy eyebrows. His look wasn't deliberately intimidating, but rather some sort of exhaustive inventory he went through and then filed under Wren, Susan. Little girl too young to know anything. From San Francisco—perverts and drug addicts. Wheedled her way into a man's job. Have a word with the mayor. Let her talk with Ella. Give the womenfolk something to do.

Susan gazed back unflinchingly, but couldn't stop her heart from beating faster. That's power all right. It seemed to emanate from him in invisible waves.

"Let's go," he said, and strode toward the door.

Parkhurst fell in behind and Sheriff Holmes nodded to Susan before he went after them. She didn't read any disapproval in his demeanor and wondered if he'd bowed to the times and hired a female deputy or two, then discovered, to his surprise, that they were quite competent.

Walking the length of the room, she sat in the chair next to Ella and felt herself sinking deep into burgundy leather. Ella sat rigid, staring at the door through which her husband had gone, her blue-green eyes sharp with anger.

"Tell me about Lucille," Susan said.

"She's been gone for hours." Ella turned her gaze on Susan, then looked down at her hands and plucked at a mangled handkerchief.

"When did she leave?"

"She didn't sleep here last night. I didn't know, not till Martha told me. This afternoon! So much time."

"Martha?"

"She thought I knew. That Lucille had planned a trip or—" Ella's voice caught and she bit her lip.

"Who is Martha?"

"Martha, my housekeeper. Why didn't she tell me?"

"When did you last see Lucille?"

"When I went to bed. I don't know. Ten-thirty. It must have been ten-thirty."

"Mrs. Guthman, your husband doesn't seem very worried."

Ella stared at her. "Dan was shot here, and now Lucille is missing. Something's happened. I know it."

"Do you have any specific reason for thinking that?"

"Lucille wouldn't just go off."

"Can you think of any place she might be?"

Ella's shoulders slumped forward and she huddled in on herself. "I don't know," she said dully.

Susan waited.

"I think," Ella went on after a moment, "maybe they—Lucille and Otto—had a—an argument."

"What about?"

"I don't know." She looked at Susan and shook her head. "He doesn't tell me, he never tells me. Sometimes—" She shook her head again. "Sometimes they argue."

When Ella didn't say anything further, Susan asked. "Does Lucille like her job?"

"Yes, of course she does."

"It's important to her?"

"Oh, yes. She's proud to be on the paper. She writes stories and reports the news and all the activities. People need to know what's going on and they like to read about their neighbors. Weddings and christenings and about themselves."

Ella spoke with a forced enthusiasm, as though she'd been challenged to prove Lucille's commitment to her job. Susan wondered why. "And Mr. Guthman was proud of Lucille? He approved of the job?"

Ella raised her chin. "Of course," she said with too much conviction and then resided back into her huddle. "He didn't always understand what it meant to her, her job. She's twenty-five, you know. He thought it was time she got married and settled down. Fathers are—" She twisted the handkerchief.

Uh-huh. Susan could see that Lucille and her father certainly might *argue*. "Did she take anything with her? Clothing, a suitcase?"

Ella looked startled. "I don't know. I never thought— I'll go and look."

They went up a stairway and into a corner room with windows on two sides. Ruffled curtains hung over the windows; the four-poster bed had a flouncy lavender-flowered bedspread of the same print. Dolls, small stuffed animals and trinkets sat on chests and bookshelves. In the corner between the two windows stood a desk with a portable typewriter, a fluorescent lamp and a small tape recorder.

With an air of futility, Ella went methodically through the hanging clothes in the built-in wardrobe, pushing each garment aside as she went to the next. She doesn't have any faith, Susan thought, in my ability to help; she feels this is a waste of time. "Is anything missing?"

"Her heavy coat. Other things, skirts and sweaters. I can't be sure."

"Suitcase?"

"Yes." Holding aside the hanging garments, Ella pointed at the back of the wardrobe where two matching suitcases sat with an empty space for a third.

"Excuse me," she said in a tight voice, eyes blurry with tears, and darted from the room, apparently not wanting to cry in front of a stranger. Susan went to the tape recorder and found a cassette in place. She pushed the eject button and took it out. Someone, presumably Lucille, had written January on it.

After replacing it, she pushed rewind and then play. She heard Lucille's voice, faint, rewound again and turned up the volume.

"January thirteenth. One twenty."

Her heart skipped a beat. January thirteenth was the day before Daniel had been killed.

"January sixteenth. Two ten. Random schedule. Makes it almost impossible." Then nothing.

"Damn," Susan muttered, rewound and played the tape again, copied the two brief comments in her notebook, then pushed fast forward. She removed the tape and played the other side. It was totally blank.

Seated at the desk, she slid open the center drawer. Jumble of odds and ends: pens, rubber bands, scraps of paper, four small metal containers that had originally held cough drops. One now held paper clips; another, six or eight colorless plastic pellets; the third, cough drops; and the fourth was empty. The other drawers had office supplies: paper, envelopes, typewriter ribbons and carbons.

She examined the clothing in the wardrobe, sticking her hand in pockets and the toes of shoes without finding anything. The drawers of the chest produced sweaters, pajamas, scarves, underwear. In the bottom drawer, she came across a small stack of canceled checks held together by a rubber band and wrapped in a yellow scarf.

Removing the rubber band, she ran through the checks, all made out to "cash" in amounts of twenty, twenty-five or fifty dollars. The first was dated five years ago and there was one for each of the eighteen following months. A folded sheet of lined paper listed the amounts, and the figures were totaled at the bottom: $500, with an exclamation point. Beneath was written, "Now it's over."

What's this all about? A flavor of penance hung over the little pile of checks, something secretive and sad hidden away beneath the underwear, something Lucille felt she had to pay for. Whatever it was had happened five years ago.

For no reason Susan could think of, she copied the amounts, then snapped the rubber band around the stack and stuck it back in the drawer.

Nothing here told her where Lucille went or why she'd gone. Susan trotted down the stairs and, when she didn't see Ella in the living room, went back along the hallway to Guthman's office, thinking Ella might be waiting there.

Ella wasn't, but a man sat at Guthman's desk, speaking on the phone. From his resemblance to Otto, Susan assumed he must be son Jack. Jack didn't seem quite comfortable in his father's chair. She knew almost nothing about him except he taught chemistry at Emerson College. She could guess, though, that at least half his female students were in love with him. Attractive, early thirties, dark curly hair and a moustache, very professorial in a tweed jacket, white shirt and tie. He also looked very worried, nerves stretched tight.

He hung up the phone and leaned back with a heavy sigh, then noticed her and started.

"Susan Wren," she said.

He rose. "Jack Guthman," he said in a pleasant baritone and extended his hand. He was almost as tall as his father, but much less massive, and had none of the force of Otto's personality, that impact of power and presence that made everyone sit up and stiffen their spines in self-protection.

"I thought I might find your mother here."

"She's lying down. Shall I get her?"

"Not necessary. I suppose you know about Lucille?"

He nodded. "Mother called."

"Have you any idea where she is?"

Something she couldn't interpret flickered in his eyes, sensitive blue-green eyes like his mother's. He shook his head.

"When did you last see her?"

He thought a moment. "Sunday evening."

Daniel's funeral had been Sunday afternoon. "Where did you see her?"

"Here. I came for supper."

"You don't live here?"

"No," he said. "I live near campus."

"What happened Sunday evening?"

"Nothing really. Ordinary family meal. The usual conversation, the cattle business, my research, the weather." He paused. "And, of course, we talked about Dan."

"And Lucille? How did she seem? Was there something on her mind? Was she preoccupied?"

"Well—" He slid a hand in his pocket and she could see his fingers form a fist. "She was kind of quiet and certainly upset about Dan's murder. Everybody is. We're sorry—"

She nodded briskly, still unable to handle expressions of sympathy. They oozed under her defenses and threatened the whole shaky façade. "Your mother thinks Lucille had an argument with your father."

"A fight with Dad? So that's what happened." Worry seemed to drain away like an outgoing tide, smoothing the lines from his face. "She was always like that. As a kid, whenever he yelled at her, she'd go and hide."

Ah, father-daughter conflicts. Susan's way had been to stand and fight. Apparently, Lucille's was to withdraw, and maybe bind up her wounds with righteous indignation. "Where would she go?"

Jack smiled. "Usually the hayloft."

Nice smile, Susan thought. "Would she worry her mother this way?"

The tension returned, bringing anxiety back to his face, and he shook his head as though to ward it off. "Oh, I'm sorry. Would you like to sit down?" He gestured toward the chairs.

"I need to talk with your father. Do you know if he's back?"

"If he is, he's probably at the Bank."

"Bank? In town?"

"Not that bank," Jack said. "The Bank is that gray building with all the bars on the windows. That's where all the money is."

"I don't understand." Guthman had his own bank?

"Go on out," Jack said. "He loves to show people."

Out on the porch, she blinked in the cold sunlight after the gloom of the house and strode toward the gray building Jack had called the Bank. There was none of the earlier activity, nobody around; everything was quiet. A squirrel ran across in front of her and, far above, she heard a jet plane. Her shoulder muscles tensed uneasily. Lucille had, apparently, taken a suitcase and driven away in her own car. Nothing indicated she hadn't gone of her own accord. In opposition was the fact that she'd missed the sign ceremony and, according to people who knew her, that wasn't like her.

Off to the right was a large red barn with snowy white trim, the massive sliding door open a few inches: a calendar picture of peaceful bucolic charm. Someone inside looked out through the door, saw her, and immediately ducked back. Male or female, Susan didn't get enough of a glimpse to tell, but that quick withdrawal was the action of someone who didn't want to be seem. Come on. Barns are made for people to be inside of. No, this someone was hiding. She'd been a cop long enough to recognize furtive behavior.

She thought of a young Lucille hiding in the hayloft. Surely not at twenty-five, simply because of an argument with her father? And surely somebody had checked. She cut toward the barn, pushed the door further open and stepped inside. Winter sunlight slanted through the doorway and sparkled on the dust in the air, lazily swirling as though someone had just passed through.

The barn seemed empty. "Lucille?" The sweet smell of hay and the pungent odor of cattle filled her nose. She heard the restless stamp of hooves. After a moment, her eyes adjusted. The hayloft? Problem here. If she climbed up to check, whoever it was could slip out while her back was turned. She needed Parkhurst, or any warm body. While she was rounding up someone, whoever was in here would be certain to get away. Susan wanted to know who was hiding from her and why. Somebody just curious about what the new police chief looked like? Then why wasn't that person innocently working around in here?

She moved along a row of open stalls. Two cows munching hay gazed at her with soft velvet-brown eyes. Three box stalls with Dutch doors ran along the far wall; all the doors, top and bottom, were closed but not latched. A wooden plaque with "FAFNER" carved into it hung above the center stall. Susan raised her eyebrows. Someone in the Guthman family must know music. If she remembered correctly, Fafner was a giant in *The Ring*.

When Susan was a child, her mother had played violin with the San Francisco Symphony. While other kids were growing up with the Rolling Stones and Neil Diamond, she was humming Mahler and Bach.

Opening the top door of the first stall, she peered in. Empty. The partition between stalls was head-high and transversed with supports. An agile person could scale it with no difficulty. She couldn't see into the center stall, but she heard movement there.

Quickly, she side-stepped, swung open the top door—and froze. Her breath caught.

The bull inside was enormous, with a sleek hide the color of mahogany. The neck, with bulging mounds of muscle, lifted a head so huge the eyes looked tiny. The nose ring gleamed. The powerful chest rumbled with an ominous strangled bellow.

Before she could latch the bottom door, he burst through. She darted aside. He halted and snorted with savage threat, causing hairs to rise on her neck. With menacing deliberation, he lifted a foot, planted it down and lifted the other, shifting his immense bulk. The head with its great horns swayed with awesome slowness in her direction. She stood motionless. The eyes held a cold black glitter.

Jesus. When Daniel told her the bull had gotten loose, she'd thought it was funny.

Fafner scraped a forefoot at the floor. She held her breath. With a bellow of rage, he thundered toward her.

SEVEN

SUSAN RAN for the door. Hooves thudded behind her.

Chest tight with fear, she dashed through the open doorway and hooked an arm around the edge. Momentum swung her in a half-circle. Face against the rough wood, breath coming in ragged gasps, she shoved hard. The door slid, then caught the bull at his massive shoulders.

He bellowed with rage and effortlessly pushed through, halted and blinked in the sunlight. She froze. He pawed at the hard ground, humped his shoulders and lowered his head.

She backed away, edging along the barn wall and fighting for breath. Cold air bit at her lungs. Slowly, the huge head swung around and his eyes glittered as he spotted her. With incredible speed, he pivoted and charged.

She shot sideways, afraid of being crushed against the side of the barn. He thundered past so close one sweeping horn caught her jacket sleeve. It tore with a ripping sound, and the force spun her around. One ankle twisted. She lurched against his surging mahogany shoulder. The power locked inside the rippling muscles slammed her back.

She lost her footing and rolled on the ground. For a moment, she couldn't breathe; then her breath came fast and she could hear it whistling through her throat as her lungs sucked in air. She scrambled to her feet.

Fafner lowered his head and shook it from side to side, searching for her. He exploded into motion, a mass of thunder hurling down, dead on, so all she was aware of was the hugeness of his head, the flare of nostrils pouring out streams of vapor, the gleaming brass nose ring, and the precision pounding of his knees as they rose high up against his chest with each stride.

She'd better do something, and fast, before she was paralyzed with fear. She feinted to her left and when the great head and shoulders swerved to follow, she cut the other way and Fafner ran straight on, straight at a man who appeared around the corner of the barn. She yelled.

Everything happened so quickly, the events all packed into fast hard actual movements, but her mind separated each action into individual components, almost as if the bull galloped in slow motion. She could watch his legs reach and push, his neck thrust forward with the effort of acceleration.

Head down and tipped to one side, he plunged a horn into vulnerable human flesh, just above the belt buckle. He raised his great head, the man dangling from the horn, and, with an angry toss, flung him away. Blood spurted in a crimson arc.

She opened her mouth to scream, but heard no sound, yanked frantically on her jacket. Her arm caught in a sleeve. She tore at it, finally slid her arm free, and started toward the bull, waving the jacket. She could feel the slow impact in her ankles as she ran; each step took long moments to leave the ground and long moments to touch down.

Bellowing with rage, the bull trampled on the fallen man. Blood bubbled in the gaping wound, spilled out over his abdomen and dripped onto the ground. With scrabbling fingernails, he tried to drag himself away. He twisted his head toward her, eyes beseeching. A horrifying burbling chuckle came from his distorted mouth. His eyes rolled up until only the whites were visible.

She yelled, waved the jacket in an arc around her head and smacked it across the bull's rump. He snorted and whirled. She backed. His head was blood-spattered. He shook it, pawed the ground, seemed uncertain for a moment, then he charged.

She dodged to one side and he overshot her. Keeping her eyes on him, she ran backwards and stumbled. He stopped, turned, hesitated, then bore down. Clawing and scrambling, she made for a concrete horse trough and wriggled under it.

Suddenly, there was a great deal of commotion: running footsteps and men shouting.

"Hey! My God, the bull's loose!"

"Sam's been hurt."

"Pitchforks! Hurry!"

Two dogs, black-and-white collie types, barked furiously and streaked toward the bull. Circling, one on one side and one on the other, they made repeated attacks at him. He lowered his head and swung toward one dog who retreated, only to come at him again when he swung toward the other.

Over the deafening clamor, the barking dogs, the roaring bull, the yelling men, she heard Otto Guthman's strong voice. "Spread out," he shouted. "Get behind him. Keep those pitchforks ready."

She could just see him standing to her left, and the rifle he held brought enormous relief. Using knees and elbows, she started to inch out from the trough. A hand clamped her wrist in a vise grip and jerked her out, painfully scraping her back.

Parkhurst yanked her upright and gave one very hard shake that made her head snap. "You could have been killed." His fingers dug into her shoulders. "What's the matter with you?"

He pulled her around behind the trough, then abruptly released her. She staggered. He started to reach for her, then dropped his hand. "You all right?" he asked, voice totally devoid of emotion.

"Fine," she replied, her voice just as clipped and flat as his, and rubbed the back of her neck. She watched several men with pitchforks advance warily toward Fafner, intent on gently urging him toward the barn.

Guthman shouted, "Not too close. Don't let him hurt himself."

Fafner eyed the half-circle of men, pawed the ground and seemed ready to charge. Guthman raised the rifle. The bull turned to menace one of the dogs. The men moved closer. Fafner started toward one man who halted. The others edged in. Fafner bellowed, whirled, and galloped toward the road with the dogs racing after him. Two men sprinted behind the dogs.

"Get those horses saddled," Guthman yelled, striding toward Susan. Face grim with anger, he planted himself in front of her. "This is all your doing."

She felt the scrape on her cheek sting.

"Meddling in what you don't know."

Ella came running from the house carrying towels and blankets. Parkhurst trotted to the injured man and knelt beside him, took the towels and pressed one against the wound. The white cloth rapidly turned red. Ella crouched and covered the man with blankets. Saddled horses were brought from the barn and the men mounted.

Guthman ran to the riderless horse, swung astride and led the pack down the road at a fast gallop. Susan went to stand beside Ella.

"They're coming," Ella said. "The ambulance."

"What's his name?" Susan asked.

"Sam, Sam Rivers. Oh, why don't they get here?"

Sam's face was gray and he lay silent, unmoving, only the blood soaking into the folded sheet under Parkhurst's hands showed his heart was still beating.

"Oh dear, oh dear, now this," Ella whispered, hands clasped tightly against her chest. "What will happen next?"

They waited. Susan felt awkward and helpless.

The ambulance, siren wailing, lights flashing, rolled up the road, swayed at the turn past the house and came to a sudden stop. Young paramedics, two male, one female, jogged toward them with stretcher and medical bags. One young man got on his knees, slapped a blood pressure cuff around Sam's arm, put the ends of the stethoscope in his ears and pumped up the cuff. The young woman applied sterile bandages to the wound and started intravenous fluid.

With a hiss, pressure was released from the cuff and pumped up again, then released; the young man hooked the stethoscope around his neck. "We'd better move," he said softly, and ripped off the cuff.

The two males lifted Sam onto the stretcher and the young woman trotted alongside holding up a plastic bag of clear fluid as they moved to the ambulance and slid the stretcher inside. She climbed in beside it. The males raced to the front and the ambulance sped backwards in a half-turn, stopped and tore off.

Ella, shivering in the cold, watched the ambulance leave and muttered in a low voice.

Susan gave her a sharp look. It sounded as though she'd said, "I hate him."

"The bull," Ella said. "Always the bull."

"Mrs. Guthman," Parkhurst said. When she didn't respond, he touched her shoulder and told her to go inside, it was cold. Ella nodded and plodded to the house.

"Well, *Chief* Wren," Parkhurst said. "City people don't always realize the dangers inherent in a rural setting."

"*You're* 'city people.'"

"For your protection, a few facts. Farming is way up there among the most hazardous occupations, with a high incidence of serious and fatal accidents." His hands were bloody with dark streaks on the blunt fingers, dried and caked around the nails. "You shouldn't be involved in any of this, but the least you could do is stay out of trouble. I'll never get anywhere if I have to babysit you."

"My safety is not your concern."

"Otto's livid. If anything happens to that bull, anything at all, there'll be hell to pay."

"That's why he didn't shoot? More concerned about a bull than an injured man?"

Parkhurst grunted. "Fafner brings in three million a year. How quick would you be to shoot?"

"Three million? How could any animal be worth that much?"

"Right now there are higher priorities than your education." He turned to leave.

"One moment."

He stopped, turned back.

"I would appreciate it," she said, "if you would find out who was in the barn just before Fafner got loose."

"This is a working ranch. People go into barns."

"Yes, even city people are able to figure that out. Whoever it was hid from me."

He listened impassively as she explained what had happened.

"Those stall doors were unlatched, deliberately unlatched, by someone who didn't want to be seen." She rubbed a hand across her cheek. "I think he was hiding in the adjacent stall."

"Why unlatch doors?"

"It got me out of the barn, didn't it? And created enough commotion for an army to sneak away unnoticed."

"Why didn't he want to be seen?"

"I do believe you have finally asked the important question. Find out if anyone admits to being in there."

"Giving orders?"

She took a breath and let it out. "Comes of natural leadership abilities."

"Yes, ma'am." He touched a finger to his forehead. "With your permission, right now I'd like to see that the bull is caught and nobody else is hurt. Then I'll do that very thing."

She watched him walk away and hoped he was going to wash his bloody hands, then tromped back into the barn. It was warmer inside but not much, and the acrid odor of cattle stung her nostrils. Whoever had been here was gone, she told herself, but her shoulders still tensed and she looked around warily. The light was dim. There were shadowy corners everywhere. The loft above, stacked with bales of hay, was a perfectly good hiding place.

The same two cows placidly munched hay, bovine jaws relentlessly grinding. The last box stall, the one she hadn't gotten a chance to look into, still had both halves of the Dutch door closed. With a shaky hand, she opened the top and peered in, then drew a breath. It was empty.

She eyed the stall where Fafner had been. Even though he was no longer there, she felt the menace of his presence and had to force herself to go inside. The soiled straw made her nose wrinkle. The space seemed much larger with the bull gone. She paced back and forth examining the floor, looking for a rock or a dart, a wire, something that might have been used to enrage the animal.

She found nothing and went into the stall on the left. Straw was spread on the floor, but at least it was clean. Nothing here either.

She went to the stall on the right of Fafner's. A pitchfork lay in the corner. Used to goad the bull, she thought, kneeling and tapping a finger against the point of a tine. Again she paced back and forth, kicking at the straw. She found a clump of mud, still damp, that had fallen from somebody's boot.

Picking it up, she leaned against the rough wall and gazed at it. Somebody had hidden in this stall and jabbed the bull with the pitchfork. Why couldn't he or she afford to be seen? She pictured the injured man, ashen-faced, with blood soaking into the white towel. Whoever she was dealing with didn't care who got hurt.

Hearing footsteps, she raised her head.

Someone ambled into the barn, carrying a pitchfork. He wore blue jeans, an unbuttoned checked jacket, a bright green shirt. He walked with a free, easy stride.

He was a kid, about sixteen, she thought, with a pale, pinched face. A clump of tawny hair beneath a billed cap, slightly askew with ear flaps dangling, hung in his eyes.

"Hello," she said, walking toward him.

He froze, then turned with taut wariness to face her, his soft brown eyes wild and suspicious like those of a deer hearing a twig snap, ears strained to assess the danger, muscles bunched in readiness. She stopped four feet away, afraid he would whirl and bound out the door.

"I'm Susan Wren."

"Seen you," he mumbled. "Name's Nat." He tossed his head, throwing the hair from his eyes.

Speak softly, she told herself, and make no sudden movements. "Do you work for Mr. Guthman?"

He nodded. "Should have been here. Came as soon as I heard."

"About the bull?" Backing to a partition, she raised herself to sit on it, put a hand palm-down on either side and let her legs dangle.

"Wouldn't have happened if I'd been here. I can make him quiet. He trusts me. Poor old Fafner, he can hurt himself. Get caught up in wire. He's gonna be scared. Might try to jump a ditch. Fall and break his leg. Nothin' be done for him, he break his leg."

"Why weren't you here?"

Nat ducked his head, embarrassed. "She wouldn't let me."

"Who?"

"Betty. Sister. Said I had the flu. Had to stay in bed. He's gonna need me when they bring him back."

"You must know Lucille."

Head tilted to one side, he looked at her as though he couldn't believe anyone was that dumb. ''She lives here, doesn't she?''

''Did you see her yesterday?''

''Betty said I had to stay in bed.'' His glance slid away.

Ah, she thought, he disobeyed the sister. ''So you stayed in bed?''

He nodded and gazed with longing toward Fafner's stall. ''I need to get it ready for him.''

''You stayed in bed all day?''

He hesitated, then nodded again.

''All day you stayed in bed. What about at night?''

He shot her an uneasy look.

''Last night,'' she said persuasively. ''Weren't you here last night?''

He tossed his head and restlessly shifted his feet. She smiled encouragingly.

He moved the handle of the pitchfork to his other hand. ''Sometimes I do, just to see he's all right. Old Fafner, he misses me. Gets edgy.''

She nodded as though she understood perfectly. ''Last night,'' she repeated. ''You came to see him?''

Nat hesitated, a sheepish expression on his face.

''Did you see Lucille?''

He looked away as though searching for some escape. Susan wondered what sister Betty was like.

''I only saw her drive away,'' he said.

''What time was that?''

''Don't know. Late. After midnight. I think— It looked like she was crying.''

''You often come to see Fafner at night?''

''Sometimes,'' he admitted. ''Sometimes I see her driving away real late.''

''When does she come back?''

''Don't know.''

''Have you ever seen her with anybody?''

He shook his head. "I need to rake out the stall, get clean bedding down."

"You never saw her with anybody?"

Again he shifted and inched away. "Once."

"When was that?"

"Can't remember. After Chief Wren was shot. Maybe Friday, maybe Saturday."

"Who was she with?" Susan spoke too sharply and he gave her a startled glance.

"Don't know. It was dark."

She took a deep breath and kept her voice soft. "Yes, I understand, it was dark, but I'd like you to help me."

He eyed her warily.

"Tell me about coming to see Fafner. Sometimes you come here, late, when everybody's in bed?"

Nat nodded reluctantly. "Nobody knows. I just— Fafner, he needs me. He gets lonely and there's nobody. And then he gets mean. And he can't be free to run. He's locked in."

The lonely kid and the caged beast giving comfort to each other. He obviously loved the massive, powerful brute and poured out tender care and affection. "How do you get here?"

"Walk," Nat said as though she'd asked another dumb question.

"How far is it?"

He shrugged. "Not even five miles. I got short cuts."

"Yes, that's good. Now tell me about the night you saw Lucille with somebody."

Nat looked worried, as though he might be asked for something beyond him. "I don't remember was it Friday or Saturday," he said earnestly.

"Where did you see them?"

"About three miles over that way." He gestured with a thumb. "On the road. And Lucille leaning in like, talking to somebody in the car."

It had been too dark to see the other person and he didn't know if it was a man or a woman.

"I think," he said, "she was mad like, arguing."

He didn't know the make of the car or even the color. He simply wasn't interested and he hadn't wanted to be seen. She thanked him and left him working with his pitchfork.

For how long had Lucille been in the habit of going out late at night? What was she doing? Last night she went out late, and this time she hadn't come back yet.

EIGHT

SEATED AT Daniel's desk, she read the note Hazel had left. The injured man, Sam Rivers, had a ruptured spleen, several broken ribs and a punctured lung. His condition was critical.

Osey stuck his head in the door, Adam's apple bobbing, and cleared his throat. "Ma'am?"

"Yes," she said sharply.

He came in, enormous feet treading warily as though he were afraid of breaking something. Standing in front of her desk, he cleared his throat again. "Ben was on the phone."

"For heaven's sake, Osey, sit down."

"Yes, ma'am." He collapsed into a chair.

She sighed. "Osey, do you think you could just call me Susan?"

"Uh—no." He swallowed and his mouth twitched. "Ma'am, I couldn't."

She eyed him suspiciously, wondering if there was a spark of humor behind his deliberate flatness, but saw nothing in his guileless blue eyes except the stunned sappy expression that always came over him in her presence. He swallowed nervously.

She made a conscious effort to keep irritation out of her voice. "Osey, what did Parkhurst say?"

"They caught the bull. The vet's out there now, but they don't think he's hurt any."

The bull, she assumed, not the vet. Thank God for that. She felt enough guilt about the beast's getting loose; she didn't need the added burden of a multimillion-dollar property getting injured.

"And he said, Ben said, nobody admitted to being in the barn."

She wasn't surprised. She nodded and looked at her watch: almost six-thirty. Her first day had been a long one and vastly overloaded with livestock. She pushed back the chair and stood up. "Thank you, Osey. I'll see you in the morning."

With uncoordinated jerks, he shot to his feet. "One other thing. Miz Wren called."

Susan slipped into what was left of her jacket after it had been savaged by pigs and ripped by bulls.

"She wants you to come and see her this evening," Osey said. "If you could."

Oh, hell. The last thing she wanted to do tonight was see Daniel's sister. She wanted only to take her battered ego and bruised muscles home to a hot bath.

HELEN NO LONGER lived on the Wren farm. Several years ago she'd moved to town, into a small white house with dark gray shutters and white picket fence, just the sort of house expected of a middle-aged spinster who had taken care of two aging parents until their deaths.

There was nothing frilly about the small living room: uninspired furnishings, everything plain and practical with an intimidating neatness. The row of silver trophies across the bottom shelf of the glass-fronted bookcase was the only incongruous note.

Helen was the librarian for Hampstead's library. Like Daniel, she was tall and thin; she had short dark hair streaked with gray, a narrow face and glasses, and she wore a brown skirt, a tailored white blouse and a loose brown jacket. Unlike the stereotypical unmarried lady, she didn't have a cat or even a dog, and in the summer there would be no flowers blossoming around her house. Maybe she didn't want the responsibility for anything dependent on her or the possibility that something might tap a locked-up source of affection. Everything about her was plain and practical. Susan had the wild desire to buy her red lace underwear.

Mouth tight, as it always was around Susan, Helen sat in a beige chair in the corner. Lamps burned on small tables, one near Helen and one on each end of the beige couch where Susan perched uncomfortably. She'd been in this house only once before. It didn't give off an aura of being loved, simply lived in.

"I was expecting to talk with Dan the day he died," Helen said.

Dan. Susan never called him Dan, always Daniel. She liked the nice biblical sound of it, even though she wasn't religious. Neither of her parents were religious; her Dutch mother came from a long line of Lutherans and her Irish father from a family of Catholics, but both parents were skeptics and hadn't laid either faith on her. "Did you see him?"

Helen shook her head. "He was going to drop by the library, but—"

Susan hadn't had time to work out what kind of relationship existed between Daniel and his sister. There hadn't been any demonstrable warmth, no hugging or kissing—she couldn't imagine anyone hugging or kissing Helen—yet there were close ties. Helen had them for dinner—supper— the day they arrived and took special care preparing a roast and the rhubarb pie that was Daniel's favorite. And he had felt a strong sense of responsibility toward her.

"What did you want to see him about?"

"I got another offer for the farm. I want to sell. I've wanted to for quite a while and Dan was always holding back."

Susan nodded. He'd wanted to keep the family farm for the son he hoped to have, and he'd tried to figure some way to buy Helen's half.

"Now I suppose you own his share."

Susan was startled. She supposed she did. It never occurred to her. Once she and Daniel had borrowed horses and ridden through the fields and across the pastureland. He'd shown her the apple tree he'd fallen from and broken his arm when he was eight, the pond where he used to swim. They'd had a cold picnic in the winter sun on the edge of the pond.

Although he hadn't wanted to work the land, he had loved it, knew every inch of it, and the soil seemed to nourish his soul just as it did the wheat. Strongly and unexpectedly, she did not want to sell Daniel's farm.

"It's a good offer," Helen said. "I want to accept. I want the money."

"I understand, but I haven't really thought. I'd like—"

"I don't think you do understand. I want to travel, go places. The only way I'll ever be able to afford it is to sell the farm. I've never been out of the state of Kansas."

The vehemence in Helen's voice startled her. Did Helen want to sell so badly she'd kill her own brother?

"Maybe there's some way I could buy it." Susan didn't know how and wondered fleetingly if her father would like to invest in however many acres of Kansas farmland. She could see Helen wasn't taken with the idea; her mouth was tucked even tighter.

"I'll need to know soon," she said.

Susan rose. "Let me have a few days to think about it." She might as well agree. What did it matter? Daniel was never going to have the son he wanted, and what would she want with acres and acres of Kansas farmland? She hated the place: the endless wheat fields, the cows, the pigs, the foreign people. The *bulls*. A kid whacked on the latest shit was easier to deal with. As soon as she found Daniel's killer, this place was history.

Sticking one hand in a glove, she savagely pushed on the fingers and turned to leave, then turned back. Helen had risen to show her out. Susan stared at the older woman. "Why don't you like me?"

Helen seemed taken aback, and her gaze wavered for a moment as though she considered denial; then she looked steadily at Susan. "You weren't the right wife for him."

"I loved him."

"Oh, love," Helen said disparagingly. "You were enthralled with something new. Painting walls and playing house. You wouldn't have stayed. Not for long, not after the shine dulled down."

Helen had fanned the little coals of guilt Susan hadn't understood. "What do you know about love?"

"Enough to know it doesn't last and you would have poured it out with the scrub water and waltzed back to where you came from."

Know the truth and it shall make you seriously pissed. "You don't know anything about me."

"Enough, missy."

Missy?

"I know you're pretty," Helen said, "and smart and got everything you ever wanted. Parents pampered and spoiled you, bought you pretty things, paid for your schooling. They didn't say, 'You can't go. The money's for Dan's education.'"

Helen's voice was harsh with old resentments. "All my life I've been trying to leave here. As a young girl, I knew better than to get tangled up with any of the young men who looked at me with calf's eyes. It's not like that for you. You don't have to stay."

"I'm still here," Susan said. "I've got Daniel's job."

"Oh yes. You wanted that and you got that too. How long are you going to stay with it?"

Helen's dark eyes, so much like Daniel's, gazed at her with knowing malice. "You going to stay here and work at the job? Worry about the town? Care about the people? Or leave soon as you get what you want from it? You shouldn't have married him. He deserved better.''

Hot fury flooded over Susan and she concentrated on the silver trophies, read the engraving to keep from shrieking.

They were all old, the most recent dated twenty years ago. They were for—

She looked at Helen, this frustrated, bitter, middle-aged woman in her tailored clothes. This librarian.

The trophies were all for sharpshooting.

Helen was a crack shot.

NINE

RAISING HER stuffed-up head from the pillow, Susan looked at the glowing red digits on the clock: five-thirty on a dark, bleak Wednesday morning. Wednesday's child is full of woe. And also coming down with a cold. She rolled onto her back with complaints from stiff, protesting muscles and groped for Kleenex. Last night she'd gone to bed thinking about Helen, and thirty minutes ago she'd awakened still thinking about her.

"You shouldn't have married him," Helen had said. "He deserved better."

Clutching the extra pillow to her chest, she mentally informed Helen, "He knew." He knew what kind of odds were stacked against us. Seventy-five percent of all cops' marriages ended in divorce. The odds were even greater for us because of the wide differences in our backgrounds.

It was on a Wednesday she'd decided to marry Daniel. She was late getting off work and by the time she got home, she was in a panic and furious at him, because she loved him, because loving him forced her to make a choice.

She'd slammed into her apartment, thrown her purse with as much force as she could at the couch and was taking off her shoes when the doorbell rang. She yanked open the door to let Daniel in.

He carried a dozen long-stemmed white roses. With an overly hostessy voice that set even her teeth on edge, she explained she was a little late. "Please make yourself comfortable. It'll only take me a moment to change."

He raised an eyebrow and offered her the flowers.

"Thank you." She looked around blankly, then shoved the flowers, paper and all, into a vase on the hearth.

He disappeared into the kitchen and she heard doors open and ice rattle. When he came back, he handed her a tumbler of Scotch. "Get some alcohol in your bloodstream and then tell me why you're so pissed at me."

"Who gave you permission to weasel your way into my heart?"

Placing his fingertips under the bottom of the glass, he raised it to her mouth.

She sipped, turned, took six paces to the fireplace, turned again. "Did you know I was in the hospital for a month?"

He nodded, leaned against the wall and crossed his arms.

She paced six strides toward him. "I was shot."

"I've seen the scar."

"One of those stupid things nobody could foresee. We were going to bring in a sixteen-year-old suspect for questioning." She turned, took six strides.

"You told me," he said. "Armed robbery. Grocery clerk killed."

"The kid's eleven-year-old brother shot me. The gun turned out to be the one that killed the clerk." Six strides back.

"You told me that, too."

"Have I told you what I think about love at first sight?" She shook a finger under his nose. "It's nonsense. You don't even know me."

"I see."

"For all I know there is no such place as Kansas." She noticed her voice had gotten rather loud. "You asked me to marry you," she said accusingly.

"I did that, yes."

"Did you mean it?" she demanded.

"I never ask beautiful women to marry me unless I mean it."

"I accept," she snapped and stared at him, terrified.

He went very still, then pushed himself from the wall and took back the Scotch. He drank it. "Really warms my heart to see you so thrilled about it," he said mildly.

"I'm scared."

He nodded profoundly. Silence ticked by.

"What made you decide?" he asked.

She smiled a quick, embarrassed smile. "That bullet came close. I'm thirty-four years old. I love you. I'd like to have a husband, a child, a—" She waved her hands, brushing at confusion. "Oh, Daniel. This is crazy. How is it ever going to work out?"

Catching one hand, he kissed the palm. "We'll just have to see," he had said.

"Just have to see": his way of saying "One step at a time."

She fumbled on the bedside table for the pack of cigarettes, shook one out and struck a match. The bright flare made her squeeze her eyes shut. Daniel was dead, there would be no child, the dreams were all ashes. She blew smoke at the dark ceiling and thought about the row of silver trophies on Helen's bookshelf, Helen's dream of travel, her fierce desire to sell the family farm, her anger and resentments. Did she kill him? She had motive and she certainly had the skill.

AT THE POLICE DEPARTMENT, Susan said good morning to Hazel and went straight to George Halpern's office. In a dark-brown suit, white shirt and carefully knotted tie, he sat at his desk working on personnel assignments and organizing patrols. He was doing a lot of the work that should have been hers, except she didn't have the knowledge that should go with the title. It was only because he'd agreed to help that she thought she might pull off this charade of being police chief.

She liked George, a genuinely good person, kind and compassionate. He was in his early sixties, with a square face and thin gray hair, bald in back. He'd been born in Hampstead, lived here all his life and spent over forty years with the police department.

He looked up when she walked in, assessing yesterday's effects on her and probably wondering if she was strong enough to stick it out or if she would fold her tent and slink away.

He smiled as she plunked down on the chair in front of his desk. Heavy lines bracketed his generous mouth and radiated more lines that hinted at his quick and quirky sense of humor. Even forty years as a police officer hadn't shaken his faith in the innate goodness of most people, a vast difference from a forty-year veteran of big-city crime.

"Tell me about Helen Wren," she said.

"What do you want to know?"

"She wants to sell Daniel's farm."

"It's her farm, too."

Susan sighed. "I guess now it's partly mine." It was an unwanted responsibility, this feeling she must do right by Daniel's farm.

"Legally," George said mildly.

She darted a quick look at him, wondering if he were implying that morally the issue wasn't so clear.

The chair squeaked as George leaned back, rested his elbows on the arms and clasped his fingers across his chest. "Her dreams never came true, and one frustration piled on top of another from the time she was thirteen."

"What happened?"

"Till then she was an only child with a doting father; then Dan was born and Arthur had a son. All that attention went to him. The mother was never strong. City girl from Atlanta. Kansas and farming just seemed too much for her."

Susan grinned. "That I understand."

"Allura needed parties and fancy dresses and people taking care of her. She had a hard time when Dan was born and never seemed to get her strength back. Running the house fell on Helen and every time she tried to get away something happened to keep her here. Usually her mother took sick. One time, bad time, it was Arthur. Tractor ran over him and darn near killed him. Then Helen had to run the farm, too.''

"Uh-huh." Susan sneezed and grabbed a tissue from the box on the desk. That explained a lot about Helen. She was fifty-eight years old, and for forty-five of those years she'd had one disappointment after another. She would feel the years going by one by one as she stayed, dutifully accepting the responsibilities that fell on her shoulders, and with each year seeing her opportunities get fewer and slipping away to none, anger and frustration and bitterness growing greater. She must have resented Daniel from the day he was born. He usurped her place in the family and then grew up able to lead his own life while she was forced to give up hers.

Susan felt sorry for her. Sell the farm, let Helen have her dream. But not till I'm damn sure her hands weren't on the rifle. "Did she kill Daniel?"

George leaned forward with a squeak, folded his hands on the desk and looked at them for a moment, then realigned the framed photos of his three grandchildren. "She shot a man once.''

"Who?"

"When her father was laid up, she was doing the farming, plus looking after him, plus taking care of Allura who wasn't ever much use. Dan was in the army then and had a wife of his own. Lot of things were going wrong around the Wren place. Livestock injured one way and another. Fences down. Cattle getting at the crops and causing damage. Machinery breaking down.''

"Who did she shoot?"

"Late one night, Arthur's dog was missing and she went looking. She caught Billy Don Kimmell setting fire to the wheat field.''

"Kimmell?" Susan said. "There's a Floyd Kimmell who works at the hardware store. Big man with red hair and the smell of a bully."

"Billy Don's son. It's not been easy for Floyd around here. Country people have long memories. He feels he's been cheated some way and like he was owed. Comes out of all this past. Back then it didn't look like Arthur was ever going to get well. Billy Don wanted to get the land cheap and was causing all that misery hoping they would sell out."

"Helen killed him?"

"She did."

"What happened?"

"This was all over thirty years ago. There was an investigation and talk of bringing charges. Folks all felt sorry for her, felt she had no choice but to do what she did. Most everyone of them would have done the same. Crops are their livelihood. Can't survive without 'em. What it came down to was, authorities decided not to charge her."

So Floyd Kimmell had a grudge against the Wrens, a thirty-year-old grudge. After all that time, had he decided on revenge? It was Helen who had shot his father, not Daniel. If he was out for revenge, why not shoot Helen?

He might have a motive that had nothing to do with all this past history. She recalled the smirk on his face yesterday morning, and somebody in the crowd teasing him about Lucille. "What kind of relationship does Floyd have with Lucille?"

"If you mean romantic, none that I know of. They know each other, but that's the extent of it."

"Any word on Lucille?"

"Not yet," George said with a worried sigh.

"Has anybody questioned Floyd about her?"

"Not specially." George eyed her, waiting for her to explain.

"Just a feeling," she admitted.

He nodded, as though that was reason enough.

"Would you send somebody—Parkhurst—to lean on him a little?"

"Osey'd be better. Floyd'd clam up when he saw Ben coming. Osey has a way of just easing information along like a lazy current moving a duckling."

"Well—" She wasn't sure Osey would recognize information if it was handed to him with a label.

"I'm going to see Lucille's editor. What do you know about him?"

THE *HAMPSTEAD HERALD,* according to a brass plaque on the front of the building, had been founded in 1886. It was a square brick structure, painted white, directly across the railroad tracks from the depot.

Henry Royce had bought the paper five years ago after a heart attack at age forty-two forced him to retire from one of the Chicago papers. He was an outsider, too, but according to George, more readily accepted than most because nobody wanted to do without the *Herald.* His office was at the rear of the building, and he sat writing copy behind an old oak desk cluttered with file folders, magazines, notes and old newspapers.

White shirtsleeves rolled up, garish red-striped tie loosened, he looked up at her and scowled. It was a scene straight out of *The Front Page.* She wondered why he didn't wear a green eyeshade. The heart attack probably accounted for the absence of a haze of smoke.

He had a heavy face—jowly—sharp black eyes and black hair, mottled with gray, that was overdue for a haircut. Thirty pounds overweight, with an ulcer, he was a short-tempered man who quickly reached a hot rage when things went wrong, which happened with great regularity on a small-town daily.

Tossing down the pencil, he leaned back in the chair. "Well, you must be Chief Wren." He spoke with a soft Southern accent.

She was getting a little tired of the sarcasm everybody loaded onto *Chief* Wren. "Where is Lucille?"

"If I knew, I wouldn't be sitting here writing this drivel. I'd haul her in and have her doing it."

"Drivel?"

"My readers are more interested in who got married and what the bride wore than hard news."

"Surely you knew that before you came."

"Yeah, well, knowing and experiencing are two different things."

He crossed his arms, tipped back his head and peered at her with cynical amusement in his beady eyes. "Maybe you know about that. Want to give me an exclusive interview?"

"No."

"Human interest," he drawled. "Romantic dreams, biological clock—career woman gives up all, then lands knee-deep in reality."

She wasn't sure she liked Henry Royce; he seemed to carry antennae that zeroed in on the weak spots. She raised her eyebrows and gave him a supercilious nod in acknowledgment of his accuracy.

Since he made no attempt to provide her a place to sit, she scooped a tottery pile of papers and files from the only chair, swung it around in front of the desk and planted herself on it. "Where do you think she is?"

"Ah, honey, she's young. You know how it goes, most likely a hot-and-heavy love affair with some sweetheart."

Susan looked at him, wondering if he believed that. She couldn't tell; his face was bland, eyes opaque. "Is she a good reporter?"

"She might be in a few years." His voice held a fond wistful quality. Nostalgia for his own reporting days? Or fondness for his pretty young reporter?

"She's green and what she's doing isn't what you'd call reporting, but she works hard and she's ambitious. Her instincts are right. That all-important nose for news all us good reporters have," he said sarcastically.

Reporters weren't the only ones with instincts. Cops had them too, and Susan's instincts told her Lucille was into something "hot and heavy" related to Daniel's death. Victim? Perpetrator? She didn't know, but she was sure Lucille wasn't in the arms of a lover. "For instance?"

He lowered his chin to his chest, narrowed his eyes and said ominously, "Cattle rustling."

"Lucille thinks that's going on?"

He nodded.

"Is she right?"

He shrugged. "On a big scale, no. On a small scale, she's convinced, yes. Anywhere you have a lot of cattle, the odd bovine can be stolen and slaughtered by somebody who likes beef and doesn't want to pay for it, or likes to make a little money selling it for less than market price."

"I see. Anything else she was interested in?"

"Toxic waste."

"What about it?"

He shrugged again. "Lucille has this flea in her ear that somebody is dumping it somewhere in the county."

"She right about that?"

"I doubt it. On the other hand, there's a lot of that going around lately."

"Did she talk about Daniel's murder?"

"Of course." He picked up a pencil, held one end in each hand and rotated it.

"Does she suspect anyone?"

"If she does, she hasn't said so."

Susan eyed him steadily and waited. When he didn't volunteer anything further, she said, "I assume you're concerned about her, that you'd rather no harm came to her. I'm trying to find her, see she's not in any danger, and I need a little help here."

He expanded his chest with a large breath and let it out with a gusty sigh. "I think she did suspect somebody."

"Who?"

"I don't know. She denied it flatly."

Again Susan waited.

"Honest truth," he said. "I don't have any idea."

"What makes you think she suspects somebody?"

His mouth twisted in a crooked smile. "Old firehorse hearing the distant clang of bells." He tapped the pencil against the back of his hand. "This was her first real crime. A lot different from covering 4-H exhibits. She's never seen a murder victim before."

She stared at him. "Lucille saw the body?"

His black eyes stared back. "She was there almost as soon as Ben was."

She hadn't known Lucille had been present at the crime scene. Had Lucille spotted something Parkhurst missed? Picked up something? Thursday night after Susan had seen Daniel's body on an autopsy table, Lucille, agitated, tried to find out what Parkhurst knew. She had stuck her hand in her pocket and very quickly jerked it back.

What was in that pocket? Something that identified the killer? Why not turn it over to Parkhurst? Protecting the killer? Why? Unless she had killed Daniel, was protecting herself and now had lit out for parts unknown.

"Where is Lucille's office?" she asked.

Henry pointed with the pencil. "Across the hall, second door."

When he made no move to stop her or come with her, she realized he must have searched already and expected her to find nothing.

Lucille's office was a smaller, neater version of Henry's: battered desk, filing cabinet and bookcases. The one grimy window looked out on an alley with tire tracks cut into the snow and across to the rear of Pickett's Service Station and Garage. She watched one of Osey's older brothers stop to light a cigarette before going inside. She didn't know which one; Osey had four older brothers and they all looked alike.

Turning from the window, she blew her nose and then slid open file drawers: paper supplies, folders of notes and expenses, clipped articles attached to typed copy. She pulled one, dated two months ago, and read about Joe Calvin, salesman for a car dealer, moving permanently to Kansas City. Henry had edited it heavily before printing and rightly so, she thought, shoving the drawer shut with a clunk.

The top of the desk was clear except for a computer, a coffee mug bristling with pens and pencils (the mug read, "NEWS MAY BE HAZARDOUS TO YOUR HEALTH"), and a telephone with an answering machine. She rewound the tape for incoming messages and pushed the PLAY button. There were two hang-ups, then Ella's voice. "This is your mother. Lucille, are you there? I wish you'd call."

The fourth was a woman with a birth announcement, then another woman, with particulars about an anniversary party hosted by the family of the Marsdens. Fifty years of marriage. Not bad. An unidentified male voice, "Returning your call again. We keep missing." A repeat call from a more distraught Ella.

Then, "It's Doug." Very angry. "What the hell's going on? You said the Drake. I've called five times. You're never in, you never return messages. Call me."

Who was this Doug person? She reset the machine for incoming calls. The Drake. A hotel? She looked around for the phone book, found it on the bottom shelf of the bookcase and turned to the listing for hotels. No Drake. She tried restaurants. Still no Drake.

She wasted some time slipping disks into the computer and scanning the contents. In the center drawer, along with paper clips, rubber bands and Scotch tape, she found a small spiral notebook with five entries. October 27, 2:10. November 12, 1:50. November 29, 1:30. December 27,

12:13. January 5, 12:32, Floyd's truck (underlined, with a question mark).

The two dates and times on the cassette in Lucille's bedroom weren't included. She probably used the tape recorder in the car and later wrote the information in the notebook.

Okay, Susan thought, Lucille took late-night excursions and on these dates she found indications to support her theory. What that theory was, Susan didn't know, but she was willing to bet Lucille was avidly on the trail of cattle rustlers or dumpers of toxic waste.

A tie-in with Daniel's murder was another thing she didn't have, unless he had run across evidence of one or the other. He had seen something that troubled him, that he wanted to talk over with Parkhurst.

She copied down the dates and times, including Floyd's name with the question mark and assumed Lucille had seen Floyd that night but wasn't certain whether he was involved in whatever she was trying to find. So far Floyd was all Susan had that even resembled a lead.

She put her own notebook in her shoulder bag and Lucille's back in the drawer. When she tried to close the drawer, it caught half way and she stuck a hand in to level the jumble. It still wouldn't close. She pulled it out all the way and a crumpled envelope fell to the floor. Crawling under the desk, she retrieved a phone bill, glanced at it, started to drop it on the desk, then sat down and copied the numbers Lucille had called in December.

On her way out, she stopped in the doorway of Henry's office. "You know anybody named Doug? Friend or acquaintance of Lucille's?"

"Nope."

When she left the newspaper building, an ice-cold wind tore the door from her grasp, and she had to lean hard into it to get it closed. The sky was a dreary gray and rippled like a washboard. Shivering, Susan jammed her hands deep into the pockets of her trench coat and clenched her teeth to keep them from chattering.

I hate this weather, she thought as she got into the pickup. Why would anyone live here? She wondered what the temperature was at home. Sixty degrees probably, rain maybe, at the very worst hard rain, but not nine hundred degrees below zero.

Her stomach growled and she realized she hadn't eaten yet today. Food had never been high on her list of important things. On the job, she'd grabbed a quick meal as she could. At home, she'd gone with the frozen dinner, cheese and bread routine. Cooking took up a lot of time that could be used for something interesting. Since Daniel's death, even though she felt hungry, she found it hard to eat. It was two-thirty and so far today she'd had only coffee. From Main Street, she turned left at Second and pulled up at the Coffee Cup Cafe. The sign above the door pictured a gigantic gold cup with mud-colored contents sending up billowing clouds of steam on which bounced happy doughnuts and sandwiches.

Inside was blessedly warm. A row of booths ran along the fogged-over front windows, and opposite was a counter with stools. Except for a couple in the end booth and a man hunched over the counter brooding at a plate of french fries drowned in catsup, the cafe was empty.

She slid into a gold vinyl booth, and a young woman with short brown hair and a snubbed nose, "Phyllis" stitched on her gold uniform, came up with a smile and a menu.

Susan asked for coffee and lit a cigarette while she studied the menu. Once she'd met Daniel here for lunch; he claimed this place served the best barbecued beef ever made.

When Phyllis brought the coffee, Susan ordered a barbecued-beef sandwich, then wriggled out of her coat. The heat, so welcome when she came in, was now overwhelming and made her nose drip more. Rubbing a clear spot on the fogged glass, she watched the people going by, heads down, bent into the wind. A small boy, submerged in a red parka, grinned at her and stuck his tongue out. She smiled back and gave him a hideous grimace. His mother, with a yank on his arm, towed him away and she was left making gargoyle faces at an affronted matron.

Phyllis slid a plate in front of her, asked if she needed anything else, then left her responsible for a barbecued beef sandwich. She stared at it. Maybe this hadn't been such a good idea. She cut it into quarters and remembered she didn't like barbecued beef. Out of the corner of her eye, she saw Phyllis and the other waitress murmuring to each other, with now and then a glance in her direction.

She set her teeth. Talk away, she thought grimly, picked up a piece of the sandwich and took a bite. She chewed, then had a panicky moment when she was afraid she couldn't swallow. She gulped hot coffee, pushed the plate aside.

A few minutes later Phyllis brought the check and laid it on the table. "Excuse me, Mrs. Wren," she said hesitantly. "But Pam and I were talking. About Lucille? We heard, you know, that you were looking for her, and ever since Bess broke her leg she hasn't been coming in to work. My Aunt Bess? She owns the cafe?"

Susan nodded, not sure what she was nodding at.

"Well, Pam and I thought maybe you'd like to know. I wasn't sure it was important, but she said I ought to tell you anyway, because it might be, you know."

"Tell me what?"

"About Bess, and her seeing Lucille's car."

You need to watch that paranoia, Susan thought. "When did Bess see the car?"

"I don't know exactly. Different times, I think."

Susan's hopes fell. Any number of people had seen Lucille's car at different times. What she wanted was someone who had seen it Monday night. She thanked Phyllis and took down Bess Greeley's address and directions so she could find the woman.

TEN

THE TEMPERATURE HAD dropped even lower when she left the cafe, and snowflakes, whipped by the wind into mad frenzy, whirled around her exposed face with malicious intent. As she opened the pickup door, the side mirror reflected a black scarecrowlike figure with flapping coattails dart around the corner of an office building across the street and disappear down the driveway. Oh hell, what now? She slammed the door, crossed the street and tromped down the driveway to a small parking lot.

Four parked cars sat there gathering snow; there was no figure, either scarecrow or human. Apparently, Sophie could disappear at will. Movement behind the shrubs along the back of the building caught her eye.

"Sophie?"

Agitated trembling of the shrubs, and the old woman rose through the froth of snow like a spirit from the vasty deep. The long black coat covered her from her chin to the toes of her laced boots; the black watch cap covered forehead and ears. Only her cheeks and sharp nose were visible and red from the cold. She carried an orange-and-yellow tapestry bag that bulged and weighed heavy on her arm.

"What's in there, Sophie?"

The bag roiled. Sophie clutched it to her chest and the churning increased. "Ha. My knitting. Excuse me, I need to find my nephew."

Bloody hell. Sophie had somebody's cat in the bag. Probably something ought to be done about it. Susan had promised to uphold and enforce. And she used to laugh when Daniel came home fuming about Sophie and spending half his time with irate people and their damn cats.

"There he is," Sophie said, and called, "Brenner!"

Coming up the driveway, emerging from the falling snow like the hero in a movie, was a man in a tan overcoat. The theme song from *The Third Man* came to mind and she wondered why, all of a sudden, everything reminded her of old movies.

Up close, he *looked* like a hero, blond hair blown by the wind in disarray across a high forehead, a clean-cut face and an air of city polish.

"This is Dan's widow," Sophie said with a crafty look. "Our new chief of police."

Brenner Nieman regarded her with surprised pleasure, as though she were the very person he wanted to meet. He smiled. Oh yes, very handsome indeed.

"Haven't seen him for ten years," Sophie said with asperity. "My own nephew, and I'd never even have recognized him. Too busy to visit his old auntie." Growls and grumblings came from the orange-and-yellow tapestry flouncing around under her arm.

"Sophie," he said. "Give me that bag."

She scowled. "You're interfering."

He held out his hand. With a hiss of resentment, she relinquished it. As he opened it, a highly indignant white cat shot out, raking his hand in launching a jump. Swearing, he dropped the bag. The cat streaked across the parking lot.

"You ought to be more careful." Sophie bent to snatch up the bag. "I have to get home. This storm's going to be a bad one." She marched off, black coat fluttering around her ankles.

Brenner watched her with a harried look. "Probably going after the damn cat again." Taking a handkerchief from his back pocket, he held it against his bloody hand. "I feel guilty as hell for being away so long. I had no idea Sophie had deteriorated so much. I don't know what I'm going to do about her." He smiled a rueful, appealing smile.

She felt herself smiling back.

"The cats are one thing," he said. "Then there's her habit of wandering around by herself, anywhere, any time of the day or night. She's an old lady," he said with exasperation. "I'm terrified she's going to hurt herself."

"I can appreciate the problem. Are you staying long?"

"As long as I can. I only planned a quick trip down and back. I've got a business deal that needs attention."

"Where do you live?"

"I move around a lot. Right now, Kansas City. You must be cold standing here, and I'd better go find Sophie before she gets into more trouble."

He led her across the street to Daniel's truck.

"What business are you in?" she asked.

"Oh, I do a little bit of everything," he said lightly. "Anything that might turn into money." Then he sobered. "Any word on Lucille?"

"How did you know I was looking for her?"

"Sophie told me." He opened the truck door for her. "I'm very sorry about Dan."

"Did you know him?"

"In a place this size," he said with a small smile, "everybody knows everybody."

She got in the truck and, with a murmur of nice-meeting-you, he strode away through the falling snow. From the side window, she watched him, a veritable picture of a man worried about an elderly relative, worried about the difficulties she posed, worried about what she was doing at this moment.

Why this squirmy, uneasy feeling that something had slipped by that she should have noticed? Probably just this lousy cold. She shook her head, pushed the heater to high, switched on the windshield wipers and mushed off to find Bess Greeley.

Five miles outside of town, the small white frame house sat just off a narrow road. Bess opened the door with a big smile of welcome. She was a large-boned, stout woman with brownish hair and wore a loose red-and-blue flowered dress that zipped up the front. She had a cast on her right leg. "Come in, come in. Would you look at that snow? You must be near froze. Come in."

Awkwardly, she maneuvered herself with crutches into the living room. "I'm just so pleased you came. I'm downright tired of my own company. Now you just sit right down over there, right by the furnace and warm yourself up."

Susan sat on the dark green couch with lace doilies across the back and arms. Doilies were everywhere, ruffled and starched under table lamps, flat on chair arms and the top of the upright piano covered with framed photos. It reminded her of Grandmother Donovan's living room, crowded with too much large furniture, knickknacks and family snapshots everywhere. Even the plaster religious icons seemed the same. Her grandmother's had always terrified her as a child.

"Well now, what can I get you? A cup of coffee?"

"No, thank you."

"A nice hot cup of chicken broth. I just made some fresh. Just the thing. Warm you right up. Are you sure? Won't take a minute."

"No, no, I—"

"Wouldn't want you to catch your death. I'll just turn up that old floor furnace a little. Not like central heating, I know, but it does the job."

"No, no," Susan said again quickly as Bess started toward the thermostat. "I'm fine, thank you. Really."

"Are you sure you're warm enough?"

"Quite sure." In fact, too warm. She was barely able to survive outdoors, but inside, she'd found, everybody kept their homes too hot for her comfort. She was accustomed to less heat and much more moisture content in the air.

Bess dropped heavily, with a breathless whoosh, into the overstuffed green chair by the window, propped the crutches against the side and used both hands to lift her leg onto the footstool. "Can you imagine anyone being so clumsy?" She slapped the cast. "I fell on my own front steps, slipped on the ice and went rolling all the way down. I thought I was gone for sure."

"Your niece Phyllis mentioned you had seen Lucille's car."

"Well, I have, you know. My goodness, where do you suppose that young lady is? With this leg of mine, I have trouble sleeping and I sit right here so I can look out the window. Not that there's anything to see most times, but I look at the stars and the moon and sometimes the night creatures go by, owls and foxes, you know. That's how I come to notice her car."

"Did you see it Monday night?"

"Monday...no-o, no, not Monday."

"When did you see it?"

Bess rubbed her chin with thumb and forefinger. "Three weeks ago today that I fell. Doctor says I have three more weeks to go with this fool cast. So it would be three, four days after that I started having trouble sleeping."

She laughed. "First few nights, no problem. Pills, you know, but a body can't take pills all her life. Goodness gracious, I'd turn into one of those drug addicts. Then where would I be? I have a business to tend to. I don't know about those girls. They're good girls, of course, but—"

"How often did you see Lucille drive past?"

"Oh dear now, let me see. Maybe two or three times. What could she have been up to?"

"You never asked her?"

"Well, I didn't, you know. I didn't see her to talk to. It's hard for me to get out much with this confounded leg."

Susan asked if Bess had seen Lucille on January seventh or fifteenth, the two days on the cassette tape.

Bess wasn't very clear on dates. She might have. On the other hand, it might have been the day before or the day after, or maybe some other day entirely.

"But it's odd, you know," Bess said. "Always so late I'd see her, two or three in the morning sometimes. And once, maybe on the fifteenth, around there, I saw that nephew of Sophie's."

"Brenner? You recognized him?"

"Well, no, not to say recognized, but I saw a car I didn't know and I heard he was coming to visit, so it must have been him."

Couldn't have been, Susan thought. He hadn't arrived until yesterday, the nineteenth.

"About time, too," Bess was saying. "Can you imagine? All those years, treating Sophie like that, and her like a mother to him. I just don't know about young people these days."

"This car was following Lucille?"

"Oh, I don't think anything like that. I saw her go by and then a while later I saw this other car. Of course, Lucille knows him. Or did, anyway. He used to work for her father, but that was a long time ago. I can't remember exactly how many years. My goodness, it must be ten or twelve. How time goes. And used to be I could remember all these details, but my memory just isn't what it was."

She smiled. "But there now, I guess I'm getting on just like everybody else. There was some kind of trouble."

"Trouble with what?"

"About Brenner when he worked for Otto. I don't know what it was. Otto never spoke of it and Brenner never said. Nobody knows. Only that he was fired and wasn't to ever go back."

"You're sure you didn't see Lucille last Monday night?"

"Well, I didn't, no. But then I wasn't watching Monday. I got a blessed night's sleep. She might have driven by. I wondered, you see, where she could possibly be going.

That's a road doesn't really lead anywhere. Well, of course, Vic Pollock's out that way. But surely she wouldn't be going there in the middle of the night, would she? He has a new car, you know.''

''Who?''

''Vic. Big black thing.''

Bess rambled on contentedly and Susan interrupted to ask how she could find Vic Pollock's farm. Bess obliged with detailed directions and numerous digressions.

SUSAN DROVE FOR MILES, past empty fields with barbed wire fencing and bare trees, headlights barely able to penetrate the gauzy curtain of billowing snow, without seeing a house or a barn or even a mailbox. Already, snow covered the road and obscured the shoulders. She hoped Aunt Bess hadn't left out a vital part of the directions.

At the next crossroad, she turned right and spotted the glowing red taillights of a car some distance ahead. Increasing her speed slightly, she pulled close enough to make out a large, black car. Vic Pollock? Well, good, a little piece of luck. All she had to do was follow.

He turned left, right, left and two more rights. She did the same, leaning forward with her eyes glued on the taillights so she wouldn't lose him.

Suddenly, he sped up and slewed through turns. The truck fishtailed as she rounded corners to stay with him. What kind of idiot would drive like that in weather like this?

His taillights swung left. She came around and hit a patch of ice. The back wheels slid. She tapped the brakes gently and turned into the skid.

The truck skated to the edge of the ditch and hung there. She pressed the accelerator. The motor strained. The truck teetered, almost pulled out, then with a fast lurch the rear end slid and the truck dropped backward and down eight feet into the ditch.

She bounced, struck her head and swore. The front wheels were just below the shoulder of the road, the headlights aimed upward like searchlights. Swearing again, she turned off the lights and ignition, and watched the windshield rapidly become opaque. She rubbed her forehead.

Well, Daniel, now look what you've gotten me into.

With the heater off, cold seeped in quickly and she listened to the wind howl. Dammit, she'd have to radio for help. She reached for the mike, then stopped, dropped her hand, and let her head fall back.

Oh Lord. She pulled in a long breath.

She had no idea where she was. She had not kept track of those turns, left and right. It hadn't been necessary. As long as she was mobile, she could head the truck generally in the right direction and sooner or later she'd get to town.

Well, she wasn't mobile, knew only vaguely where she was, and a blizzard raged around her. She was lost, lost in the wilds of Kansas. A giggle rose in her throat. Out here where there was a road every mile, absolutely straight and true, north–south, east–west, one-mile intervals, laid out like a checkerboard, and she was lost.

She was to call and inform the citizens of Hampstead that their police chief not only couldn't find a killer and a missing woman, but couldn't find her way home either?

No. She'd stay here and freeze to death.

ELEVEN

HER HANDS were numb, her feet were numb, and her face felt cold enough to crack if she touched it. Freezing to death was a real possibility here unless she did something. Oh shit. She took a breath, exhaled with a frosty puff and reached for the mike.

"Hi, Hazel. It's Susan. Could you let me talk with George?"

"Sorry, he's not in. Anything wrong?"

"Well, I've managed to drive the pickup into a ditch."

"Are you hurt?"

"No. I just can't get the damn thing out."

"Hold on. Osey's here. I'll let you talk to him."

"No, Hazel—" Oh damn. She wanted somebody who could help, not Osey.

"Ma'am?"

"Yes, Osey. I've got a little problem."

"Where are you?"

"That's part of the problem. I haven't any idea."

Silence. Then Osey said, "Could you describe the area?"

"Empty fields and barbed wire fences."

"Yes, ma'am. If you could do a little better than that. Can you remember what you passed? Any mailboxes?"

"No."

"Any buildings?"

"Not that I could see."

"What about trees? Any where you are now?"

"It's hard to see with the snow, but I think there are two just ahead of me by the road."

"I don't suppose you know what kind they are?"

"I'm afraid not."

"Have you seen any ponds?"

"One, but it was a long time back." Trees and ponds, for God's sake. They were all over the county and nearly identical as far as she could see.

"Can you remember anything else? What about gates, wood slats or wire?"

"I didn't notice," she snapped.

"Okay. Was there anything you did notice? Any fallen trees or a herd of Holsteins—uh, black-and-white cattle?"

Her teeth began to chatter and all she could think was stupid. Stupid, stupid, stupid not to pay attention to what she was doing. Stupid to be sitting here getting colder and colder, answering questions about trees and Holsteins. "No. I only remember a couple of goats."

"Are you uphill or downhill from the crossroad?"

"Just downhill."

"Don't worry, I'll find you. Is the truck okay? I mean does it run?"

"Yes." Don't worry. Osey is going to find me. Osey. My life depends on Osey. Oh dear God.

"How much gas do you have?"

She switched on the ignition. The needle hovered just above empty. She switched it off.

"Ma'am?"

"Not very much," she said flatly.

"Okay. Keep the motor running and the heater on. Oh, and you probably know to crack a window and check the exhaust pipe is clear?"

She replaced the mike and gazed out the side window at the swirling snow. Taking a breath, she struggled to open the door against the wind, clung to the steering wheel, then dropped into the ditch. She landed hard and felt a sharp pain in one ankle. The wind tore at her trench coat, wrapped it around her legs and hurled snow in her face.

Snowflakes stuck to her eyelashes and she brushed her eyes with the back of a gloved hand. As she staggered through drifts to the rear of the truck, snow made its way inside her boots. She scooped a clear space around the exhaust and floundered back to the door.

Getting in wasn't as easy as getting out. She grabbed at the seat; her hands slid and she fell. She clutched at the steering wheel and hauled herself inside. Puffing like a dragon, she slammed the door and rolled the window down a hair.

When she reached for the ignition, she felt a momentary fear it wouldn't start, but the motor caught immediately. She turned on the hazard lights, thinking they would help if Osey managed to get anywhere near.

She waited.

Minutes crept by. Wind whistled at the crack in the window. The heater droned. Warmth slowly seeped over her. The gas gauge stayed just above empty. She waited. Closing her eyes, she leaned her head back and let her thoughts ramble over what she'd found out in the last two days.

Helen wanted to sell Daniel's farm. She desperately wanted money to get out of here, and there was Daniel in her way, recently married and hoping for a child. If he got his child, he might never agree to sell. She had shot and killed a man years ago.

The man's son, Floyd Kimmell, was pleased with himself, smugly felt he had gotten away with something. Susan was certain of it. She had seen that smirking expression too many times to be mistaken, but she wasn't so certain it meant he had killed Daniel. She couldn't believe, if he had, that the motive was related to his father's death, but he might have killed Daniel because Daniel discovered what he was up to.

Lucille. Lucille. On the trail of cattle rustlers. Evidence of cattle rustling was the bait used to lure Daniel into a trap.

Lucille, last seen about ten o'clock Monday night. Missing now for almost two days.

The motor coughed, sputtered and died.

Coming alert with a jerk, she squinted at the gas gauge. Empty. So much for Osey's rescue. How long does it take to freeze to death? She had a vague memory victims felt cozy warm just before expiring. If that were true, she had nothing to worry about; she'd never been so cold in her life.

She heard Daniel's voice saying, "Now, Susan, don't get dramatic. You'll be okay." She smiled to herself.

He'd said those words to her the day he went back to work and left her alone for the first time. The day had been a long one and by midafternoon panicky thoughts of "Oh my God, what have I done?" scrabbled in her head like wailing demons.

She'd opened the bottle of white wine chilling in the refrigerator and sat at the kitchen table. When Daniel came in, she raised her glass. "Hail, wedded love. Stay me with flagons, comfort me with apples."

He grinned. "I don't think you got that quite right."

"Whatever." She poured him a glass.

"Susan, have you already had a little of this?"

"Only a little. I'm saving the other bottle for dinner. I didn't want to be tipsy when you got home."

"Uh-huh. Moderation." He touched her glass with his and sat beside her.

"Did you marry me for my moderation?"

"I did. And to discourage single ladies from bringing me casseroles."

"Your casserole days are over, buster. I slaved over a roasted chicken from Dilly's Deli."

"You mean Dilman's Delicatessen?"

"Is that what I mean?"

"Nah, probably not." He ran the back of one finger lightly down her cheek. "You probably mean to ask if you love me."

"Do I love you?"

"Yes, you do. I'll prove it."

"How?"

He kissed her neck, softly, just below the jaw. "Come with me. We'll see about the chicken later."

A horn blared. She opened her eyes and blinked. A patrol car sat on the road above. Osey got out and shouted. She rolled down the window.

"You all right?" he called anxiously.

"A lot better now."

Grinning, he turned back for a gas can and slithered down the side of the ditch. He poured gas into the tank, then tromped around to the window. "I tried to get Dad's tow truck, but it's on a run and I didn't know how long it'd be gone. People stuck everywhere. I hoped maybe I could get it out for you. No chance."

"Can you pull it out with the squad car?"

He shook his head. "Transmission's not too good. Better not try. If you'll come with me, we'll get help."

He scrambled up the side of the ditch, then turned, held out a hand to help her and tugged her up and out with ease.

"How did you find me?" she asked after they had gotten into the patrol car.

"Goats. Only one place you could be. Nobody keeps goats except the Henningers. They got a baby allergic to cow's milk."

Ah. Like a magic trick, simple when you knew the answer.

He drove with more speed than she was comfortable with given the weather; it had her clutching the door handle and stomping imaginary brakes. "Did George ask you to see Floyd Kimmell?"

"Yep, but Floyd wasn't working today. I went out looking and he wasn't home either."

She wished she'd insisted on Parkhurst. He would have poked around for whatever he could find. "Did you think to take a look around?"

"Yes, ma'am. Went through the barn, walked around the house, peered in all the windows. Didn't spot any blood or any bodies. And nothing else either, like Lucille tied up in the kitchen."

She shot a quick look at him with a sneaking suspicion he knew her opinion of him and was deliberately playing the country bumpkin. His face was deadpan. Immediately, she looked back at the road; not watching what they might slide into was more than she could bear.

The headlights gleamed on a mailbox and she glimpsed the name Pollock as it flash by. "You didn't stop there."

"No, ma'am. Vic Pollock isn't somebody you ask for help unless there's no other way. There's been Pollocks around here just about forever and they've never been very friendly. They usually don't bother anybody as long as they're left alone, but you never know what they're apt to do."

"What kind of car does he drive?"

"Just lately, a new black Caddy."

So it probably had been Vic Pollock she'd been following.

"Vic's mean as a snake. Meaner since Emma Lou's been gone," Osey said.

"Emma Lou's his wife?"

Osey nodded. "She's a pretty little thing, kind of timid. I saw a movie once about a lost little dog. Emma Lou always reminds me of that little dog."

"Where is she?"

"Visiting her family is what Vic said when folks started asking."

"How long has she been gone?"

"Two months or more maybe," Osey said. "It was a while before anybody noticed they hadn't seen her for a spell. We'll go to Henningers'."

They drove another mile before Osey slowed and turned in to a farmyard. A small black-and-tan dog rushed at the car, barking and trotting alongside. Osey stopped at the rear of the house and the dog backed off, but continued to bark. An outside light went on and a man, pulling on a yellow slicker, came out the back door.

"Gene Henninger," Osey said, and got out of the squad car, leaving the motor running and the windshield wipers going. The two men spoke briefly; then Gene bent to look at her through the window. She rolled it down.

"Evening," he said. "Understand you left the road a ways back."

"I'm afraid so."

"No trouble. We'll get 'er right in no time." He straightened, slapped Osey on the shoulder and went back into the house.

Osey slid behind the wheel and in a few minutes Gene came out carrying a lantern. Osey shoved the car in gear, made a wide circle and headed for the road. He paused until he heard the clatter of a tractor behind them, then drove back to the pickup with Gene following on the tractor and the lantern swaying like a beacon in the falling snow.

When they reached the truck Susan stood on the road while Gene slid into the ditch and attached chains to the axle.

"Okay," he shouted to Osey over the noise of the tractor. "Get in, keep a hand light-like on the wheel."

Osey did as he was told. Gene climbed on the tractor. The motor roared, the tractor strained. The truck balked, then with a lurch was pulled, lumbering, up and onto the road. Osey stuck his head out the window and waved. Gene collected the chains. Susan thanked him.

"Glad to help. Had to pull Lucille out pert near the same place not long ago."

"When?"

"Believe it was the same night Dan was killed. Sorry about your husband."

"Thank you. What was Lucille doing out here?"

"Don't know. Saw her one other time. Got the idea she was keeping an eye on Vic Pollock for some reason." Gene touched his hat, got back on the tractor and disappeared into the snow.

Osey jumped down from the pickup and helped her in. He told her to go right at the first crossroad, left at the next, then another right and straight into town. "Will you be okay?"

"Yes. Thanks for the help."

He grinned, stepped back, and she drove off.

WHEN SUSAN CLUMPED into the police station, Hazel jumped up and rushed toward her. "Hazel, it's after seven. Why are you still here?"

"I was worried about you."

"I'm just nifty peachy, except for a large dose of humility." Susan shrugged off her trench coat, trudged into Daniel's office and flung it at the coatrack. She blew her nose.

"Hoo, because you slid off the road? Listen kiddo, that happens. Who are you trying to be, Superwoman?"

"Yes," Susan hissed. "How'm I doing?" She flopped in the chair, tugged off her boots and massaged her wet, cold feet.

"Hey, not to worry. Even God made mistakes. Look how many bones he put in catfish."

"Oh, right. That makes me feel better."

Hazel grinned. "Well, to take your mind off it, would you be interested to know we got a call about a stolen cat?"

"Oh, Lord. A white cat, I suppose."

"Yep. Marley and Koontz went out to see about it."

Susan exhaled with a sharp sigh. Obviously, Brenner hadn't gotten to Sophie in time, and she'd managed to get her hands on that cat again.

Tucking one foot under her, she leaned back in the chair. Brenner hadn't been here in years; why had he come now? A reason more specific than visiting his elderly aunt?

"Hazel, do you know anything about Sophie's financial situation?"

"Not really. Why?"

"I assumed she was poor, sort of a bag lady. Instead of collecting trash, she collects cats."

"Oh heavens, Sophie isn't poor. When she sold out her land, she got some money. Who knows what she did with it though. Maybe buried it in Mason jars in her backyard. Why?"

"I wonder about Brenner. He's her only relative. Does he expect to inherit?"

"I imagine so. Unless she spends it all before she dies. Anyway, she's the kind that lives forever."

"How well do you know Brenner?" Susan stretched out her legs and wiggled her toes.

"Not at all now. When he was a kid I knew him as well as the others. He was one always in trouble."

"What trouble?"

"Kid stuff. Cutting school, fighting, reckless driving. Like that. Nothing real serious. If he gets anything from Sophie, it'll be his second inheritance."

"Second?"

"Well, not exactly, I guess. There was some insurance money after his parents died."

Maybe Brenner had squandered all the insurance money and come back to check on the state of Sophie's health. So what might that have to do with Daniel? Nothing that Susan could see.

"You'd better go home, Hazel. You should have gone hours ago."

"I'll get you some coffee first."

Susan padded to the window in her stocking feet and looked out. On the street a car drove by and the headlights turned a zillion snowflakes into tiny silver stars. This had been another long day. Her head ached and she gently rubbed the tender knot on her forehead.

"Pretty, isn't it?"

She turned with a start. Parkhurst in gray pants, newspaper folded under the arm of his blue sport coat, came in with a mug of coffee.

"Invigorating," he said. "Makes you want to take off cross-country. Explore winter wonders. Throw caution to the winds and drive a truck in the ditch."

"Ha ha," she said and leaned back against the window ledge. His dark eyes flicked over her and rested on her stocking feet. Without her boots, she was two inches shorter than he was.

"Hazel said you could use this." He handed her the mug. "It's been cooking all day, should be just about done."

She took a sip: sludge, worse than what her father used to make.

"You're probably used to hot buttered rum after a frolic in the snow, but we do what we can." He rested one haunch on the edge of the desk. "Far be it from me to question the actions of the chief, but would you mind telling me what you were doing out there?"

She gave him an icy look and wrapped both hands around the mug. Undrinkable the coffee might be, but at least the container warmed her hands. She told him about Bess Greeley, her broken leg and her spotting of Lucille's car. "According to Bess, that road only leads to Vic Pollock's place. I wanted to ask him if he had seen Lucille, knew what she was doing out there. Osey said Vic has a wife nobody's seen for over two months and Vic claims she's away visiting her family."

Parkhurst smiled. She was so startled she took another sip of sludge. She'd never seen him smile and was astounded at the change; it took away the flat, hard look and made him seem almost human.

"You think Vic killed Emma Lou and buried her out there somewhere?" he said with a raised eyebrow.

"I think it's possible."

Parkhurst rolled the newspaper and tapped it against his knee. "Emma Lou's not too bright. She's young and pretty and not very happy with Vic. The Pollocks are hard on their women. If she's not back with her relatives, then somebody interesting wandered across her path and she took off with him."

"Wouldn't Vic go after her?"

"He might be glad to see her gone."

Even so, Susan thought, he'd probably do something. Males seldom felt indifferent when a wife or lover walked out.

"Find out if Emma Lou is with her family."

Parkhurst raised the rolled newspaper and touched it lightly to his temple. "Anything you say." He stood up.

"How is Sam Rivers?"

"Still alive, still critical."

"Parkhurst, why is that bull so valuable?"

"He'll be valuable long after he's dead."

"That's a good trick."

"Frozen semen," he said. "It's shipped all over the world."

"Oh, to improve the quality of beef."

"Well, that, but more important is the quantity of milk from superior dairy cows. Otto's bull has a proven record of siring daughters who produce five or six times more gallons of milk per year than other diary cows."

"I see."

"This is Money we're talking about here," Parkhurst said. "Bull semen is big business, on a multibillion-dollar scale for Otto and others like him. Speculators can buy so many hundred units of semen and sell months later when the price goes up, or buy percentages in specific bulls."

"Like the stock market."

"Now you're beginning to understand."

Money, she thought, always a potential for murder.

Parkhurst unrolled the newspaper and dropped it on her desk. "You might want to take a look at this," he said as he walked out.

Shoving herself away from the window ledge, she padded to the desk and stared at her picture on the front page. Oh Lord. Great picture. She lay face down, arms clutched around her head, with her posterior pinned down by a gigantic sow whose snout was lifted victoriously. Headline: NEW POLICE CHIEF ROLLS INTO ACTION—REARGUARD ATTACK ON UNDERBELLY OF CRIME.

Ah, another perfect end to another perfect day in paradise.

TWELVE

SUSAN BLEW HER NOSE and started pulling open desk drawers. She found a bottle of aspirin, swallowed two with a minimal amount of coffee and then found the phone book she was looking for. She slapped it on the desk, paged through, ran a finger down the *R*'s and then punched the number.

"Royce," the editor answered in his soft Southern drawl.

"Good evening, Henry."

"Ah, Chief Wren." His voice faded as though he'd changed the receiver to his other ear, and in the background the voices and canned laughter of a television program were cut off.

"You must have seen the paper," he said. "Wasn't that some pic?"

"Splendid. I'll put it in my scrapbook. I just wanted to let you know I owe you one. If I'm ever in a position to respond in kind, you can count on it."

He gave a wheezy chuckle. When he got over his mirth, he asked, "Any trace of Lucille?"

"Not yet."

He growled irritably, which she interpreted as uneasy concern. His little theory about a lover must be wearing thin. "Jack Guthman called a little earlier, wanting to know if I'd heard from her," he said.

"I assume that means he hasn't."

"Yeah, I guess you can assume that."

"Are they very close, Jack and Lucille?"

Henry grunted. "I don't know how close they are, but Lucille has a big dose of hero worship for brother Jack.

From listening to her, you might think he was the next thing to God.''

"Um. Well, if you do hear from her, let me know." She hung up and stared at the picture. Three or four names leaped to mind, of former colleagues in San Francisco who would have howled with delight at it. What had crossed the mayor's mind when he saw it? Damn, damn. She blew her nose again and then called the hospital to ask about Sam Rivers. No change.

Snow was still falling heavily when she slithered off for home, and the streetlights glistened through the frenzied swirls. She put her mind to Jack Guthman, wondered if Lucille had confided in him about her suspicions of cattle rustling or toxic waste, mentioned Floyd Kimmell or Vic Pollock. Or Doug.

Pulling over to the curb, she snapped on the interior light and scrounged in her shoulder bag for her notebook to find Jack's address. Sixteen twenty-nine Hawthorne. Near the campus, she thought. She made a left, cut across town and did some zigzagging, squinting in the darkness for street names, before she ran into Hawthorne, a wide tree-lined street in the oldest section of town. This was Hampstead's swanky area. Many of the homes were large and some looked out of place under the falling snow, as if they'd have been more comfortable on a plantation in the Deep South.

Jack's house was a small one-story with brick facing, and it appeared dark. Not home? She parked anyway, climbed out of the pickup and plowed through snow drifts to the porch. He might be in the back where she couldn't see a light. She rang the bell, waited and then knocked. Irritated, she plodded back down the steps.

A car slewed into the driveway and Jack got out, slammed the door and hurried toward her. "What's happened? Lucille—?"

"No," Susan said with a shake of her head. "I didn't mean to startle you. I haven't any news, only more questions."

"Oh." He let out pent-up air with a long sigh. "Sure. Okay." He ran a hand through his hair, brushed at the snowflakes on his face and looked at her uncertainly. "Could I interest you in something to eat? A problem came up at the lab and I haven't had supper yet. We could get a meal at the inn. It isn't far."

She hadn't had anything to eat either since her attempt at the Coffee Cup. Maybe food would relax him and he'd be able to answer questions. She said a meal sounded fine.

Fifteen minutes later, she walked into the Wethertime Inn. Jack had led the way and was already chatting with a young blond waitress in a white blouse and long black skirt as if they were old friends. They probably were. In small towns it seemed everybody was an old friend, something she didn't always remember.

Jack introduced her and Aby, the waitress, smiled. "I know who you are, of course."

Of course. I'm the only one around who isn't everybody's old friend. She wasn't sure she liked this standing-out-like-a-sore-thumb stuff.

The dining room was dimly lit and almost empty. Only a few people, brave enough or stupid enough to venture out in heavy snow, sat in the curved red-leather booths that lined three walls. The tables in the center, with white tablecloths and flickering candles in red glass globes, were all unoccupied. The ceiling was timbered with wide beams, and the pictures on the rough textured walls were scenes from the Old West.

Aby chided Jack flirtatiously about not being in for so long as she led them to a booth and placed menus in front of them. The candle flickered shadows across his face, highlighting the lines of fatigue and deepening the dark circles around his eyes.

"You look tired, Jack," Aby said. "Have you been working too hard?"

"Yes," he said with mock solemnity, and ran a thumb and forefinger down his moustache. "Have to keep scrambling, have to keep on top of the research."

Aby laughed and floated away.

"What kind of research are you doing?" Susan asked as she opened the menu.

"Plastic hay."

She looked at him over the top of the menu. "You're joking."

"Funny, that's what my colleagues all say." He smiled and the smile emphasized the gray tiredness in his face.

"What's it for?"

"Cattle feed."

"Plastic isn't digestible."

"It doesn't need to be."

"It's a synonym for shoddy. You want to push this fake, shoddy world right into the stomachs of the poor cattle?"

"It's superior to hay." He started patting and poking his pockets. "Usually I have some," he muttered. "It gets in my pockets in some mysterious way. Never mind."

Leaning his elbows on the table, he spoke like a teacher. "Cows are ruminants. They need roughage. If they don't get about fifteen percent hay, serious problems develop in the rumen."

"Rumen, I assume, is the stomach."

"The first of four. Feed initially gets digested there and then is regurgitated as cud and rechewed."

Aby floated back and Jack recommended prime rib. Susan settled on tarragon chicken with noodles. With all this talk of cows, she didn't feel she could look at a slab of red, bloody beef. He ordered prime rib, then handed back the menus and went right on with his instruction. She let him. The lines of strain eased as he talked.

Underneath his easy lecturing manner was a note of steel determination. Obviously, this research was important to him; he believed in it. Plastic hay sounded like nonsense to her, but what did she know? She hadn't even known that cows had four stomachs.

"Hay doesn't have the nutritional value of grain, but it's essential. It forms a floating mat that scrubs the papillae and prevents buildup of bacteria. Otherwise, bacteria enter the bloodstream and cause liver abscesses."

Papillae. That awful-looking stuff in the supermarket labeled tripe? He intended to make a name for himself in this rigorous work at revolutionizing the feeding of cattle. She wondered how much his determination had to do with proving himself to his father. Jack hadn't gone into breeding cattle like Otto, but chose chemistry. Like I didn't want to be a lawyer? Powerful fathers had a lot to answer for.

"The plastic substitute is more efficient. Hay is bulky and heavy, dusty. It has to be ground and mixed with grain and it's difficult to send through mechanized feed-delivery systems. My biggest problem, aside from constantly running out of funds, is finding the right shape."

Salad bowls were placed in front of them, and she picked up a fork. "This plastic has to be the right shape?"

"You wouldn't think so. What do cattle know, right? But that seems to be the case. Originally, I tried disk-shaped pellets. No good. Then cylindrical. No good. Cattle detected them in the feed and wouldn't eat them. Too slippery, maybe. But I think I've got it now."

"Is it harmful?"

"No, that's why it's so great. When the pellets are chewed they get shredded, and after they're swallowed they float in a mat just like hay. Nothing is absorbed into the bloodstream. I've traced it with carbon fourteen."

He chased a tomato around his plate and finally stabbed it. "After an animal is slaughtered, about twenty pounds of the plastic can be recovered and recycled. What's lost through elimination is biodegradable. Plastic roughage is cheaper and more efficient than hay. Each animal needs about four pounds of hay per day.''

He popped the tomato in his mouth, chewed and swallowed, then pointed the tines of his fork at her. "Only one-tenth of a pound of the substitute accomplishes the same end. The money saved is tremendous.''

He looked at the fork, looked at her and gave her a rueful grimace. "Are you finding all this fascinating?''

"Yes, indeed,'' she said with a smile, and actually she was. Somewhat. People with enthusiasm were infectious, and she thought he must be a good teacher, but all this wasn't helping her find Lucille.

Aby removed the salad bowls and put down Susan's chicken and Jack's prime rib. "I've heard Brenner Nieman is back,'' she said to Jack. "You two plan to get into some escapades while he's here?''

"I hope not.'' Jack rubbed a knuckle down one side of his moustache. "I think we're a little too old to be sneaking a calf into the bell tower.''

Aby grinned. "Well, I hope you come in for a meal. It'll seem like old times.''

"Calf in the bell tower?'' Susan said after Aby left.

"Kids. It seemed like a good idea at the time.'' He shook his head in a half-appalled, half-amused memory of adolescent antics. "You can lead a calf up long flights of steps, but there's no way you can lead it down. It caused quite a ruckus. The poor thing had to be carried down in a sling, bawling and struggling.''

"You and Brenner are friends?''

"When we were kids. I haven't seen him for a long time, haven't even heard from him.'' Jack broke open the baked potato and added butter.

"He had some trouble with your father. What was that?''

"With Dad?'' Jack looked startled. "Oh, a long time ago. Brenner was paying too much attention to Lucille to suit

Dad. She was only fourteen or fifteen. I wasn't around. I'd already left home and that kind of left Lucille all by herself." He seemed suddenly to lose vitality and tiredness settled back over his face.

"By herself?"

"Usually it was me that took Dad's wrath."

"You were a rebellious child?"

"I guess you could say that." He smiled. "I'm sure Dad would."

That explained Henry's comment about hero worship, she thought. No wonder Lucille adored Jack, the older brother, bigger and smarter and braver. He must have seemed very heroic, disobeying their father, blazing trails, pushing everything as far as he could and taking punishment with arrogant swagger. Susan wondered if Jack, as she herself had done, had formed an alliance with his mother to get around his father and create enough margin to survive and make choices.

He cut off a chunk of meat, then took a sip of water and looked at her. "You're not at all like Cathy."

"No? What was she like?" She'd seen pictures of Daniel's first wife and knew Cathy had been small and blond and pretty. She hadn't thought much about her until after Daniel's death; then she experienced a fierce jealousy, because Cathy'd had twelve years with him.

"She was sweet, kind of quiet. Didn't Dan tell you about her?"

"I know she was killed when a tree crushed the car she was driving."

"A tornado came up fast. It happens sometimes."

"Sweet and quiet" was probably the kind of wife Helen thought Daniel deserved. Susan jabbed a carrot and ate it. "Did Lucille ever discuss her job with you?"

"Not often. She likes to keep things to herself." He spoke reluctantly, obviously more comfortable discussing rumens and papillae. "Until she's accomplished whatever it is. Then she likes to dazzle everybody with the results."

"Did you know about her late-night drives?"

"Drives?"

"She drove around at night, after midnight—one, two in the morning. Her car was seen going out the road toward Vic Pollock's. Why would she do that?"

He looked puzzled. "I haven't any idea."

"Romantic interest?"

"Good God, no."

She chewed on a piece of chicken. They were now the only people in the dining room; all the others had finished and gone. "Could she have been running some sort of surveillance on Vic?"

"Spying on Vic? Why?"

"Can you think of a reason?"

"No. It doesn't make any sense."

It might, Susan thought, if Vic had killed his wife, and Lucille suspected; perhaps suspected Vic shot Daniel because he found out. "Who would Lucille talk to? Friends?"

"Well—" He poked at the baked potato as though he might find the answer there.

Despite Lucille's hero-worship of her brother, they apparently weren't very close. She didn't discuss with him the things that were important to her.

"Sophie," he said. "She always thought a lot of Sophie."

"What about a man named—" Susan was going to ask him about Doug, he of Lucille's answering machine, when Aby bustled up.

"Excuse me. Jack, there's a phone call for you. They said it was important."

He murmured an apology, dropped his napkin on the table and slid from the booth. Susan went on with her meal, and in a few minutes Aby came back.

"Jack said to tell you he's sorry, but there's some kind of problem. At the lab? He apologizes, but he said he really had to go and see about it."

"Problem?"

"Oh, you know, with those cows he's always going on about."

"I see." Susan reached in her bag for her wallet.

"That's all right. Jack already paid. He said he'd call you in the morning if there was anything else you wanted to know."

Susan nodded. "Aby, do you know Lucille?"

"Sure. I know Jack better, of course. Lucille's younger and she was always just one of those little kids."

"Any idea where she might be?"

Aby shook her head. "Can't understand what's wrong with her, worrying everybody like this."

"Do you know anybody named Doug?"

Aby thought a moment. "No, sure don't."

Snow had stopped falling by the time Susan left the Inn, and it was bitterly cold, but the world looked soft, rounded and beautiful in the dark with lights picking out iridescent colors. She headed for home and would be glad to get there; her head ached, her ankle hurt and her nose felt raw. Her mind picked away at the snarl of exasperation and worry about Lucille. You damn fool, where are you?

THIRTEEN

IN DANIEL'S OFFICE, Susan sat hunched over the desk reading the stacks of reports gathered in the search for Lucille, looking for something, anything that might give a hint where to look next. Her cold was in full bloom and she'd pulled the wastebasket near the desk for tossing in soggy tissues.

Osey had questioned Floyd Kimmell. Floyd claimed he didn't know anything and hadn't seen Lucille. Floyd was nervous.

George had questioned Vic Pollock. Vic hadn't seen Lucille; stuck to the story his wife was visiting relatives. He was belligerent.

Otto Guthman thought he might have some cattle missing. He wasn't positive, was still trying to get an accurate count. He had no idea where Lucille was, insisted she was fine, she'd be back any time now. Ella Guthman was frantic about her daughter, but couldn't suggest any place Lucille might be.

Susan arched her back and stretched, then lit a cigarette, moseyed to the window, and yanked on the cord to raise the blinds higher. The glass was fogged with ice crystals on the outside; the sky was gray and overcast. Snow covered the rooftops and the street was a mess of churned-up slush. Three or four people tromped by, all muffled up and trailing streams of vapor.

Why hadn't anybody seen Lucille in the last sixty-two hours? In a town this size, where everybody knew everybody, where could she hide?

Long ash formed on the cigarette; Susan turned from the window, went back to the desk and tapped it against the ashtray. Near the ashtray sat a small framed snapshot of herself in an orange life jacket, hair windblown, taken on the deck of a friend's boat. Daniel had liked that picture. She pitched it in the bottom drawer, then sat down and read Parkhurst's interview with Sophie. Sophie hadn't seen Lucille, had no idea where she was and thought Parkhurst ought to be looking for her instead of wasting time asking questions. The latest missing cat was still missing.

She put out her cigarette, leaned back and gazed at the fluorescent fixture in the ceiling. Could Sophie be hiding Lucille? According to Jack—and he still hadn't called, as he had promised—Lucille considered Sophie a friend, and Sophie was certainly unconventional enough. Susan shook her head. No, couldn't be. Brenner was staying with Sophie. He'd notice. Sophie might hide Lucille, for reasons only understandable to herself, but surely Brenner wouldn't go along.

Susan wondered about the injured man and checked with the hospital. Still alive. Still no change in his condition. She remembered the phone bill she'd seen in Lucille's office and shoved around papers to find her notebook, then cleared a space and studied the list of calls Lucille had made in December. Two numbers had been called several times each.

Osey ambled in. "Ma'am?"

She looked up.

"Ben asked me to tell you he's talking to neighbors about Emma Lou Pollock, trying to pin down more how long she's been gone and where she might be."

She nodded. Two missing women? One dead, one missing? Two dead? "Osey, do you recognize either of these phone numbers?"

He bent over the desk. "This here's the *Kansas City News*." He put a finger on the bill. "Don't know this one, it's Kansas City too, by the prefix." He straightened, stepped back and waited.

She reached for the phone, then, aware he was still waiting, said, "Thanks, Osey. That's all."

"Right." He ambled out.

She punched the number he couldn't identify and got a recorded message. "This is Doug McClay. Leave your name and number and I'll get back to you."

She left her name and both police department and home numbers, then broke the connection and cradled the receiver against her shoulder. Doug McClay. Kansas City. She pushed a button to get Hazel.

"Yes, Susan?"

"Hazel, do we have a Kansas City phone book?"

"Sure do. White pages or Yellow?"

"Both, I guess."

Hazel brought in the phone books and eyed Susan with concern. "You don't look so good. You should be home in bed."

"It's just a cold. As long as I breathe through my mouth I'm fine." Susan looked up the *Kansas City News*. Osey was right about that number. And a Doug McClay was listed in Kansas City, with an address on Morganhill Drive.

She called Jack and the phone rang, unanswered. She tried Emerson College and was told Dr. Guthman was teaching a class. Thinking maybe Lucille's mother would know Doug McClay, Susan phone the Guthmans'; the housekeeper said neither Ella nor Otto was home.

She thought a moment, then flipped through Yellow Pages to hotels. Hotels, hotels. Drake, Drake. Yes. Drake Hotel. She reached for the phone again.

"Drake Hotel, may I help you?"

"Do you have a Lucille Guthman staying there?"

There was a pause. "Yes. Ms. Guthman is a guest here."

"Would you ring her room, please." She let it ring until the receptionist broke in to say, "That number doesn't answer."

Susan broke the connection and pushed the button for Hazel. "I don't suppose you happen to have a street map of Kansas City."

"I might. Let me check."

A moment later, Hazel came in and handed her the map.

IT WAS AFTER THREE by the time she found Morganhill Drive, a quiet residential street of mostly new homes, with spindly trees and bare front lots. She had crossed the river into Missouri before she came to Doug McClay's address.

It was a small two-story house, red brick with white trim and a steep, peaked roof. She pressed the doorbell and waited, then stepped to her right for a try at looking through the window. The curtain covered it completely. Irritated, she rang the bell again. Well, not surprising, since he hadn't answered the phone, but some people let the machine pick up calls and she'd thought it worth a try.

The garage sat at the end of a long driveway with two narrow paths shoveled clear of snow. Why bother to shovel the whole driveway when all you really need are two tracks to get the car in and out? Hands shoved in her pockets, she walked up a cleared path to see if a car was inside the garage. The overhead door was shut and locked, the only window too high to look through. She scribbled a note asking McClay to call as soon as possible and stuck it in the mailbox.

THE DRAKE WAS a small hotel and as Susan tromped up to the entrance, an elderly man with a cane struggled with the door on his way out. She held it open for him. He smiled, wound a scarf around his throat and said, "Got to keep moving."

Quite right, she thought, and smiled back.

The lobby had green couches and gold chairs with potted plants lurking in the corners. The young woman at the reception desk reluctantly placed her paperback romance face down on the counter and fixed her gaze on Susan. A mass of frizzed brown hair obscured a small face, giving the impression of a timid animal sheltering behind a thicket. A white pin with the name Patsy was attached to her red sweater. Susan asked for Lucille Guthman's room number.

"She has three-ten, but she's not in."

"How do you know?"

"Because you're the second person this afternoon who's asked."

"Who was the other?"

Patsy raked back her hair and as soon as she let go, it fell over her eyes again. "He didn't leave his name."

"What did he look like?"

Patsy gave her a suspicious look. "Why did you want to know?"

"Maybe I know him."

"Oh. Well. Nice." Patsy smiled a dreamy smile and seemed to drift off in a fugue.

Whoever he was, he'd certainly had an impact on her. "Was he tall?"

Patsy nodded. "Blond hair. And handsome, you know? He was real mad about something. I could tell. But nice anyway."

"What was he wearing?"

"Black pants and a white sweater. One of those fisherman's sweaters with all the cables? Oh, and he had black gloves."

Susan thought of Brenner Nieman and his slick, blond handsomeness, then decided that was pretty farfetched. How would Brenner know Lucille was here, and why would he come to see her even if he did know? There must be more than one blond, handsome man in this part of the world.

"He said he'd try again later," Patsy said. "Would you like me to tell him you were here?"

"When did you last see Lucille?"

"Oh, gee. That would have been yesterday." Patsy thought a moment, then nodded.

"Did she say anything?"

"No. Well, hello or like that."

"Was she going out?"

"I guess so."

"Where was she going?"

Patsy shrugged.

"What time was that?"

"About three o'clock."

"When did she check in?"

"Monday night," Patsy said.

"What time?"

Patsy shrugged again and her fingers strayed toward the novel. "I don't work the night shift."

"I'll just go up and see if she's come back."

"Okay, but I know she isn't there."

Patsy snatched up her book and Susan went to the elevator. On the third floor, she knocked on the door of room three-ten and got no response.

No sounds from inside and the door was locked; a DO NOT DISTURB sign hung from the knob. "Lucille? Open the door. I need to talk with you." She waited. "Come on, Lucille. This is silly."

A couple came out of a room further along the hallway and went past chatting about where they might go for supper. Susan dabbed at her drippy nose with a tissue, shoved it in her pocket and looked at her watch. Almost four-thirty. She got back in the elevator and it groaned and grumbled its way down to the first floor.

Putting down the novel, Patsy gave her a smug smile. "I told you she wasn't in. She went out early this morning."

"How do you know that?"

"Because she left a wake-up call for seven and she didn't answer. So she must have gone before then."

"Maybe she was in the shower."

"Pretty long shower. She was called at seven and then at eight and then at eight-thirty. She just got up earlier than she planned."

"Did you see her leave?"

Patsy shook her head. "She could have had breakfast in the coffee shop, I guess."

In the coffee shop, Susan found the manager, a man in his forties, behind the cashier's desk and asked if Lucille had been in for breakfast. "Twenty-five," Susan said to jiggle his memory. "Pretty. Blond curly hair, blue eyes."

"Oh yeah. I think she was here."

"This morning? What time?"

"No, yesterday."

"You haven't seen her today?"

"I don't think so. We get kind of busy around here." His voice trailed off and he thought a moment. "Guthman, yeah." He shuffled through a pile of order cards. "Three-ten. She left a request with room service yesterday evening. Coffee at seven this morning."

"And you took it up to her?"

"One of the girls did. Hey, Joan," he called to a waitress who hustled over. "You take that coffee to three-ten this morning?"

Joan nodded. "I knocked, but nobody answered so I just left the tray by the door. Anything wrong?"

"You picked up the tray later?" Susan asked.

"I didn't. One of the maids brought it down. I guess she didn't want coffee after all, because the pot was still full. The cup hadn't been used."

"Guests." The manager's shrug said nothing a guest ever did would surprise him.

Susan took the groaning elevator back up to the third floor. She was getting a bad feeling about all this. A laundry cart stood outside the open door of three-twelve and sounds of a vacuum cleaner drifted out. At three-ten, the DO NOT DISTURB sign was still on the doorknob. Lucille still didn't answer a knock. Susan wondered what she should do. A sneeze had her groping for Kleenex. Damn cold. She could just camp outside this door and wait. Another part of her mind said something was wrong.

Lucille hadn't been seen since yesterday afternoon. She didn't meet Doug McClay when she was supposed to. She didn't answer her wake-up call, didn't drink the coffee ordered yesterday evening, didn't return any of Doug's five calls, didn't answer the phone.

Susan thought about taking all this to the Kansas City police. To get in the room, they'd need a search warrant; to get that, they'd need to show probable cause. Could she do that? Missing person. *Who said she was missing?* Her mother. *Nothing illegal about not telling your mother what hotel you're at.* I'm worried. After they stopped laughing, they'd tell her to fuck off.

She tried to tell herself she could be wrong. All that did was make her worry more.

The hum of the vacuum cleaner stopped, and after a moment a maid came trundling it out of the next room. Her name tag read Delores; she was a middle-aged woman who walked as though her feet hurt.

"Have you cleaned this room today?" Susan asked her.

"Not yet. It's been there all day." Delores nodded at the sign hanging on the doorknob. "I can't go home until I clean in there."

"I'm a police officer." Susan flipped open her ID case. She had no authority here, but most people don't scrutinize police identification. "Would you unlock the door, please?"

Delores gave her a dubious look, then with a shrug pulled a key from her pocket and inserted it in the lock. She pushed the door in, stepped away and took her laundry cart and her vacuum and her tired feet off down the corridor.

The room was dark inside, the curtains closed. Running a hand along the wall, Susan located the light switch and turned it on. Brown carpeting, double bed made up but rumpled, long, low desk-chest combination across one wall with a television set on one end. An easy chair and a small round table in the corner with a hanging lamp above; a spiral notebook on the table.

She turned on the bathroom light. Hum and rattle of the exhaust fan. Unused towels, paper-wrapped glasses, cosmetics on the countertop and a toothbrush, dry. Shower curtain pulled across the tub.

She jerked it aside, then let out a breath. The tub was empty, clean and dry. No dead body sprawled on the white porcelain.

The closet had one small suitcase and a few items of clothing on hangers. She started to worry about having gotten the maid to let her in here. She'd be in trouble if Lucille or the hotel filed a breaking-and-entering or illegal-search complaint. As nearly as she could tell, nothing seemed amiss. No sign of any struggle.

On her way out, she picked up the notebook from the table. Nothing but blank paper with thin strips twisted in the spiral where pages had been ripped out. She tossed down the notebook and noticed a small white triangle of paper stuck between the edge of the carpet and the wall behind the table. She bent to retrieve it; a corner of lined paper with two penciled words, "like sleet."

As she straightened, her eye caught a quick glint of something small and shiny beneath the bed. She went to the bed, leaned down to lift back the spread and stared into a blue, mottled face.

Blood roared in her ears, air got trapped in her lungs, an acid taste filled her mouth.

Lucille lay on her back, head twisted to the right. A blue scarf cut into her neck; her eyes bulged; her tongue protruded. The light sparkled on one silver earring.

Susan dropped to her knees and braced herself on both hands. Oh Jesus.

Blowing out air with a long breath, she stood up.

There was a loud pounding on the door.

"Police! Open up!"

FOURTEEN

SHE FROZE.

More pounding. "Police! Open up."

When she opened the door, the two uniformed police-men eyed her with carefully bland faces. One was tall, with sandy hair, the other slightly shorter and stocky, with short black hair.

"Would you mind telling us what you're doing here?" The taller man spoke to her.

"Don't get excited. I'm a cop."

He raised skeptical eyebrows. She started to get identifi-cation from her shoulder bag and the stocky man took a step closer. "Don't move."

"What's your name?" the taller man asked.

"Susan Wren. Yours?"

"Riley." He inclined his head at the other officer. "Brandelli."

"Well, Officer Riley, the young woman who rented this room has been strangled." She paused. "Her body's under the bed."

Riley tensed, looked at Brandelli and gave a short nod. Brandelli squatted by the bed, lifted the bedspread, looked up at Riley and nodded in return.

"Have you any identification, Miss Wren?"

She patted her bag. Brandelli held out a hand. "If you don't mind."

He took the bag and dumped the contents on the table, then grinned at her, a flash of white teeth in a dark face. "Got a permit for this?" Taking a pen from his shirt pocket, he isolated Daniel's .38.

Funny man. She glared at him and pointed out her identification.

"Hampstead," he said with not quite a sneer, and handed it to Riley. "What we have here is a chief of police."

Riley glanced at her identification, then said to Brandelli, "Call it in."

AN HOUR LATER she was perched on a hard wooden chair in Captain Dayton's office. She was alone. He'd left her to stew, a trick she'd used many times herself, and now she was realizing just how effective it was. The professional part of her mind pointed out she'd been very stupid and just might see her career as a cop swirl and disappear down the drain with a glug.

The door opened behind her and she jumped. Captain Dayton strode to the desk, stood there and regarded her with cynic's eyes. She sat up straighter; she was in the presence of authentic authority. He was a large, square man in a rumpled brown sport coat, with a heavy jaw and a dark stubble of beard, thick dark eyebrows and a receding hairline. He tossed her ID on the desk. It landed with a slap. They both stared at it.

"Says here"—he leaned forward and obliterated her picture with a blunt thumb—"you're Susan Wren." He had a deep gravelly voice.

She nodded.

"Says you're chief of police of Hampstead, Kansas."

She looked up at him.

"That right, young lady? You really Hampstead's police chief?"

"Yes, sir."

He grunted and threw down her driver's license, tapped her picture with his thumb. "Says here you're Susan Donovan."

"Maiden name. I . . . uh, I've not been married long."

"Says here San Francisco. San Francisco, California? That right?" He glared at her, then hooked an ankle around the chair leg, pulled it out and dropped into it. "So, Susan Wren or Susan Donovan or whatever your name is, what were you doing in that hotel room?"

She took a breath and let it out slowly. "Lucille Guthman's been missing for three days. I've been looking for her, to question in connection with a murder." She gave him a succinct and coherent report of the investigation into Daniel's death.

Dayton listened without comment except for an occasional grunt or lift of his dark eyebrows. It might have been her former boss she was facing with queasy apprehension. Chase Reardon was smoother and slicker, soft-voiced, and communicated with words rather than grunts, but the atmosphere and its effect on her were the same. She'd been called in to get her ass chewed, and the awful part was she knew she deserved it.

When she was finished, Dayton crossed his arms over his broad chest and glowered from under his dark eyebrows. "Why did you go in that room?"

"I don't—"

"You ever hear of a goddamn search warrant? You ever hear of probable cause? I don't know how you do things in your area, but around here we don't illegally enter hotel rooms. Citizens have rights." His voice held no sarcasm; captains didn't need to be sarcastic.

"She was dead."

"So she was. You claim you didn't know that when you went in."

"Yes, sir."

"You left Hampstead at what time?"

"Twelve-thirty."

"Uh-huh."

There was an uncomfortable silence.

"Coffee?" he asked.

She took a breath, then nodded.

He leaned forward with a jerk of the chair, picked up the phone and growled at somebody. Replacing the receiver, he leaned back again.

An officer brought in two Styrofoam cups and put them on the desk. Dayton leaned forward, removed a plastic lid, sailed it toward the wastebasket and offered her the cup.

She took a sip. "I'm out of cigarettes."

He fished a crumpled pack from his shirt pocket and tossed it on the desk. She shook one out and lit it. It wasn't her brand, and the smoke was harsh against her dry throat. She coughed. Well, Daniel, what do you think? Presumptuous of me to assume I could handle your job, and serves me right?

Dayton raised his cup and eyed her over the rim. "How did you know Miss Guthman had been strangled?"

"What?"

"You told Riley she was strangled. How'd you know?"

"I saw her. I lifted the bedspread and there she was with the scarf around her throat and her face blue. Strangled is strangled, Captain, whether it's my area or around here." Her voice dripped with sarcasm and she regretted it immediately. His expression told her if she worked for him she'd be back on patrol in a minute. Reardon would have reacted the same, if she were lucky.

"You entered the room shortly after five. Riley got there at five-ten. You were in there with the body for about ten minutes. What did you do?"

"I didn't know *the body* was there. I went in and I looked around. I only found her just when Riley got there."

"You searched the room."

She hesitated, nodded.

"Find anything?"

"No, sir."

"Destroy anything?"

"No, sir. How long has she been dead?"

Silence. Then he said, "A while. We won't know until after the autopsy. Probably dead somewhere around twelve to sixteen hours."

Lucille had been killed then, Susan thought, Wednesday night or early this morning.

"You ought to be charged," he said.

"With what?"

Shark's smile. "How about impersonating a police officer?"

Ha ha. "How did you know I was in there?"

"The maid. Who got to worrying about her job. Who told the receptionist, who told the manager, who called us."

He stared at her, black eyes pinning her stiffly to the chair. "There are a number of legal possibilities here," he said. "Like accessory after the fact. Obstructing—"

"I'm not an accessory to anything. I've obstructed nothing. Are you going to charge me?"

He grunted and shoved the phone toward her. She raised an eyebrow.

"Get somebody down here with proper credentials to vouch for you."

She picked up the receiver and punched a number. Parkhurst answered. Damn, damn. She'd hoped for George.

"This is Susan," she said crisply and explained where she was. "I'd appreciate it if you'd come here."

When she hung up she said to Dayton, "A man named Parkhurst will be here as soon as he can. He will tell you I am who I am."

"Ben Parkhurst?"

"You know him?"

Dayton gave a bark of laughter. "I've worked with him."

Bloody hell, of course he had. She might have known.

Again, Dayton left her alone in his office. The same officer brought her more coffee and her own brand of cigarettes. She asked him if he could find her some Kleenex and he brought those too. It was almost nine when Dayton returned; Parkhurst, darkly angry, was with him. She stood up. Parkhurst, dressed in black pants, gray sweater and a black jacket with the collar turned up, looked at her with a hard, flat expression. Dayton's fleshy face held an expression of amused malice; he had, no doubt, been enjoying jokes at Parkhurst's expense.

"The hotel manager," Dayton said, "is more bothered by a guest murdered than a room entered illegally." He glowered at her, then finally said, "Get out of here."

She took a breath, removed her trench coat from the back of the chair and slipped it on.

"Been interesting running into you," Dayton said to her, then gave Parkhurst a wolfish grin. "Good to see you again, Ben."

A muscle twitched in Parkhurst's jaw. "I'd appreciate it if you'd let me know what surfaces in the investigation, and I'd like a copy of the autopsy report."

Right. *I'd* appreciate that too.

Dayton nodded. "You'll get it."

She could feel Parkhurst seething as he followed her down the stairs. She had committed an unforgivable sin, embarrassed him in front of his colleagues.

At the front desk, a man stood talking to two uniformed officers; a tall man with blond hair, straight eyebrows and square jaw. His gaze caught hers and held it for a moment; then one of the officers spoke to him and he turned away. She didn't know him, but there was something intense about his scrutiny of her. Had he been brought in for questioning in Lucille's death? She started toward him.

Parkhurst caught her arm. "Where're you going?"

"To find out who that is."

"Come on."

"I just want to—"

He hustled her out the door. She went along with him, furious with herself for doing so. When they reached his Bronco, she felt the effort it took for him to refrain from shoving her inside. Her chest was tight with her own anger: anger at herself for letting him drag her away, anger at him for rescuing her and anger at Lucille for getting killed.

"Why the hell did you do a stupid thing like that?" he said as he started the Bronco and sped out.

"Like what?" The dark streets were empty and glistened under the headlights, trash fluttered around the frozen slush along the curbs.

"Don't be obtuse. If you're going to play at being chief, you'd better stick to the rules."

Rules. Rules of the game. Games and rules. She knew the game and she knew the rules just as well as he did, but Daniel was dead and now Lucille. "I didn't plan on getting caught."

"Every dumb shit who holds up a gas station thinks like that."

She took short, fast breaths; the tension in the car seemed to burn up all the oxygen. It was too warm and the thrum of the heater resonated through her head.

"You're getting yourself in trouble and making Hampstead look like a joke." Streetlights threw flickering shadows across his dark face, briefly highlighting his cheekbones and upper lip.

Not Hampstead, him. Making *him* look like a joke. She wanted to tell him to go to hell, but he was right. In the line of duty, he could inform the mayor, and Bakover could justifiably dismiss her. She'd behaved like a civilian and had no right to be angry. "I found Lucille."

His upper lip pulled flat, giving her a glimpse of white teeth. "Yeah, you did that."

"I'll have to tell the family."

Parkhurst pulled into the hotel parking lot where she'd left the pickup. "I'll go with you," he said as she got out of the Bronco.

She slammed the door; cold air hit her like a fist. Shaking, she climbed into the pickup and drove too fast, came into a curve with the tires screaming and a slow motorist just ahead. She swerved around and dropped back to a much safer speed. Parkhurst stayed three car-lengths behind and once they reached Hampstead, he followed all the way to the Guthmans'.

FRIDAY MORNING in Daniel's office, her eyes felt gritty, and even coffee hadn't much affected her sluggish brain. The only good news, her cold was getting better. It had been late by the time she'd gotten home after telling the Guthmans of Lucille's death. When she finally went to sleep she dreamed. Over and over, she bent to lift the bedspread and stare into the dead blue face.

She glanced through the reports Osey had left on the desk. Perfectly typed, no errors or strikeovers, but that's all she could say for them. Floyd Kimmell claimed he hadn't gone to Kansas City Wednesday night. He'd been at home, in bed, asleep. He hadn't strangled Lucille. Vic Pollock, with a great deal of bluster, claimed much the same.

She rubbed her eyes. Inconclusive. Either could be lying. Floyd lived alone and, with his wife gone, so did Vic. Either could have driven to Kansas City, strangled Lucille and driven home. Why had Lucille gone to Kansas City?

She tried to reach Doug McClay, with no luck. Even though the Kansas City police were investigating Lucille's murder, her death was connected with Daniel's, and Susan intended to question McClay.

She lit a cigarette and smoked in short, frustrated puffs, wondering what Jack Guthman could tell her about McClay. Crushing out the cigarette, she rang Jack's number, then tried the Guthmans'. The housekeeper informed her Jack had gone into Emerson.

She slid on her white trench coat, slung the strap of her bag over her shoulder and went out to the pickup. When she pulled out of the lot, she had to brake quickly to avoid a dusty gray Mustang that turned abruptly in front of her.

Emerson College, founded in 1858, now covered 320 acres with buildings including dorms, labs, chapels and a small theater, all settled into gently rolling hills with large ancient trees: bare-limbed maples, elms and walnuts. The buildings were a mixture of old and modern, many of them made of the warm, creamy-colored limestone. Pathways cut across snow-covered slopes that sparkled in the bright sunshine, and students in jeans and down jackets hurried along heading for classes.

Susan turned into an oval street with a canopy of giant maples and stopped in front of the administration building. It was one of the older buildings, rectangular, three-storied with a flat roof and three imposing stone arches guarding the main door.

The office seemed dark after the bright sunshine; she blinked to help her eyes adjust, then asked a young woman behind the counter where she could find Jack Guthman. The woman consulted a schedule and said Dr. Guthman was at the Rumen Metabolism Laboratory in the rear of Lehman Hall. Susan asked for directions and set off on one of the pathways, slushy with trampled snow.

A student ran flat-footed toward her, papers clutched between his outstretched hands, and muttering, "Oh God, oh God." He gave her a wild-eyed stare. "I didn't hear the alarm," he said, and plunged down the path.

She smiled sympathetically. Her student days at the University of California in Berkeley were long in the past, but not so long that she'd forgotten the late nights finishing assignments and the frantic scrambles getting to class in the morning. Back then, she was working for civil rights and calling cops pigs. Things do change.

At Lehman Hall, she wandered down a corridor and stopped in the doorway of a lab to ask a student in a white smock where experiments in bovine nutrition were being done. She was told the doorway at the end.

The large metal door held a sign that read "EXPERI-MENTS IN PROGRESS. DO NOT ENTER." She knocked. Jack, wearing a long white lab coat and carrying a clipboard, opened the door. He looked terrible, face haggard and gray, dark shadows under his eyes. There seemed to be less of him, as though he'd lost weight overnight.

"A few questions," she said gently.

A spark of emotion flashed briefly in his eyes, but was gone before she could interpret it. Anger, probably, at the messenger who'd brought the bad news.

He hesitated a moment, then looked at his watch. "I have a few things to check."

"I'll wait."

The large, high-ceilinged room was windowless and dimly lit. Four cows, mahogany-colored with white faces, stood placidly in head stanchions. Each one had a round, black object like half a tennis ball protruding from its side. A student in a long black apron, with an elbow-length plastic glove on one arm, waited by the cows, looking at her with interest.

"Eric," Jack said as they walked toward him, "this is Chief Wren. My assistant," he said to Susan. He made a notation on the clipboard, then nodded to Eric, who reached for the black cap and pulled, removing it like a cork from a bottle and exposing the interior of the cow's stom-ach. Susan felt her own stomach muscles tighten and she swallowed.

"It was done surgically," Jack said. "So we can see what's happening in the digestive tract."

Inching closer, she bent to look at the deep inner secrets of the animal: dark, humid reservoir, gurgling sounds. A mass of partially digested hay floated on liquid.

Jack nodded again at Eric, who reached into the cow and pulled out a handful of grayish-yellow hay. The cow seemed sublimely unconcerned. Eric held out the steaming, drip-ping mass for Jack's inspection.

He made a notation on the clipboard. "This one's healthy. Nice mat of hay for the scratching action that's vital."

Delicately, like an ornithologist replacing a hatchling in its nest, Eric reinserted the sodden hay and put back the rubber cap. The next cow seemed listless. It was swaybacked and stood with its feet spread as though to keep from falling. When Eric removed the cap, the animal wheezed and lurched. A dirty gray froth bubbled up from the hole.

"This is the result of a high-starch diet and no hay. Bacteria overproduce and create the foam." Jack made notes on the clipboard and, when he finished, went to a deep sink in the corner to wash his hands.

Taking off the lab coat, he hung it in a cupboard and pulled on a tweed jacket. "My office," he said, and she nodded.

They walked along the dim corridor and out into the cold air and bright sunshine. She squinted. He didn't speak as they took a pathway down a slope to another building, but she could sense some strong internal struggle going on in his mind. As they passed the admin building, she noticed a dusty gray Mustang pull up in front.

In his office, she sat in a chair by the metal desk piled with exam papers. He sat behind it, as though it were a barricade that might protect him, with his back to the window, which looked out over the path they had just walked down. Chemistry textbooks and bound copies of professional journals jammed all the bookshelves except one in the middle that had a neat row of plastic bags. A poster of Swiss Alps and a framed sketch of an old man peering through a microscope hung on the wall.

Wearily, he rubbed his eyes that had the slightly unfocused look of shock, then ran a thumb and forefinger down his moustache. "I canceled my classes, but you can't just cancel experiments. They don't wait. You have to—" He shook his head and shoved his hand in his jacket pocket.

"Yes." If he thought she disapproved of his working on the day after learning of Lucille's death, he was wrong. Whatever gets you through. "I believe Lucille was killed because she knew something about Daniel's murder."

"I keep seeing her. Lucille. I was eight when she was born. Red-faced squalling little thing. Seeing her. The new bike she got for her birthday. She was ten, I think. Always following me around. Graduation from high school. First job. First day at the newspaper."

"What did Lucille know?"

He shook his head.

"Think, Jack. She knew something. What was it?"

"I've tried to think. My mind just—"

The neat, efficient mind, so good at solving problems with cows' stomachs, was unequipped to cope with his sister's death.

"Anything, Jack. A comment, a question, an odd response."

"I— No," he said. "No, nothing."

"She knew something, suspected something that made her death imperative. What was it?"

His face seemed even grayer and he looked at her blankly, then shook his head, more as though trying to clear it than in negative response to her questions.

"Why would she go to Kansas City?"

"I don't know."

"What reason could she have?"

"Maybe—maybe simply to get away."

"Why, Jack? Why would she want to get away?"

He slumped back in his chair and she could feel him drawing further in on himself, putting up protective barriers against her probing.

"What do you know about Doug McClay?"

"He's a reporter for the *Kansas City News,* doing the kind of thing Lucille wanted to do." Jack took his hand from his pocket and bounced five or six small colorless pebbles on his palm.

"He was a friend?"

"Yes."

"Close friend? A lover?"

Jack turned to stare out the window and let the pellets trickle through his fingers. "I expect so. He asked her to marry him. She told him she wasn't ready to get married."

"Have you met him?"

"Once. He didn't like me."

"Why?"

Holding the pellets in one palm, he rubbed his thumb over them. "Just one of those things."

Not surprising maybe, jealousy of the adored brother. None of this was getting her anywhere; her shotgun questions weren't penetrating his shock and grief. Maybe he didn't know anything to tell her. She watched him toss the pellets from one hand to the other.

"What are those?"

He looked at the pellets as though he didn't know how they'd gotten there. "Artificial roughage." He let them dribble through his fingers onto the desk. "They always seem to be in my pockets. I'm not sure how that happens." He tried a smile that didn't work.

She picked up a pebble that looked like a miniature ten-gallon hat.

"I think that's it," he said.

"What?"

"The right shape." He rose, collected several plastic bags from the shelf and lined them up on the desk.

"This is what I started with." Opening a bag, he poured out a handful of dish-shaped pellets. "This has all taken so long because I've had to hustle around for grant money."

He opened another. "I had high hopes for this shape, but cattle wouldn't eat them." Picking up a handful of cylindrical pellets, he let them slip through his fingers like a prospector handling gold nuggets.

"After it's been chewed and swallowed, it looks like this." From another bag, he pulled out a clump of grated material that looked like some sort of weird seaweed that might accompany a Japanese dinner.

He flipped a hat-shaped pellet toward her. "Try it."

She looked at it dubiously.

"Go ahead. It's not harmful."

She stuck it in her mouth and tried to bite down. It felt like chomping on a toothbrush handle.

"It's incredible," he said. "It works fantastically better than I ever expected. It's going to make great changes in the cattle business."

She chewed. Gradually, the pellet flattened and became the consistency of the jujubes she used to get at the movies when she was a kid. Her jaw muscles ached. She took it out and stuck it in her pocket.

"Jack." She was sorry to bring him back. "If you think of anything that might help, please let me know."

The lines of strain returned and a look of pain crossed his face. She thought he was again seeing images of Lucille.

"I—" He picked up a handful of pellets. "Yes, of course."

She stood up. "I will find out who killed her," she told him quietly.

"Will you?" His voice was distant. His hand scooped up a few pellets and he pushed them into his pocket.

"Oh yes," she said softly.

She trudged back up to the admin building where she'd left the pickup. A dusty gray Mustang was parked next to it. Waste of time, she thought as she started the truck. She'd made Jack think about Lucille's death and gotten nothing. Better if she'd spent the time tracking down Doug McClay. Why was he so hard to get hold of? She stopped at Erle's

Market and bought soup, cheese and bread and went home to have lunch.

Taking the mail from the box, she tucked it under her arm and unlocked the door. She turned up the heat and glanced through the mail. The letter from her mother brought a rush of homesickness. The rest of the mail she added to the pile on the desk in the small room with French doors off the living room.

In the kitchen, she put away groceries and opened a can of chicken noodle soup. While it heated, she read the letter. Tears puddled up. She saw her mother's face looking down at her with great tenderness. She was six years old and miserable with some kind of flu. She wanted to rush right home and give herself up to her mother's care.

Across the bottom, her father had written, "When are you going to stop this nonsense and get back here!" That did it. A perceptive man in so many ways, he had never learned that pushing his only child was guaranteed to make her go the opposite way.

She stirred the soup, then stared out the window over the sink at the bird feeder on the elm tree. A pair of starlings perched briefly and then flew away. Daniel liked to feed the birds. The feeder hadn't been filled since he died, one week and one day ago. Maybe she ought to buy birdseed. Just as she poured soup in a bowl, the door bell rang.

The tall blond man on her doorstep was the man she'd seen at the Kansas City police station last night. He wore a dark blue jacket, corduroy pants and black gloves. Parked in the driveway was a dusty gray Mustang.

"Chief Wren?" It was a statement more than a question, and he gave her a diffident smile. "My name is McClay. I've been trying to catch up with you all morning."

FIFTEEN

"I GOT MESSAGES you wanted to see me." He sprawled in one of the blue-flowered curved-back chairs near the fireplace.

Indeed, she did, and nice of him to oblige, she thought with mild suspicion. No tracking him down, no insistence, no taking herself to him at his convenience. What did he want?

"Thanks," he murmured when she handed him a cup of coffee.

She took a sip from the cup she was carrying, settled in an identical curved-back chair and put the cup and saucer on the small table between them.

Winter sunshine slanted through the window and made a bright rectangle on the silvery-gray carpet. He stared at it, blinked and rubbed his eyes. He looked tired, as though he'd been up all night. He probably had.

"I want to know what happened to Lucille," he said.

She could see anger in his eyes and tension in the tightness of muscles around his mouth. Another male grappling with paralyzing emotions. Jack tried to insulate himself with work; Doug was apparently handling grief and anger by trying to comprehend, make sense out of the senseless. She understood that. "The Kansas City police are investigating Lucille's death."

He brushed that aside with an impatient gesture. "The answer is here and so is the killer."

"Why do you say that?"

He shot her an irritated look. "Don't play games with me. I want to know who killed her. Whoever it was murdered your husband. You've been investigating his death for over a week. Are you getting anywhere?''

"Did you know Daniel?''

''No,'' he said sharply, then took a breath and gave her a diffident smile. "Look,'' he said more softly, ''I'm sorry, I'm not doing this very well. Let me start again. I don't know anybody here. I've been talking with the Kansas City police, and they said you found her body. I'd just like to hear about it.''

"You don't know Jack Guthman?''

''No.'' He started to shake his head and then said with a heavy sigh, ''I met him once. What does it matter?''

It probably didn't, but Jack had said they'd met and if Doug thought of lying about that, he'd likely lie about other things. ''Jack said you didn't like him. Why not?''

She could see him make a great effort to control his impatience. He shrugged. ''I just didn't see why Lucille idolized him.''

"When did you last see her?''

"Tuesday evening. We—'' He hesitated, then said flatly, ''Argued.''

Now there's an understatement. The argument had probably been a bitter fight, leaving behind regrets for harsh words spoken in heat that could never be apologized for.

"She was obsessed by your husband's murder. It was all she thought about or talked about. Goddammit, if she'd left it alone, she'd still be alive.''

"What did she know?''

''Know?'' Distractedly, he ran a hand through his blond hair, which glinted gold in a shaft of sunlight. ''She didn't *know* anything.''

Wrong. Lucille knew something, at least suspected something. Susan was certain of it without having any hard evidence. Maybe Lucille hadn't told Doug, or maybe he was keeping the information to himself. Reporters tended to treat information like a savings account, not to be used indiscriminately but invested only where it would bring a good return. What kind of return was he looking for?

"Why did Lucille go to Kansas City?" she asked.

He took a gulp of coffee, put the cup on the saucer with a clink and pulled a glossy folder from his pocket. She took it from his outstretched hand and glanced at a prospectus for something called Meadow Manor, with artist's sketches of three different homes, lush lawns, a profusion of flowers, swimming pools and stately trees that seemed to sway to seductive breezes. She gave him a questioning look.

"That's why she went to Kansas City," he said. "To check into that housing development."

"Why?"

"The development was started by leasing the land. The speculator got enough cash and credit together to print up these brochures, rent a fancy office, hire an architect and get three model homes built. Stage One. Then he sold limited partnerships to finance the construction of homes. Stage Two. So far so good, except he had to use that money to make lease payments and pay the architect in Stage One. Now we move to Stage Three, the golf club and golf course."

Turning over the brochure, she looked at the artist's rendering of clubhouse and fairways, so lovely she could almost hear the swish, swish of sprinklers. "Why was Lucille interested?"

He ignored the question. "More partnerships were sold on the proposed golf course and that money used to shore up the housing construction in Stage Two."

"Mr. McClay—"

"This whole house of cards is about to come tumbling down, unless he can figure out a Stage Four to keep Stage Three from going belly-up. The money's gone, credit's gone, construction has stopped and the site looks deserted. The fancy office complex has one little receptionist and lots of closed doors so a potential customer won't see the offices are empty.''

"Mr. McClay, this is all very fascinating, but what does it have to do with Lucille?"

"The speculator is Brenner Niemen."

"Brenner," she repeated.

"He needs money, lots of it, and in pretty good time."

"Maybe you could explain why Lucille was so interested in Brenner's business affairs."

Doug stared at her. "Lucille believed he killed your husband and she was set on proving it."

Susan lit a cigarette and stared at him through the smoke. "Why did Lucille believe that?"

He swirled the coffee, tipped up the cup, and drained it. "I don't know," he said slowly. "It was more a case of deciding the guy was guilty and working hard to find a reason."

All this stuff about Meadow Manor might make an interesting article on the back page of the newspaper, but he was a journalist; his job was to make interesting stories. She had no idea whether she believed him or not.

He gave her a hard look. "Tell me about Lucille."

She told him a carefully edited version of finding the body and nothing of the investigation into Daniel's death except that she had leads which she was following.

After he left, dissatisfied with the little he'd learned, she reheated the soup, made some notes and thought about Brenner while she ate.

Lucille, if Doug could be believed, wanted to prove Brenner was guilty of killing Daniel. Didn't make sense. Even if Brenner needed money—and she was inclined to believe that much, at least—how would killing Daniel help?

It was after four when she got back to the police department, and she was sitting at Daniel's desk simply staring at her notes when George came in.

"Did that McClay fellow find you?" he asked.

She nodded and related her conversation with Doug McClay. "What can you tell me about Brenner Niemen?"

"Well now, Brenner." George pulled on the knees of his dark gray trousers and lowered his rear to the chair. What would she ever do without George? Not only was he doing a lot of her work, but he was a ready source of information on the natives.

"Grew up here," he said. "Went to school, wasn't a very good student, got into scrapes. His folks owned the dry cleaners, ran it themselves. Brenner had to help out after school and summers."

"The parents are both dead?"

George nodded. "That was a sad thing. It happened right after Brenner graduated from high school. There was a fire. The place burned down completely and they were both killed. It's been . . . oh . . ." He took off his glasses, making his gray-blue eyes seem vague and dreamy, drew a handkerchief from his back pocket and cleaned them. "About sixteen, seventeen years."

"What caused the fire?"

He put his glasses back on, bringing his eyes into focus, and stuffed the handkerchief back in his pocket. "Nobody ever did figure that out. There was some thought it was deliberately set, but no kind of proof showed up."

"There was insurance." She took cigarettes from her bag, lit one and dropped the pack on her notebook.

"There was, quite a bit. I don't recall the exact amount. Some thought Brenner Senior might have set it, just so he could collect. Mighty careless if so—got both him and Netty killed. Brenner went to live with Sophie then. Didn't stay long, less than a year, then he took off. Was back every now and then for a year, and then he was gone that long stretch."

"Could he have set the fire?"

"Some thought that, too. Insurance company finally paid off. Money went to Brenner, of course."

"Did you recognize him when he came back?" she asked.

"Recognize him? He was Brenner come back to visit."

"You're sure?"

"You got some idea Brenner isn't Brenner?"

"I wondered if that was a possibility." But even as she said it, she knew it was fancifully unlikely. "Several people have commented they wouldn't have recognized him."

George smiled. "When they say they wouldn't recognize him, they don't mean exactly that. He left here a boy and came back a man. So there's been those changes, but he's moved a long way from his roots, picked up some glossy polish. Folks think he's gotten uppity."

The phone rang, startling her, and she picked it up.

Hazel said, "Helen's on the line."

Susan felt the amorphous guilt she always felt about Daniel's sister. She asked George to have someone check Doug's information on Meadow Manor and find out if Lucille had been digging for it. When he left she said to Hazel, "Put her on."

"I've been waiting to hear from you," Helen said.

"Yes, I understand, but—"

"I don't understand why you're stalling."

Because I can't let you have Daniel's farm until I know you didn't kill him. "I've had a number of things on my mind," she said dryly.

"I'm sure. I'd like to get this settled before the buyer backs out."

"Who is the buyer?"

Silence. "Otto Guthman," Helen said with some reluctance.

"Why? He has plenty of land."

"My land adjoins his. He's been renting it to raise cattle feed."

"I see," Susan said. "I need a little more time. If Guthman's the buyer, it's unlikely he'll back out."

Reaching to put out the cigarette, she brushed her notebook off the desk and when she bent to retrieve it she saw the listed amounts of Lucille's little stack of canceled checks. "Helen, do you know who might lend Lucille money?"

"What?"

"Who would have lent Lucille five hundred dollars several years ago?"

"What on earth for? Otto has plenty of money. She wouldn't need to borrow."

But she had. For something she couldn't ask her father for. It probably had nothing to do with anything, just one of those little nagging loose ends that would never get tied up.

"I'm tired of waiting," Helen said. "I want to sell the place."

Before Susan could respond, there was a click.

With a grimace and a shrug, she replaced the receiver. Poor frustrated, unhappy Helen. Just when it looked like she had a chance to get what she wanted, there was Susan standing in the way. Soon, Susan thought. If you didn't kill him, the farm is all yours and I hope the money you get from it brings you some joy. Bring you joy. The words set a tune running through her mind. They were a phrase from an old Tom Paxton song.

Hazel stuck her head around the doorway. "Ben called while you were on the phone. He asked me to tell you he went up north to see about Emma Lou. She's not with her family and they don't know where she is."

So *nobody* has seen Emma Lou for two months. "Where is Parkhurst?"

"I'm not sure. You want me to get hold of him?"

"Not necessary. I want to get a look at Vic Pollock. I just need a couple of uniforms."

"I can bring in Yancy and Camarco."

Dropping cigarettes in her bag, Susan rose and retrieved her coat from the rack. "Have them meet me out there."

HER BREATH MADE frosty clouds in the pickup, and even
with the heater turned on high she didn't notice any appre-
ciable difference until she'd reached the outskirts of town
and was driving past open fields with barbed wire fences.
The radio crackled at her and she picked up the mike.

"Traffic snarl-up," Hazel said through a great deal of
interference. "Yancy and Camarco got tied up with—"
Static cut in. "I got Ben. He's on the way. He said—" The
rest was lost.

The ramshackle house, a small house of weathered shin-
gles, warped and pulling free, with a swaybacked roof, sat
far back from the road. Light glowed in one window. A
floodlight atop a pole illuminated a yard littered with rotting wood, twisted metal, discarded and broken furniture,
all covered with snow.

An overturned bathtub nosed up against the foot of the
light pole, and the light picked out piles of bird droppings.
Parked at an angle to the sagging porch was a mud-spattered
Cadillac, new and shiny black with one crumpled fender. An
old battered pickup, paint rusted off, was next to it.

Oh my. Except for the Cadillac, what we had here was
straight out of *The Grapes of Wrath*. What kind of fellow
was this Vic Pollock?

The floodlight allowed enough brightness to read her
watch. Six-thirty. Come on, Parkhurst. I want to see what
this guy looks like. The radio caught her attention and she
picked up the mike.

"Parkhurst," he said through a lot of crackle. "Where
are you?"

"Pollock's."

"I've got—" static garbled his words "—and I'm at—
enge—s corner."

Henninger's, she thought, the good Samaritan with the
tractor. Not more than five minutes away. Fumbling in her
shoulder bag, she found the pack of cigarettes, shook one
out and lit it. She cranked the window down a bit to let out

the smoke, and looked over this vision of neglect and decay.

From the house, she heard a bellow of rage. "I'm gonna kill you!" And then a high-pitched cry.

For a moment, she froze. Automatically, she grabbed the .38 from her bag and slid out of the pickup. She tossed her cigarette in a snowbank and raced to the house.

"Kill you, stupid bitch!"

She tromped up the crumbling porch steps and, standing to one side of the door, pounded on it. "Police!"

Inside, a dog set up a clamor and when the barking stopped, she heard thumping around and muttered curses. She banged again.

The porch light went on and the door opened. The man stared stupidly at her .38.

"Police," she said. "What's going on here?"

He was about forty, a large man with broad shoulders, powerful arms and greasy blue-black hair. He wore filthy khaki pants and a red plaid shirt, unbuttoned; thick black hair covered his chest. "Can't say anything's going on. You gonna shoot me for it? With that little bitty gun?"

"Who's here with you?"

He scratched his head, perplexed. "Nobody here but me."

"Who were you threatening to kill?"

He looked blank, then smiled broadly, and the friendly grin crinkled the skin around his small eyes, but didn't quite reach them. "See what you done, Lulu? Scared this nice lady bout half to death." He opened the door wider as he spoke over his shoulder and she saw a sandy-haired dog, the size of a labrador, standing a few feet behind him.

"Spilled my beer," he explained. "Clumsiest bitch that ever was."

The dog came forward, teeth bared and neck hair raised. Vic aimed a kick and Lulu dodged, made the same high-pitched cry and slunk into the kitchen.

The sudden burst of adrenaline jangled uselessly through her bloodstream, and she felt foolish. Her hand trembled as she awkwardly stuck the gun in her bag. "Are you Mr. Pollock?"

He nodded.

"I'm Chief Wren."

He nodded again.

"I'd like to talk with you for a few minutes."

"Don't know what we might talk about. Come in and we'll see."

It was unbearably hot inside. Pungent odors, like the smell of a predator's den, assaulted her nostrils. The only light in the living room came from the flicker of the television screen—a big, expensive new set. The sound was turned off. Empty beer cans surrounded a lumpy couch. Near a black vinyl recliner, one can lay on its side and beer puddled around it.

Bright light came from the kitchen. She could see a refrigerator, large and new, with black fingerprints around the handle. The dog huddled beneath the table. Vic closed the kitchen door, shutting out the bright light and the television flicker played across his face with a strobe effect on the amiable smile, hiding the small eyes in shadow.

Watch yourself, Susan. Osey'd said Vic was unfriendly. That was on a par with calling a Bengal tiger Kitty.

"Have a seat." He nodded toward the filthy broken-down couch, which at one time might have been beige.

She perched gingerly on the edge. Three rifles were propped, butt down, in one corner; all three looked shiny new; anything that didn't look new was battered and squalid. All along she'd been operating under the premise that Daniel was shot for some specific reason, not because a psycho happened to have a rifle. Well, this man had a rifle and she wasn't so sure he wasn't a psycho. She could see him snugging the butt to a broad shoulder and squeezing the trigger with a blunt finger.

He smiled at her, the small eyes all crinkly. "Have us some beer." Dropping into the recliner, he reached down to grab two cans from the row along one side of the chair. He popped them open; beer foamed and sloshed.

"Celebrating." He gave her one of the dripping cans, wiped his hand on his pants and took a long swallow from the other.

The can was slimy beneath her fingers. With the heat of the room and the feral smell, the thought of taking a sip made her gag.

"Better to celebrate with someone," he said. The animal intensity he exuded was hair-raising, but right now he was just drunk; the sloppy, I'm-so-smart kind of drunk that leads to a loose tongue.

"What are you celebrating?"

"Life is better for ol' Vic." He laughed. "Might get better yet."

"How could it get better?" He wasn't seeing her as a police officer, only as a woman. They don't count.

"Always on at me, clean up the place. Get her things. Refrigerator won't keep milk. Whole outside a refrigerator." He made a sweeping gesture with the beer can, then looked at it and grinned. "Need it to keep beer."

In the stifling-hot room, she was beginning to sweat. "And you got a new car, too?"

"Caddy. Best one they had. Never get to ride in it."

"Who?"

"Slut. Showed her. Good riddance. Nothing left now. Plenty of nice little ol' gals around. All sweaty palms and willing when ol' Vic gets to 'em." He popped open another can. Beer spurted and dripped on his pants.

Drunks could change moods in a flash. What was holding up Parkhurst? Just keep ol' Vic talking until he gets here. "Do you know—"

"Nobody knows. Nobody's business. Nobody's but mine. Not Lucille's. Watching. Thought I didn't know. Ol'

Vic always knows. Thought she could find out. Prying eyes. Lucille had prying eyes."

"Lucille?" she murmured.

"Rid of her. Just like Emma Lou. Won't give ol' Vic any more trouble." He laughed; the harsh bark became a choking cough. Leaning forward, he hacked and gasped, finally cleared his throat and poured more beer down it.

"Prying eyes," he muttered. He drank and gazed at the can. "You're not drinking," he said with soft menace. "Beer not good enough for you?"

Her heart raced at the sudden change. He now had an alert intentness, as if he were listening, as though somewhere far back in the tangled jungle of his mind a twig had snapped. The sleeping beast lifted his head and tested for scent.

Raising the can to her mouth, she let the tepid beer touch her lips but swallowed only her own saliva, and gauged the distance to the door.

"Prying eyes. Things happen to pretty ladies with prying eyes. Look what happened to Lucille. Would you have prying eyes, pretty lady?" There was an oily intimacy in his voice.

He emptied his beer and placed the can very quietly on the floor, then smirked and rolled his shoulders. Chuckling with a little snorting rasp like a stallion, he placed his hands on the arms of the chair. "Been a long time since I had a pretty little thing like you."

She was aware of the black hair on the back of his hands, the thick black hair on his chest, the rank smell mixed with alcohol fumes. Very slowly, she moved the can of beer to her left hand.

"We're gonna get along just fine." His obscene smirking face leaned toward her. "Think you're too good for ol' Vic?" He snorted.

She imagined flaring nostrils and stamping hooves. Even more slowly, her right hand went toward her bag resting against her thigh.

"I like snotty ladies." He winked. "Nothing more fun than teaching 'em to be nice. You're wanting it. Been a week since your man got himself killed. Been missing it. Don't know what kind of man ol' Dan was when it come to pleasurin' you, but no way he could compare with ol' Vic."

Her hand slid into the bag and curled around the .38.

He lunged at her.

She threw the beer at him and drew out the gun. The full can struck his cheekbone. She jumped up, twisting to face him as he sprawled on the couch. She backed a step.

He sat up, touched fingers to the cut on his cheek and looked at the blood. "Now, that's gonna cost you. Till you'll be pleadin' with ol' Vic."

"Just sit right there." She held the gun in both hands and backed another step. Her foot came down on an empty can. It rolled and she fell. Her elbow hit the floor and pain rushed up her arm.

Quick as a snake, he threw himself at her and knocked her flat. She tried to roll, but his upper body, at an angle to hers, weighed heavy on her chest and squeezed the air from her lungs. He tore the gun from her fingers and with a side-hand fling, tossed it away.

She panted, trying to catch her breath.

He grinned. "That's right, pretty lady. You gonna be just fine. Ol' Vic gonna teach you some fun."

SIXTEEN

His GRIN BROADENED, flesh all crinkled around his eyes, his foul breath came in hard gusts against her face. A knee pinned one arm, at her side, his heavy weight crushed her chest, and his hand held her other wrist to the floor beside her head.

She lay very still, sucking air into her lungs. Goddammit, I can't move my arms. Don't panic. My legs are free. Wait. In a minute. Air.

He raised himself slightly, shifting his weight to his knees, causing agony in her arm but allowing her to pull in a welcome breath.

With his free hand, he caressed her throat, then squeezed gently. "Gonna teach you like you never knew."

Filthy creep. Taking a breath, she drove one knee into his ribs and smacked her forehead against his nose. He grunted, released her arm and clapped her on the side of the head. Lights spun behind her eyes, sound rushed in her ears.

She drove a fist into his neck and felt a numbing sting go up her arm. He pulled his head aside.

Twisting her body, she got a knee against his ribs, smashed the heel of her hand up under his nose, then pushed with her knee in a desperate panic.

She managed to unbalance him enough to scramble free. He grabbed an ankle. She kicked with her other foot, kicked again. His grip loosened. She scooted on her rear. Bending forward, she got on hands and knees, then stood up fast.

He leered at her and came up on the balls of his feet in a gangly crouch. Light from the television flickered on his heavy face. In the kitchen, the dog barked.

Vic moved around her in a shambling circle. Relentless, like a freight train. She kept turning to face him.

The dog barked louder.

Over the grunting rasp of Vic's breath, she heard a noise. Car? She listened, straining to hear. Vic reached for her. She slashed down at his arm and kicked his knee.

Someone pounded on the door.

Jumping to one side, she kicked hard into the back of his knee and jerked down on his shirt collar. He fell with a thud.

With a splintering crack, the front door flew open and banged against the wall. Parkhurst came in, handgun drawn.

She stared at him, breathing in short gasps. By God, the cavalry. She had never been so pleased to see him. His cold eyes stared at Vic and she got the impression of strong emotion held under tight control.

With a slight turn of his head, Parkhurst flicked his glance at her. "You damn fool—"

Vic exploded into a shambling lunge—awkward as he looked, he was cat-quick—and slammed a shoulder into Parkhurst's hip. Parkhurst flew back against the door jamb. Vic was on him in an instant. Grappling for the gun, he smashed Parkhurst's hand against the wall. The gun dropped. He planted a fist under Parkhurst's ribs; Parkhurst slumped. Then that tight control shattered and Parkhurst came boiling up, face twisted with naked fury.

"Parkhurst—"

Vic swung with both fists. Parkhurst tucked his jaw into a curled shoulder and raised a forearm. Vic hammered away at arm, elbow, and shoulder, each hit accompanied with a hard explosive *uff*. Parkhurst, in a loose crouch, dodged and sidestepped and maneuvered away from the doorway to the center of the room. He landed a blow under Vic's ear.

"Knock it off!" The television flickered light and shadows over sweaty, grimacing faces.

Vic, smile frozen on his heavy face, brought a fist up under Parkhurst's protective forearm, and Parkhurst's head flew back. He snarled and pounded right fist and left fist fast into Vic's midsection.

She edged around them, flicked on the overhead light, then knelt by the recliner and clawed through dust for her gun. Her fingers touched the wooden grip; she grabbed it and stood. Leveling it at the two grappling, grunting men, she yelled, "Freeze!"

Parkhurst ground a heel into Vic's instep and smacked an elbow up under his jaw.

"Parkhurst!" She grabbed at his arm and he brushed her away like a bothersome gnat. She staggered back and fell.

In continuous motion, he whipped a backhand across Vic's eyes, gouged a thumb in his throat and slapped, palm open, against one ear. With a grunt of effort, he jammed a fist just below Vic's belt.

Oh Jesus, Parkhurst was going to kill him. She scrambled to her feet.

Parkhurst grabbed a wrist, spun Vic around and jerked his arm high up between the shoulder blades, then ran Vic three steps into the wall. Vic's head smacked with a force that shook the house. He dropped, made one effort to get up, then sprawled, resting his cheek on the grimy floor.

Parkhurst stood over him, breathing hard, fists clenched, jaw set and eyes glazed with hatred. He turned to her. Just as volatile, just as scary as Vic. "Why the fuck didn't you wait?"

"What's the matter with you?" Half afraid of him, she crossed her arms, turned to face him.

She saw him regain control. It happened in seconds, as though he pulled a shield around himself; his face smoothed into an expressionless mask, his eyes became opaque and he unclenched his fists. The only remainder of his uncontrolled fury was a muscle twitch in his jaw.

"You ever heard of unnecessary force?"

"It's the only thing he understands."

"What he understands won't cut it. What I understand is you cannot knock around suspects."

Parkhurst looked at her. "You sorry I showed up?"

She took a breath. No, she wasn't sorry, she'd been damn glad to see him. "That doesn't excuse your behavior."

"Well, ma'am—*Chief*—if I promise, scout's honor, I'll never do it again, with that satisfy you?"

"This isn't a joke, Parkhurst. Assault charges against Vic could be dropped because of your actions."

Parkhurst raised an eyebrow. "Are you saying to me, ma'am, stick to the rules?"

God damn him. She felt her face flush with anger. She took a breath. "What took you so long. Henninger's is five minutes away."

He closed the front door, retrieved his gun, then fingered his ribs and rolled his shoulders. "I told you I was at Engle's Corner."

"What's that?"

"Truck stop thirty miles north. I've been busy." From an inside jacket pocket, he withdrew a search warrant and slapped it into her hand.

She studied it for a long moment; duly signed by a judge. "How'd you manage this?"

"It took a little doing. Emma Lou's parents were glad to see me. They've been worried. She always phoned every two or three weeks and they haven't heard from her. They tried to call and Vic always told them she was out somewhere, shopping, at a neighbor's. They're afraid he killed her and they jumped on filing a missing-person's. That had to go through the sheriff's department. There's a deputy right behind me."

Parkhurst looked at Vic. "His habit of beating up on Emma Lou had her at the doctor's office a few times, once in the hospital. And we managed to find one woman willing to swear she heard Vic threaten Emma Lou."

Vic stirred, thrashed around and got himself into a sitting position. He shook his head, then shook it again. "Like to broke my eardrum. Can't hear nothing but fizz."

When the sheriff's deputy arrived, he escorted Vic out, to be taken to the county jail and booked for assault.

"Look around at this place," Susan said after they left. "Everything is broken-down and grubby, except for some very expensive new items. Like the Cadillac in front, and this." She tapped the television set. "And those." She nodded at the rifles propped in the corner. "You think maybe Vic has gotten his hands on some money lately?"

Parkhurst's dark eyes took inventory of the room.

He grunted, and they searched the small house, being very careful not to get in each other's way, not to look at each other, like two dogs who weren't obliged to fight as long as they didn't acknowledge the other's presence.

Dirty dishes caked with rotting food teetered on the kitchen counters and sink. The dog curled up under the table as far away from them as she could get.

"This is Lulu," Susan said.

Parkhurst squatted on his heels, spoke softly, and stretched out a hand. The dog crept forward and licked the hand, then rolled over so Parkhurst could rub the exposed belly.

"I'll take her to a neighbor," he said, as he rose to his feet. "Probably better off there anyway."

The bathroom sported a tub and basin coated with grime. The bedroom, tangle of dirty sheets on the bed, exuded an even stronger odor of predator's den. One room was filled with junk. Parkhurst was efficient and thorough, and she understood why Daniel had appreciated him. They found nothing that belonged to Emma Lou—no clothing, jewelry or cosmetics. No pictures, letters, bills. Nothing. Every trace of her presence had been removed.

"How much land does he own?" Susan asked.

Parkhurst smiled, one of those rare smiles that dramatically changed his dark looks. "Over three hundred and fifty acres."

THE SKY WAS a sullen gray on Saturday morning when she drove back to Vic's farm. Parkhurst and Osey, standing inside the dilapidated barn, both turned to look at her as she crunched through ice-crusted slush toward them. Parkhurst, in faded denims and black leather jacket, acknowledged her presence with a short nod; Osey, collar of his sheepskin jacket turned up, grinned and hitched up his blue jeans. Beside the barn sat a pickup and horse trailer with two saddled horses.

"Whose are they?" she asked.

"Otto's," Osey said. "Borrowed. Always lets us if we need to."

"Nothing in the barn," Parkhurst said.

Good. She didn't relish clambering around through junk in a structure that looked as if it might come crashing down if anything was disturbed.

Behind the barn was a small shed that held a jumble of tools: spades and shovels, ropes and chains, empty gas cans, odds and ends, all rusted and uncared-for.

Several feet from the shed was a large rectangular pit, eight feet long and four feet wide, filled with burned, blackened refuse. A new layer of garbage had been thrown over the top, and it was covered with snow. Parkhurst crouched on his boot heels at the edge of the pit and with a gloved hand brushed away snow, picked up a handful of ashes and let it filter through his fingers.

"Vic doused this with gasoline," he said. "I'd guess he threw a mattress on top, soaked everything and set fire to it." He looked up at Susan with a gleam of malice in his dark eyes. "We need to go through every inch of it."

She nodded.

"We're looking for bones," he said. "Human bones."

"Indeed, I did know that."

Osey loped to the pickup and brought back a tarp, which he spread over the snow at the side of the pit. Then he began to shovel out small mounds of debris and tip them onto the tarp. He whistled softly while he worked.

She sifted through muck. Beside her, Parkhurst did the same, working carefully. They didn't speak, and Osey every now and then threw them an anxious glance, like a child upset by friction between the grown-ups. As the morning went on, the sky turned a brighter gray and the chill of the wind softened. She felt gritty with ash; it blackened her gloves, got in her eyes, coated her mouth and grated against her teeth.

For their trouble, they found metal belt buckles, metal hardware from a suitcase, a few melted lumps that were probably buttons, and pieces of jewelry. They also found bones: small bones and pieces of bones. Each item was put into a plastic bag and labeled. As the pit got deeper so did Parkhurst's look of dissatisfaction.

It was past noon before they finished. She stretched and twisted her aching back. Osey cheerfully shoveled the mess back into the pit.

"Well?" she asked Parkhurst.

"Nothing."

"The bones?"

He shrugged. "I'm not a pathologist, but my guess is animal bones."

Yeah, she thought so too.

Squinting, he looked past the barn and across the hills. "A lot of space to dump a body, if there is a body."

She brushed filth and ash from her jeans, then washed her hands and face in the icy water from the outside pump. Osey washed, drifted away, and ambled back with a paper sack and a thermos.

"Sandwiches," he said. "Hazel thought we might need them."

In Parkhurst's Bronco with the motor running and the heater on, they munched through thick ham-and-cheese sandwiches and drank coffee. The relief from the cold was welcome.

"Vic still isn't talking," Parkhurst said. "Probably by this afternoon he'll have sobered up enough to want a lawyer. Then he'll get out on bail." Parkhurst's mouth tightened against his teeth in a smile. "For our own safety, any searching ought to get done before Vic gets back. Let's go."

They all climbed out of the Bronco and traipsed to the horse trailer. Osey was eager, like a Boy Scout on a camping trip, but Parkhurst, she felt, had some reluctance and it puzzled her. He was a hunter and the closer he got to the quarry, the more coldly satisfied he became, so why the reluctance?

Osey backed out a trim chestnut mare with a white blaze. Skittish after the long confinement, she arched her neck, tossed her head and pranced sideways with her white stockings flashing. She was a beauty.

Osey dropped the reins and the mare stood, but couldn't resist a waggle of her rear with a fast up and down of back hooves. Osey cinched up the girth, then backed out the other horse, a placid bay gelding.

Parkhurst stood well back, his face impassive, making no offer to assist, and she suddenly understood his reluctance. He didn't ride, or at least was uneasy about his ability. Well well, so you can't do everything. Ha. All those riding lessons she'd wheedled from her father had just paid off. Osey tightened the girth on the bay, picked up the reins and handed them to Parkhurst.

"Drive along the access roads," he told her. "Take any possible side tracks and keep an eye on the terrain. Look at anything suspicious. I doubt Vic would want to lug a body very far. He'd pick a spot fairly accessible by vehicle."

"You take the roads, I'll take the horse."

He looked at her, then with a caustic twitch to his mouth, held out the bay's reins.

"I'll ride the mare," she said.

Osey looked worried, and stammered. "Oh well— I don't— The bay is—"

She winked at him and he blushed. Gathering the reins, she swung lightly into the clunky western saddle and the mare danced with eagerness.

Osey, moving fast, caught the bridle. "Ma'am, this little horse is . . . frisky. I don't think— You could get hurt. Have you ever ridden before?"

"Yes, Osey, I can handle her."

"Take the bay," he pleaded. "He's a nice easy—"

"Osey, for heaven's sake, if you want to do something, adjust the stirrups."

He did so, slowly, dragging the job out, and the mare shifted impatiently. When he finally stepped back, Susan gave the horse her head and the mare took off with a leap that nearly unseated her. Probably serve her right. It had been years since she'd done any riding, and getting dumped on the rear would be mighty embarrassing after her great show of authority.

She brought the mare to a controlled canter and, looking back, saw Osey, white-faced, streaking after her on the bay. She waved at him and smiled with reassurance, then she simply rode. Despite the clunkiness of the saddle, she enjoyed the feel of the animal beneath her and the wind whipping in her face. She wanted to ride forever, cantering across the shallow hills on the responsive, sure-footed mare with those powerful muscles bunching and stretching.

Concern for the animal made her bring the mare to a trot and then a walk. There might be patches of ice or small holes beneath the snow, and she could hardly hope to spot anything like a grave while skimming across the landscape.

Osey trotted up beside her and grinned. "I guess you're all right."

She smiled and patted the horse's neck.

"If you want to go that way," he swung his arm to the south, "I'll do the other way."

Nodding, she reined the mare off at an angle and realized how difficult this would be, only a matter of luck if they found anything. If Emma Lou was killed over two months ago, the ground would have had time to settle and there wouldn't necessarily be any noticeable evidence of digging. The snow made it even harder: Any spot that might look suspicious would be covered.

She scanned the horizon. In the distance was a clump of trees and she made her way more or less in that direction. When she came to what looked like a track, she dismounted and brushed away snow. She found tire marks, remounted and followed the track. After a mile or so, either she lost the track or it petered out. Angling back and forth, she tried to pick it up again and came to a fence with the barbed wire sagging and hanging loose. She turned the mare and rode along the fence.

They neared a ravine and the mare gathered muscles to jump, but Susan held her back and walked her along the edge. It was eight feet deep and three across at the widest section, with nothing inside but snow. At one point, she saw Parkhurst's car several miles away and after a time, she reached a gravel road and saw his tire tracks.

Crossing the road, she trotted the mare up to a stock tank with a huge windmill, tank half full of scummy, dirty water, frozen in the center. The windmill wasn't moving and obviously hadn't worked for some time. Above the trees in the distance, a hawk circled in the gray sky and she wondered what kind it was. Daniel would have known. Riding gradually uphill, she saw a small black-and-tan dog trotting toward the trees. Cottonwood trees?

Purposefully, the dog went about his business, stopping now and then to investigate an interesting scent. She followed and he stopped once to look at her and wave his tail,

hen disappeared over a rise. When she reached the top, she
headed for the trees and then made her way through them.
She saw the dog again, busily pawing at the ground at the
base of a tree.

The mare stopped, pointed her ears, snorted and pranced
sideways. Susan urged her forward. The mare balked. Susan nudged her. The mare took dainty, mincing steps and
tossed her head.

"Where did you learn to ride?"

Startled, Susan lost a stirrup and almost lost the mare,
who reared and wheeled. She tightened the left rein, forc-
ing the animal into a tighter and tighter circle, finally getting her under control.

"Sophie, what are you doing here?"

"Sorry. Stupid thing, frighten a horse. Know better."

"How did you get out here?"

"I can still get most places I want to be." Sophie had on
the long black overcoat and a black scarf around her head.
No wonder the mare had spooked; she was an eerie figure
standing by the tree.

"Found anything yet?" the old woman asked.

"How did you know we were looking?"

Sophie snorted. "Won't work with me, child. I'm nosy
and don't intend to change or apologize. What are you
looking for?"

The mare, dancing and fidgeting, was difficult to restrain, and Susan fought with her.

"Emma Lou?" The old woman smiled slyly. "Trash. Do
better to look for her in Kansas City. If you're expecting to
find something, you're looking in the wrong place."

"What?"

"Over there." Sophie pointed. "Try in that hollow."

The mare tossed her head and made an unexpected sideways jump. When Susan again got her under control, the old
woman had gone.

"Sophie!"

Susan nudged the mare, coaxed her forward. She planted her feet, but Susan convinced her they were going on. A creek gurgled along at the bottom of the slope, and across it was a barbed wire fence with wire missing in one section. Sophie had disappeared; she could have slipped behind any of the trees.

"Dammit," Susan muttered. Turning the mare, she allowed a canter toward the area Sophie had indicated and came to another track so deeply rutted beneath the snow, it had obviously been used by a heavy vehicle. She followed it to a point where the ground sloped steeply down to an irregular, depressed area. A few stunted trees grew around the rim.

Dismounting, she tethered the mare to a tree and clambered down the slope. Tumbled into the floor of the hollow were about twenty metal drums partially covered with dirt and snow. She brushed at the snow and examined a drum. It had no marks of any kind to identify it.

"Ma'am?"

She looked up. Osey dismounted, dropped the reins and slithered down. He tossed straw-colored hair from his eyes. "I saw the mare, wondered if you fell off. What have you found?"

"Not what we were looking for."

Osey ambled around looking at the drums, now and then thumping them. "What's in 'em?"

"I can make a pretty good guess. Can you find Parkhurst?"

Osey nodded, trudged up the slope, jumped on the bay and trotted off. She stared at the drums. Toxic waste; she hadn't a doubt. Was this why Daniel had been killed? She shivered. The temperature was dropping, the sky was turning a darker gray, and the wind was no longer soft as daylight began to fade.

SEVENTEEN

WHEN SHERIFF HOLMES took off to sort out a fatal accident involving a drunk driver, Susan went to his office window and looked out at a cold gray sky, the color of frozen pond water. Late yesterday afternoon, Vic Pollock had been released on bail. Parkhurst and a deputy were bringing him in for more questioning. The street outside was empty with Sunday morning quiet, and somewhere bells rang, summoning all the good folks to church.

And then there was Vic, she thought, turning from the window as the door opened and a deputy herded Vic Pollock into the office. Parkhurst was right on his heels. The deputy closed the door and leaned against it. Vic leveled on her a gaze of rancorous resentment. She wrapped herself in a cloak of cool poise, crossed to the sheriff's desk and stood behind it.

"Sit," Parkhurst said to Vic, and nodded at the chair in front of the desk. She shot Parkhurst a cautionary look, but he seemed to have himself well in control; after Vic lowered his bulk to the chair, he went to the window, propped his rear on the ledge and folded his arms. Silhouetted against the gray sky, he looked like a short-tempered guardian angel.

The dissonance between them was, to say the least, intensified after his attack on Vic. She was angry and he was white-lipped and defensive.

Vic leaned his broad shoulders against the chair back and it creaked in protest. What was going on in his head, other than resentment at being here, she had no idea. He gave no

indication he'd ever even seen her before and certainly no
evidence of guilt or contrition at his assault on her.

He'd spruced himself up some in cleaner khaki pants and
a red plaid shirt, and his greasy blue-black hair was slicked
back, but his fingernails were rimmed with dirt and he still
gave off a faint odor of the predator. She'd brought in a
grizzly bear and felt there ought to be bars between them.

"Where's your wife, Mr. Pollock?" she asked as she sat
down.

"Don't rightly know."

"You've been telling people she's visiting relatives. Why'd
you say that?"

"None of their business." He stared right through her as
something stirred deep down in the wilderness of his mind.
"Emma Lou'll be back." Anticipation flickered across his
fleshy face.

Plans for Emma Lou when she returned, Susan thought,
and doubts nibbled at her theory he'd killed his wife. If Vic
was relishing cruel punishments, Emma Lou couldn't be
dead. If she wasn't dead, where was she? Sophie'd said better to look in Kansas City. Did Sophie know something or
was she just talking?

"Toxic waste, Mr. Pollock. Who's paying you for the
privilege of leaving it on your land?"

"I purely didn't know what was in them drums."

Parkhurst made a sound of disgust. "Some slime just sidled up with a fistful of money and said, 'You take it and I'll
leave my poison right here in the middle of all this fertile
farmland.'"

Vic scooted his chair a little to one side and turned his
head to look at Parkhurst. "Weren't like that. City fella
come to talk, needed space, didn't matter out in the open.
Said nothin' about no poison."

"You didn't ask," she said, "what was in the drums?"

Vic swung his head back to her and she was reminded of
the slow menace of Guthman's bull. "What for? God an-

swered my prayers. Nothin' grow in that holler anyway and it's been hard times. Always repairs and the wheat crop failed and then them taxes. My great-great-granddaddy started up that farm. Weren't gonna lose it for them taxes.''

That had a little ring of truth behind it, and she wondered whether a jury would give it any credence. ''Who approached you?''

''I only saw him the once.''

''How were you paid?''

''Came in the mail, regular.''

''A check?''

''Cash.''

''What was his name?''

Vic furrowed his brow, signifying deep thought. ''Don't believe I can remember.''

''Uh-huh.'' She knew he was lying. He knew she knew, and he didn't care. ''What did he look like?''

''Like everybody else. Ordinary.''

''Tall? Short?''

''Uh—'' Again, Vic wrinkled his forehead. ''Medium, I'd say.''

''Hair color? Age?''

''Can't think right offhand. Maybe light-colored hair, maybe some younger than me.''

He was vague and unhelpful because that was his nature, but he was also annoyed that the easy flow of money was cut off. What passed for intelligence was a sort of animal instinct for survival; make it pay and he wouldn't hesitate to sell out his supplier.

''Where does this toxic waste come from?'' she asked.

''Don't know.''

Another lie? She couldn't tell. It was possible whoever made the arrangements carefully kept that information to himself. ''Lucille Guthman found out what you were doing.''

''Don't see how. Didn't anybody know.''

"That why you killed her, Vic?" Parkhurst said. "She found out, would have spread the word and spoiled your game. Same reason you killed Dan."

Vic swung his head to look at Parkhurst and grinned, crinkling up the flesh around his small, cold eyes. "Can't pin it on me. Weren't anywhere near Kansas City."

Parkhurst, without moving a muscle, managed to convey contempt and utter disbelief.

"Pried into a lot of things, Lucille did," Vic said. "Got into something she shouldn't of. Just like Dan."

Susan leaned back in her chair, not allowing any of her rage to show, and let Parkhurst take over the questioning. He asked the same questions she had, only rapid-fire and accusatory, with sneered disbelief when Vic gave the same answers.

Vic didn't show any of the signs of guilt most people display: no tension in his posture, no clenching of jaw muscles, no breaking of eye contact or tightening of knuckles. His large hands with thick black hair on the backs lay relaxed on his bulging thighs. The only emotion she could read was fuming irritation that his lucrative sideline was interrupted by interfering busybodies. He stuck to ignorance and gave away nothing more than that the man who paid him was maybe blond and maybe younger.

"Answered all these questions more'n twice over," Vic said. "You got nothin' on me."

Unfortunately, that was true—nothing concrete to tie him to the murders; none of his three rifles had been the weapon used to kill Daniel—but Vic was at the center of much furor. The attack on her was the least of it and probably canceled out by Parkhurst's assault on him, but environmentalists were sharpening their pencils to make lists of charges to bring against him, and neighboring landowners were rushing out to consult attorneys.

"You're free to go, Mr. Pollock." She stood up behind the desk. "That'll be all for now."

His lifted his head slowly to stare at her, and for a brief instant his eyes were unguarded. Primitive fear crawled along her scalp and she felt hair stir on her arms. As clearly as though he spoke aloud, she heard his dispassionate thoughts. *Come a time when you're all alone somewheres. Look over your shoulder. I'll be there.* Then it was gone, that glimpse into his mind, like a shutter clicking shut, and he rose, nodded to her, grinned at Parkhurst and shambled out. The deputy followed. She backed to lean against the wall.

"Sweet fellow, isn't he?" Parkhurst said.

"The stuff of which nightmares are made." She folded her arms and rubbed the upper parts. "You think he killed Daniel and Lucille?"

Parkhurst took a long breath, pushed himself off the window ledge, paced to the chair Vic had just vacated and dropped into it. "Why would he kill Dan?"

"Daniel might have known about the toxic waste. You said he wanted to talk to you about something, maybe that was it."

"How'd Dan find out?"

"Lucille could have told him."

Parkhurst slouched down, stretched out his legs and crossed them at the ankles. "Speculation. We need a few hard facts. There's somebody else who must have been just as concerned as Vic to keep this all quiet."

"Yes. The city man with blond hair who set it up. You say he might have killed Daniel and Lucille?"

"I'm saying we let the sheriff keep bringing Vic in and chipping away. If a murder charge looms, I'll bet he suddenly starts to remember a lot more about that man."

She nodded. And probably a lot more about where his wife is. If Emma Lou's disappearance wasn't connected with the murders, she wanted it out of the way. She glanced at her watch. Lucille's funeral was at three.

A FEW MINUTES before three o'clock, Susan slid into a pew far in the back of the crowded church. She wondered how many of these people were here out of liking for Lucille and how many out of the respect due Otto Guthman.

A bronze casket with a spray of pink roses sat just below the altar rail and masses of flowers were bunched on either side. The music pounded in her head and she felt dizzy with a sick sense of unreality. The casket blurred, blended and superimposed itself on the image of Daniel's. Digging fingernails into her palm, she took a slow breath and concentrated on the people in the pews in front of her.

Ella Guthman, hunched and shriveled inside a black dress, seemed propped up by Otto, face dark with anger, on one side and Jack, face waxy pale, on the other. Doug McClay, seated on the aisle midway down, looked remote with inward concentration. Cold light bled through the stained-glass windows and dusted his blond hair with a greenish tinge. What was he thinking of? Lucille? Or was he focusing hard on anything else just to get through this?

Brenner Niemen and Sophie sat just behind him, Brenner with his arms crossed and his head bent, Sophie darting glances back and forth over the congregation with avid curiosity, like a promoter counting the house. Floyd Kimmell's reddish-brown hair made him easy to spot, and his beefy shoulders strained the fabric of his reddish-brown suit coat. I sure wish I knew what it is you think you're getting away with. Maybe nothing to do with the murders. She hadn't found any evidence that pointed to him, but maybe she hadn't looked hard enough.

Osey Pickett was with his parents and the four older brothers who looked so alike she couldn't tell one from the other. Hazel, clutching a handkerchief, fixed a sorrowful gaze on the Guthmans. George Halpern and his plump, comfortable wife were just in front of Susan, and Parkhurst sat beside them. Two rows ahead Helen looked composed and attentive; next to her Henry Royce, the editor, looked grim.

When Susan came out of the church after the service, it was bitterly cold and beginning to sleet. In her little brown Fiat she followed the procession of black cars behind police escort to the cemetery and stood at the edge of the group around the open grave. Rows of weathered stones with withered, faded flowers stretched around them. A cold wind sneaked through the skeletal trees etched against the slate sky. Icy pellets stung her face.

Ella leaned heavily on Jack, her face twisted with pain. Otto stood tall, with his head high and his brows drawn together in a look of thundering rage. Doug McClay stared intently at the toes of his shoes, possibly to shut out the minister's words. Sleet hissed an accompaniment in the background like a thin keening dirge.

"I am the resurrection, and the life: he that believeth in me, though he were dead, yet shall he live: And whosoever liveth and believeth in me shall never die."

When Reverend Mullet finished, people began moving around, approaching the Guthmans with offers of sympathy and speaking to each other. Susan threaded her way through the group, intent on catching Sophie, but several people stopped to ask what she was doing about these awful murders and when would there be an arrest. Soon, she told them. "I'm following every lead and the investigation is progressing." She kept moving, not giving anyone an opportunity to ask where it was progressing to. George's wife gave her an understanding smile and a friendly pat on the arm as she passed.

"Miz Wren." Mayor Bakover, face ruddier than usual from the wind and cold, touched the brim of his hat, and led her aside, then rested both gloved hands on the handle of his cane. "I'm afraid this has gone on long enough."

She eyes him warily. What was he talking about?

"Folks weren't any too pleased about your appointment to chief and now I'm going to have to listen to them. Not only haven't you found who killed Dan, but you allowed another death to occur. This simply won't work. I'm sorry, Miz Wren, but I can't permit this to go on any longer. I'm afraid I'm obliged to relieve you of your duties."

"It's only been eleven days since Daniel was killed." She kept her voice calm. "I'm making progress."

"Do you know who killed him?"

"I will."

"Not good enough. I need somebody who'll get results now. There's no further use for you."

Why, you bastard. She'd underestimated him, felt she'd been so clever convincing him, but he'd taken one look at her and understood immediately how to use her to his benefit. Somebody had to pry into the affairs of Otto Guthman; his name had been used to lure Daniel into a trap and it was on his land Daniel had been shot.

The mayor had been in a quandary; he dared not offend Guthman—powerful, influential and staunch supporter—in case Guthman was innocent. And there was Susan. If she found the killer, all to the good. If she didn't—if she annoyed prominent citizens—well, what could you expect, she was an outsider and a woman at that. Now that Lucille had been killed, Bakover felt Guthman was innocent; he wouldn't kill his own daughter. Susan could be dismissed and somebody else brought in.

She wasn't as convinced as Bakover of Guthman's innocence. Maybe he wouldn't kill his daughter, but maybe he was just that ruthless if there was no other way. That she'd discovered no glimmer of a motive didn't mean there wasn't one.

"You knew it was only temporary," Bakover said. "This is your last day."

She was so furious her jaw ached as she tried to speak in a level voice. "You can't do that."

"Yes, Miz Wren, I can. I'm afraid this has been a mistake and now I have to rectify it."

Helen, moving past in her firm stride, stopped and gave the mayor a disdainful look. "Taking candy from babies, Martin?" she murmured and went on.

The mayor's jowls quivered and his face flushed darker. Helen coming to her defense? Or was that an insult? "Who's going to replace me?"

"George will have to do it." Bakover nodded at someone over her shoulder.

She turned to see George Halpern and Parkhurst, dark overcoats buttoned and collars turned up, standing just behind her, George with the attitude of a kindly mediator, Parkhurst with his look of icy arrogance.

"She's doing a good job, Martin," George said. "Let her get on with it. A murder investigation isn't like buying new shoes. It takes time."

"She's already had time. Now this is enough. First thing tomorrow morning you start as acting chief."

George shook his head. Dear George, she thought, he has more faith in me than I deserve.

"Are you refusing?"

"Calm down, Martin."

"If you won't take over, somebody else will have to." Bakover was furious at having his big dismissal scene blown by the bit player. He turned to Parkhurst. "Ben—"

Goddammit, just what Parkhurst was waiting for.

Parkhurst grinned evilly. "You want me to take over?"

Bakover sputtered and veins popped out in his temples. That was certainly *not* what he wanted.

"A few more days," she said quickly. "Just let me have a few more days."

Bakover, seeing a way to back down, took it.

"Five days," he said. "Until the end of the week." Making an attempt to gather his self-importance, he added, "But you'd better show me some results."

Before she could rearrange her face into some semblance of intelligence, she heard a low, angry voice and turned to see Guthman glowering at Brenner Niemen.

"... never speak to me." Guthman jabbed a blunt finger into Brenner's chest, and Brenner stumbled back a pace. "Out of my sight. Don't come near—"

Parkhurst, moving at a trot, got between them, took a grip on Guthman's arm, spoke softly and drew him away. Ella directed a look of hatred at her husband's back for a moment, before Jack, arm around her, gently urged her toward the path that led to the cars. Everyone else then began to drift along behind them.

Susan stopped Brenner as he started to follow. "What happened?"

Wind blew through his blond hair and he smoothed it back. "I have to admit I'm not sure. I've never been Otto's favorite person, but that was unexpected. I went up to offer my condolences." Brenner shook his head. "He had to do something with his grief and I guess I was handy."

"A number of people were handy," she said flatly.

He stared past her, then turned to look around behind. "Did you see where Sophie went? I better find her. Will you excuse me?"

She watched him set off for the gravel path and catch up to the few stragglers, leaving her alone in the cemetery. Sleet pattered hard and fast against the gravestones. Daniel's grave was on the other side of the path and she was suddenly very lonely and very cold, so cold she wondered whether she'd ever get warm.

When she got home, she filled the bathtub, pulled off her clothes and slipped into the painfully hot water. Five days. Could she come up with answers in five days? She'd better, that's all the time she had.

Wind rattled pellets of sleet against the bathroom window and she remembered the scrap of paper she'd found in Lucille's hotel room. *Like sleet.* With a guilty start, she realized she hadn't mentioned it to the Kansas City police, or to Parkhurst. She'd forgotten it.

What could be like sleet? Awful stuff, nasty, treacherous and cold; it coated everything with ice, made the roads dangerous, collected on utility wires and caused them to break. Nothing was like sleet.

Closing her eyes as the warmth seeped into her, she tried to focus on what she knew, follow suspicions to a certain conclusion, but names and details snarled infuriatingly with little bits of logic counteracted by conflicting evidence.

Her mind drifted and thoughts floated more and more lightly, bobbing her along toward sleep. She heard Daniel's voice saying, "Now, Susan, it's not that complicated. The giant guards the treasure when the saints come marching in and the sun shines up yonder where all that's gold doesn't glitter."

Of course. That's it. That's—

The phone rang, bringing her up with a jerk that sloshed water over the edge of the tub. Muttering, she climbed out and grabbed a towel.

"Dammit, I'm coming." Wrapping the towel around herself, she dripped on the blue carpet as she padded into the bedroom.

"Hello, love, you sound mad. Did I call at a bad time?"

"Hi, Dad." Sitting on the bed, she patted her legs and feet dry. "I was taking a bath and dozed off."

"How are you, baby?"

"Freezing. We're having an ice storm."

He chuckled softly. "It's sixty-eight degrees here. When are you coming home?"

"Well, Dad, maybe sooner than I wanted."

EIGHTEEN

"THIS IS A HOUSE of mourning." Martha, the Guthmans' housekeeper, in a black dress, iron-gray hair severely trapped in a bun at the nape of her thin neck, folded her arms and stared at Susan with unyielding disapproval.

"Mrs. Guthman is grieving," she said, plainly shocked that Susan could be so lacking in decency she would even think of intruding.

"Please ask her," Susan said firmly, "if she could see me for a few minutes."

Martha looked down her nose, said, "I'll ask," and moved away stiff-backed, leaving Susan standing in the entryway.

In a few minutes she returned and nodded curtly. "This way," she said, thin-lipped in protest.

Susan followed her rigid back along the gloomy corridor to a room at the end. The curtains were drawn against the sunshine and Ella sat in dimness in a rocking chair with a partially finished pink sweater in her lap.

"I'm sorry to bother you," Susan said.

"It doesn't matter." Ella spoke in a low, strained voice. "Nothing matters anymore."

Susan was gripped by sympathy, so unexpected and so intense her throat tightened, and with it came resentment at Lucille. How could the twit be so stupid? Didn't she realize prancing around after a killer was dangerous? Was she so young and foolish she thought she was invincible?

"I was making this for her birthday." Ella stroked the pale pink sweater. "She would be twenty-six on March twelfth."

Ella wasn't dressed in black; she wore a gray-and-ivory skirt and a white blouse with an old-fashioned cameo pinned at her throat and, for now at least, she wasn't crying, but she had been, that dreadful wrenching anguish that tears the soul apart. Susan had seen the effects often enough to recognize them; the slack face, reddened puffy eyelids, dull splotched skin. Strands of gray-blond hair lay damply against her forehead.

She had an impulse to put her arm around Ella's shoulder, but she sat down on the linen-covered couch and waited like a bird of prey to swoop down on Ella's grief. The room was large, with a television set and a sewing machine, a grand piano in the far corner, a carpet with red and pink roses, a row of shiny-leaved plants on a shelf under the window, and on the walls, framed photos of Jack and Lucille at various stages of childhood.

"Why was Mr. Guthman so angry with Brenner Niemen yesterday?" Susan asked softly.

"He's—Otto—is angry that Lucille is—is— And he can't even say how sad he is. And so he just— When he saw Brenner at the funeral, he lashed out. It was wrong of him. He shouldn't have behaved that way." Ella's voice faded. "He shouldn't have. Not at the funeral."

She rocked gently. "I knew something terrible would happen. When Lucille just vanished, I told him. I told him he had to do something. If he'd found her, she might not—" Ella crushed the sweater under her fingers. In her pain, she was blaming Otto for Lucille's death.

"Why was he upset that Brenner was at the funeral?"

"Something that happened a long time ago. A long time ago."

"What happened a long time ago?"

"It was because . . . because . . ." Ella smoothed out the sweater; pale-pink cashmere threads caught in her fingers. "Otto found him with Lucille. Kissing her and they . . . her clothes were all mussed—unbuttoned. They were in the barn. In the barn,'' she repeated with bewilderment. ''Of course, Lucille shouldn't have... it wasn't right, anyone could have found them. And Otto just went in and there they were.''

Otto finding them was probably the point, Susan thought. ''When was this?''

''Lucille was fifteen.''

''Ten years ago?''

''When it happened he was angry... angry... told Brenner to leave, never to come near Lucille again. He made it hard for Brenner, very hard.''

''Did she see Brenner after that?''

''She didn't.''

That was said so firmly, Susan assumed Ella doubted it. ''Was she in love with him?''

''She was too young.'' Ella turned over the sweater and plucked at the inside. ''What does it matter? Gossip, disgrace—they can't hurt her. Nothing can hurt her. Not now.''

''Was she hurt?''

''Of course, she was hurt. She was a young girl. Young girls get hurt.''

''Was she angry with Brenner?'' Susan asked gently. Was that why Lucille had wanted to prove Brenner guilty, because of an old wound that never healed?

''Why are you asking about all this? What's the point? It won't bring her back.''

''It won't bring her back'': that brick wall the grieving mind ran up against. Susan remembered her first investigation into the death of a child, the mother's eyes staring hard ahead with the blank glaze of denial. There were some things too awful for the human mind to accept; and revenge, finding the culprit, were not enough to get over that brick wall. ''It won't bring her back''—the cry of every despairing, anguished, grieving mother.

''Do you play the piano?''

For a moment, Ella looked blank, then looked at the piano. "Oh. No. At least not well. I studied opera as a girl. I had it in mind to be a singer. I always hoped Lucille would learn to play, but she never wanted to."

"Where can I find Mr. Guthman?"

"I expect in the breeding pen. Always so busy. That bull, that bull, always so important."

Susan left her swaying slowly, the rocker creaking softly and rhythmically.

THE BREEDING PEN wasn't a pen at all but a white frame building; inside, it was one large open area with straw on the floor, hitching posts along the walls and the strong odor of cattle mixed with the dusty smell of hay. Sunshine streamed through the doorway and sparkled on the dust in the air. Guthman, wearing blue denim pants and jacket, stood spraddle-legged giving orders to five men who wore the glazed, attentive expressions that said they'd heard it all before. Each man held what looked like a section of oversized rubber hose with a glass tube on one end.

"I don't want anything to go wrong," Guthman said. "You know what to do. Everybody be careful. I don't want any accidents, I don't want any spillage. Remember, you're holding thousands of dollars in your hands. Don't drop it."

The five men all nodded dutifully.

"Let's go." Guthman turned, noticed her in the doorway and with intense irritation strode toward her. "This is no place for you. You'll have to leave. We're just about to take collections. This isn't a picnic. You could get hurt, or likely cause somebody else to get hurt."

"I'll wait till you're free."

"I'm a busy man."

"Too busy to help me find out who killed your daughter?"

He gave her a steady, penetrating look and she thought he wanted to pick her up by the scruff of the neck and toss her out on her rear. No doubt, he would lodge more complaints with the mayor. She kept her demeanor unruffled. That high-handed attitude won't get rid of me; if Bakover's taking away the job anyway, I have nothing to lose. "I'm staying until you have the time," she said calmly.

Apparently, he believed her; he scowled, looked at his watch and seemed to conclude talking with her was the quickest way to get rid of her.

"When I can leave here." He took her elbow, jerked her aside and well back from the doorway. "Barney, get those steers in here."

One at a time, six steers were led in and tied to posts, where they stood docilely, switching their tails. Steers in a breeding pen? Steers were males, castrated males. Obviously, there was a whole lot about cattle she didn't understand. "Why not cows?"

"Steers are easier to keep clean and less possibility of losing a collection."

The bulls didn't mind?

Guthman's gaze passed over the steers, checking that all was satisfactory; then he gave a quick nod. As though the whole thing had been choreographed, the men with rubber hoses moved to position themselves near the front of the steers. Again Guthman's gaze scanned the entire assembly and again he gave a quick nod.

Stomping and snorting, Fafner swept through the door, his handler trying to control him with a rope on the nose ring. The huge bull bellowed and swung his head from side to side. The handler trotted alongside as Fafner curved and lunged his massive bulk in a menacing caper.

Four more bulls were led in and paraded in a circle past the steers. Rumbling bellows rose to a deafening level; stomping hooves kicked up dust. Grunts and muttered curses came from the handlers as they tried to restrain their charges. The steers seemed unaffected by the ruckus, but the bulls appeared to be fiercely aware of each other, and the

hreat of competition had them raging with eagerness to
each the steers. The handlers, with increasing difficulty,
maintained control and kept them moving in a circle.

Suddenly, Fafner plunged toward a steer's hindquarters
and reared on his hind legs. The handler, with great effort,
yanked on the lead rope and managed to jerk the animal off
balance. His front hooves landed with a thud.

"How much does he weigh?" she asked in awe.

Guthman continued to eye his prize bull. "Twenty-eight
hundred pounds."

My God, she thought, as much as an automobile.

Fafner reared again, and again the handler pulled him
down. The bull bellowed with rage. The other bulls got even
more avid and made repeated lunges for the steers. When
Fafner in a frenzy of lust reared a third time, he was allowed to mount a steer, who stood quite unconcerned.

A man ducked quickly to Fafner's side, slid the length of
rubber hose over the bull's penis as convulsive shudders
passed over the animal. The man stepped back and held up
the glass tube. "Good catch!"

Guthman nodded with satisfaction. "Take him back," he
said to the bull's handler. Now that the king was taken care
of, the lesser bulls were allowed to reach the objects of their
affections.

"How much is a good catch?" Susan asked.

"Above five cubic centimeters."

She wasn't sure how large a cubic centimeter was.

Guthman gave her a tight smile. "It sells for four thousand dollars a unit. A unit is a half-cubic centimeter," he
added before she could ask.

She did some rapid calculations, came up with forty
thousand dollars and mentally whistled. "What happens to
the semen after it's collected?"

Guthman watched as Fafner was taken out. "Tested and
evaluated at the lab. Then packed with egg yolks in straws

and frozen with liquid nitrogen. It's stored in the Bank. We'll talk there.''

Trotting after him, she squinted in the sunshine. The vast sky was a bright blue with not a cloud in sight, but the air was cold, and she was forced to hustle a bit to keep up as he strode toward the gray stucco building with bars on the windows. No wonder it was called the Bank.

"Egg yolks?" she asked.

"Gives protection from the shock of freezing and feeds the sperm.''

Ah yes. We surely wouldn't want the valuable little devils to go hungry.

Opening the door, he allowed her to precede him. A secretary looked up with a harried expression as they came in. Guthman, obviously proud of the efficiency and success of his business, showed her around. The pride tempered his irritation as he led her behind the reception area into a large room with the clutter and bustle of any warehouse. Two men were preparing orders for shipment.

Guthman introduced her to a third man. "Slater, my foreman here.''

Slater, a thin man with gray hair and a precise manner, briefly explained the procedures. The straws Guthman had mentioned were actually thin metal tubes; they were kept in vacuum tanks of liquid nitrogen with labels that read ANI-MAL SEMEN, DO NOT DROP, in large letters and several languages. Each had a code number that identified a specific bull. For shipping, the tanks were packed in crates.

"Everything running smooth?" Guthman asked.

Slater nodded. "No more trouble with equipment not where it belongs." He called a sharp command to one of the workers and sprinted off to supervise something that wasn't being done to his satisfaction.

"Good foreman," Guthman said, "but fussy as an old woman." He took her to his office, barking at the harried secretary for coffee as they went past.

A huge world map, dotted with different-colored pins to show where semen was being sent, took up one entire wall of the office. On the opposite wall hung an enlarged photograph, in color, of Fafner standing on a grassy hill, looking virile and gazing into a rosy, profitable future.

Guthman nodded toward two black leather chairs separated by a small table beneath a window with winter sunlight flowing through. He dropped into a swivel chair behind a heavy oak desk, bare except for in tray, out tray, telephone and pencils. She sank deep into one of the leather chairs and the sunshine spilled over her brown-trousered legs. Guthman seemed to tower over her, and like the bull, seemed virile and powerful.

He also inspired the same sort of incomprehensible awe; she was half fascinated by him, half repelled. With the semen collection a success, he was riding on the flush of satisfaction. It put him in an expansive mood and should work to her benefit, making him more apt to answer questions. The secretary scurried in with coffee pot, cups, cream and sugar on a tray, deposited it on the desk and scurried out.

"Why were you angry that Brenner Niemen was at Lucille's funeral?" she asked.

A dark, dangerous look came over his face. "Lucille's dead. My only daughter."

"Do you think Brenner had something to do with her death?"

"Huh. If I thought that, I'd do more than get angry." Guthman poured coffee, got up to hand her a cup, then reseated himself and picked up the other one. He took a gulp. "He's a bad one, Brenner. Rotten to the core. Always has been. I told him years ago, I never wanted to lay eyes on him. I meant it then and it still goes. He had no right to be there."

Guthman had been furious at Brenner for playing slap-and-tickle games with Lucille, and the anger was still strong all these years later? That kind of long-lasting rancor made her skin crawl.

"Did you know Lucille was going out late at night?"

He stared at her. She was already beginning to irritate him—vaguely, like a buzzing fly—and he wouldn't put up with her long.

He decided to answer the question and nodded, slowly and deliberately. Again she was reminded of Fafner. "I didn't like it."

"Did she tell you why?"

He picked up a pencil and tapped one end against the desk blotter. "Working. She had a job and she intended to do it."

Trying to catch red-handed the culprit dumping drums of toxic waste on Vic's land?

"I shouldn't have let her go."

"Monday night? The night she left?"

"I never should have allowed it." With the point of the pencil, he gouged small ruts in the blotter. "We had an argument. One of the mares was sick. I went to check on her. She was better. Lucille was leaving when I came back in." He spoke as though each word had to be forced.

"I told her she couldn't go out. With a killer running around, it wasn't safe. She said I couldn't give her orders. Huh. Living in my house, I give the orders." He glowered, took a gulp of coffee and went on in a harsh voice.

"She shouted all I knew was orders. Blind, couldn't see what was going on under my nose." He snapped the pencil in half. "She said that was the way I felt, she wouldn't live here any more."

"What did she mean, 'blind'?"

"Nothing," he stated flatly. "Nothing goes on here I don't know about."

Well, maybe, Susan thought, but you didn't know much about daughters. "You thought she hadn't come back because of the quarrel?"

"God forgive me," he muttered in a low rumble, "that's what I thought. I expected her to get in touch with her mother in a day or two."

"What else did Lucille say?"

"Nothing. She was crying. She ran out and got in her car." He stared through Susan, unseeing. "And I let her go."

The phone rang. He snatched it, barked a hello and listened for several seconds. "Couldn't be," he said.

She picked up a catalogue from the table at her elbow; a slick glossy, expensive catalogue, warm from sitting in the sunlight and with the same photo of Fafner on the cover as the framed picture on the wall.

"Your handlers didn't do it right," Guthman said.

She flipped through pages of colored photos of bulls with a one-page biography of each and, in the usual glowing terms of advertisements, the text pointed out the remarkable possibilities of the offspring of these animals. Udder improvement. *Oh, dear.* Two and a half times the usual quantity of milk.

"Cows not receptive," Guthman said.

She read about tall daughters with fancy rumps and good feet, superior depth of body.

"Not possible," Guthman said. "Sperm count high." He listened, grunted and made some notes. "I'll check into it," he said and banged down the receiver. "Don't know what they're doing, and then wonder why cows not in calf."

Closing the catalogue, she tossed it on the table where sunshine glinted brightly on Fafner's picture. "Mr. Guthman—"

He brushed a hand as though shooing the buzzing fly. Damn the interruption. He was back to businessman, mind occupied with whatever the phone call had brought. She'd get nothing further from him now.

As she drove back to the police department, she thought about Lucille's quarrel with Guthman. What had she meant when she accused her father of being blind? What was going on under his nose?

She was still puzzling over it that night when she got into bed at a little after eleven. The phone woke her three hours later, jerking her from a deep sleep. She snatched the receiver. "Hello?"

"If you want to catch the cattle rustler," a voice whispered, "go ten miles west of town. Take the farm road off to the right. Down by the creek, across Vic's land."

"Who is this? Sophie?"

There was a click and then the dial tone.

NINETEEN

REPLACING THE RECEIVER, she squinted at the glowing red digits on the clock—1:20—and groped for the lamp switch, then squeezed her eyes shut against the painful stabs of light. Vic's land? She shivered, remembering that glimpse into ol' Vic's savage mind, the threat she'd seen there. *You'll be all alone. Look over your shoulder.*

Come on, she told herself. "I'll get you for this"? Threats like that didn't mean anything. For the most part. And Vic hadn't even said it, she'd only imagined it.

A trap? "Rush right out here and you'll catch the cattle rustler." That's how Daniel had been killed.

After a tiny click, the clock showed 1:23. Time marching on, stop dithering around. She reached for the phone with a small, agreeable sense of malice at waking Parkhurst in the middle of the night. He answered on the first ring—must have a phone by the bed—and sounded fully alert.

"Susan," she said crisply, and told him about the call she'd just received.

"Who was it?"

"I'm not sure." Her mind didn't hum along at its best when startled from a deep sleep.

"Did it sound like Otto Guthman?"

Parkhurst's mind seemed to work quite sharply even when jolted from sound sleep: The person who had lured Daniel to his death had sounded like Guthman. Maybe Parkhurst hadn't been asleep.

The voice could have been male. She thought of Guthman's odd way of speaking, putting equal emphasis on each word and sounding as though it hurt his throat to speak. "I

don't think so," she said. "It was a whisper. It could have
been anyone. If the call's legit, we'd better not waste any
more time."

"I'll meet you at the crossroad," Parkhurst said, and
hung up.

As she splashed water on her face, she tried to recapture
in her mind the voice on the phone: calm, no indication of
breathlessness or sharp rush of adrenaline.

Hurriedly, she brushed her teeth, yanked a comb through
her hair, then dressed in black corduroy pants and black
sweater. Had it sounded like Vic? She wasn't sure; whispers
were anonymous.

Pulling a dark gray jacket from a hanger, she shrugged
into it and tried to figure why she'd thought the caller had
been Sophie. Maybe something in the cadence. She started
to leave, then grabbed a muffler and a watch cap of Daniel's and shoved them in her pockets as she trotted down the
stairs.

THE NIGHT, cold but at least above freezing, was clear, the
black sky aglitter with stars. The huge, pale, fake-looking
moon hanging just over the hills on the horizon cast long
shadows behind them. She stumbled on the rough, uneven
ground as they slogged their way across the pasture. Vic's
land. A chill settled in her spine. He could shoot them,
tumble their bodies in some isolated spot and no one would
ever know.

A sense of unreality gripped her, of forever walking across
an alien landscape of small hills under an endless sky, waiting to be shot in the back.

Parkhurst went down a slope and up the next and she
stuck right beside him, slipping a little on the way up. The
slightly warmer temperature left patches of mud. He put a
foot on one strand of barbed wire and held up the others,
allowing her to climb through.

"The nearest point of the creek," he said in a low voice, "is a quarter-mile that way, just beyond the trees. Sound carries."

She clenched her teeth and muttered, "I was aware of that."

They crossed another field, and when they reached the cottonwood trees he halted. It was darker under the trees, and moonlight filtered through bare limbs to throw a crisscross of shadows over his face. She heard the splash and trickle of water.

He raised his head, listening, and she caught a glimpse of white teeth as the intent look of a hunter closed over his face. Since he was more familiar with the terrain, she let him lead; he slipped from tree to tree like a commando. She tried to follow with the same quick silence and worried about tripping or scraping a boot heel against a tree root. The sound of running water grew louder, and far ahead, she saw the flicker of firelight.

Putting a hand on his arm, she whispered, "Can you circle around, come in from the other side?"

He nodded and was gone. She waited to give him time to work his way around, tried to control her breathing, to hear over the sounds of the creek. She could hear her own heartbeat. Daniel had been killed after receiving a phone call telling him where he could find a cattle rustler. Tree limbs swayed, constantly changing the patterns of shadows. Her feet got cold.

She began to move cautiously toward the firelight. Would she find Daniel's killer at the end of the line? Accomplish her goal within the five days the mayor had grudgingly given her? She stopped behind a tree trunk, then eased forward again. Dead leaves and small branches were underfoot. Don't step on a twig; the snap would sound like a gunshot. Was Vic waiting for them at the end of this dark trek? He hadn't shot them when they were crossing the empty fields. Was he waiting at the edge of the creek with his rifle raised?

Maybe she shouldn't have called Parkhurst; this was her private vendetta. Her heart banged against her ribs. Maybe the killer was just a few yards ahead, the bastard who shot Daniel. Her senses seemed overly sharp. She was acutely aware of the acrid smell of wood smoke, the snap and crackle of the fire, the shadows moving like live things through the trees.

I'll get him, Daniel. She crept closer. Where was Parkhurst? By now, he should have had time to get in position on the other side of the fire. He couldn't have been shot; she'd have heard the sound. His throat slit with one silent slash? Captured, with the rifle pointed at his head?

Carefully, slowly, she kept moving, then froze behind a tree. Her breath caught; hair rose on the back of her neck as she stared at a nightmare vision.

On the creek bank, the fire danced. A large bulk with steam rising from it hung from a tree limb. A man, huge and menacing, slashed out with a long knife that glinted with each stroke. Eerie, evil shadows capered around the darkness like spectators at some satanic ritual.

On the ground, a slick black pool of blood glistened. The fire shimmered and fluttered, throwing wavering light over the grisly relics of carnage; severed cow head, hooves and scattered entrails. Above it all hung that big cold moon. She leaned against the tree, feeling sick.

Directly across from her, on the other side of the fire, Parkhurst stepped into view. "Nice night for slaughter," he said.

The man spun, knife raised.

Parkhurst thumbed on a flashlight.

Floyd Kimmell, mouth open, stood spotlighted beside the hanging carcass. His red hair looked the color of blood; a sheen of sweat covered his face.

"Drop the knife."

Floyd lowered his arm, knife blade pointed up for attack, and took a threatening step.

"Now!"

He waggled the knife and began to circle around Parkhurst. Parkhurst moved only enough to keep the other man blinded by the flashlight. Floyd raised an elbow to shield his eyes and kept circling, moving nearer.

She stepped out from the tree with her gun gripped in both hands and shouted, "Floyd!"

He turned. Parkhurst closed in, made a chop at Floyd's arm, and the knife fell.

"Doggone it," Floyd said. "How'd you find me?"

Parkhurst's teeth flashed in a grin.

SINCE THEY WERE outside city limits, the sheriff's department held jurisdiction and Susan contacted Sheriff Holmes. Within thirty minutes, he arrived with two deputies, loaded Floyd Kimmell in a patrol car and carted him away. The deputies stayed behind to collect the bloody evidence, a job she was happy to let someone else handle. Parkhurst stayed with them; she trailed after the sheriff to the Frederick County jail.

Under the harsh glare of fluorescent ceiling lights in the interrogation room, she sat next to Sheriff Holmes in a straight-backed chair on one side of a wooden table scratched with initials and scarred with myriad rings from coffee mugs. Technically, it was the sheriff's arrest and he would do the questioning; out of courtesy she was permitted to sit in.

Floyd, his jeans and black sweatshirt reeking of wood smoke and slaughter, slumped in a chair on the other side of the table with one arm hooked over the back and shot her an aggrieved look. With his bushy red hair, muttonchop whiskers and reddish-brown eyes, he resembled a bungling fox.

She stared at him. Are you the one? Did you shoot Daniel?

"Well, Floyd," Holmes said with a soft-spoken, unhurried manner, "you seem to have gotten yourself in a heap of trouble."

The sheriff, with his close-cut gray hair and lined face, didn't look at all like Daniel, but that unhurried manner reminded her of him. Floyd glowered, pulled his hands from the table, let them drop in his lap and cracked his knuckles.

Holmes scraped his chair back a little, took a pipe from the pocket of his blue uniform jacket and began tamping in tobacco. "Just how many steers have you slaughtered?"

Floyd shrugged. "Don't know, I lost count."

The sheriff, pipe stem clamped between his teeth, struck a match and held it above the bowl; his sleepy-lidded eyes watched Floyd over the flame. He shook out the match and puffed on the pipe, producing clouds of gray smoke. "What did you do with the beef?"

Floyd let his gaze roam over the pale green walls as though he might find inspiration in the dirty smudges. "I sold it."

Holmes nodded encouragingly.

"I'd get a phone call, that's all. And I'd slaughter the beef and meet a guy somewhere and turn it over and he'd give me the money."

"What's his name?"

"There was no need for names."

"Who is he?" Susan asked, impatient with the sheriff's slow way of handling things.

Floyd slid a glance at her, then back to Holmes. "Don't know who he is," he said peevishly.

Holmes gave her a bland look that said, Back off. I know what I'm doing.

Get on with it then, she thought. He puffed on the pipe and eyed Floyd through the smoke, which combined with the stench of wood smoke and the too-warm temperature of the room, made her slightly queasy.

"Well now, maybe you could tell me how this whole thing got started."

Floyd shifted in the chair like a schoolboy and cracked his knuckles. The sheriff's thin, lined face held the concern of a parent waiting for a delinquent child to own up. Tell me everything, his attitude indicated, and I'll help you all I can.

"I was asked, is all. Guy from Kansas City asked if I was interested in making some money."

"Who?" Susan asked.

Floyd cracked his knuckles.

"Stupid, Floyd," she said. "You're being stupid. The whole setup was stupid, and whoever's paying you must be even stupider than you are."

Floyd shot forward and planted clenched fists on the table. "He's smart. He's always been smart. He said—" Floyd clamped his mouth shut and his face turned purple.

"You're going to end up in jail," she said, "while the man who set this up is going to go free."

Floyd threw himself back in the chair and stared sullenly.

Always been smart, she thought. He knew the man. A local person?

Holmes leaned comfortably back and propped one ankle on the opposite knee. "I knew your momma. Nice woman. How do you think she'd feel about all this, her son stealing from the neighbors?"

"You leave my momma out of this. Maybe she'd like it just fine, huh? Maybe if she was alive to know, she'd think, Yeah, about time. About time I got some of what I was owed."

The sheriff slowly shook his head. "What are you owed?"

"We shoulda had a decent place. They shoulda helped. I never got anything as a kid. None of these good neighbors did anything about that. Wasn't fair." He darted a glance of malice at her.

Had he killed Daniel because of some twisted idea of what was fair?

"Cattle rustling's against the law, Floyd," Holmes said with heavy disappointment.

"Yeah? What has the law ever done for me? Shriveled-up old bitch Helen Wren shot my father. The law do anything to her?"

"Circumstances—"

"Circumstances, shit! Just because she was big hotshot important around here."

"What did you think of Daniel?" she asked. "How'd you feel about him?"

Floyd crossed his arms, hands in his armpits, and shrugged. The sheriff cleared his throat. She ignored him. "You own a rifle, Floyd?"

"'Course I do."

"Did you use it to kill Daniel?"

Alarm flooded his face. "I never killed anybody."

The sheriff gave her one brief shake of his head and said to Floyd, "Well now, somebody's responsible. If you didn't do it, you better tell me what you know, so we can sort this all out."

Floyd cracked his knuckles.

"Serious trouble, Floyd," Susan said. "We're talking about murder."

Floyd glowered. "I don't have to say nothing."

Sheriff Holmes worked at him for several minutes, but Floyd refused to answer. Holmes, sighing with heavy regret, called a uniformed deputy to escort him to a cell.

After they'd gone, the sheriff took the pipe from his mouth, tipped his head and looked at her with mild reproach. "Ms. Susan, you're in too much of an all-fired hurry."

"Sheriff—"

He held up a hand, palm out. "Now I know you have a personal stake in this, but you ought to consider the individual you're dealing with and proceed along the most appropriate path.''

''I simply—''

''Floyd is not exceptionally bright, but he's bright enough to realize a murder charge is real serious. And by throwing that possibility at him, you sent his mind into a shutdown. If you'd kept quiet and let me work around in circles and ease up on it, we'd have gotten more from him.'' Holmes raised his eyebrows. ''Um?''

A swarm of defensive thoughts buzzed through her mind, but she didn't say anything.

''Now we'll let Floyd simmer for a day or so and then I'll talk with him again. I'll let you know what I get out of him.''

''Thanks,'' she said with as much deference as she could muster.

THE COLD NIGHT AIR sent tired muscles into shuddering spasms and she had to make a conscious effort to lift one leaden foot and then the other, push and cajole her body to the pickup. For a while she slumped over the steering wheel. The adrenaline-fired energy from the phone call, the eerie tramp across fields and the bizarre scene of slaughter had worn off. Driving twenty-five miles through the dark seemed a chore beyond her ability. Lethargy closed over her and all she wanted to do was go to bed. Finally, sluggishly, she turned the ignition and shoved the truck in gear.

As she drove away, a memory surfaced from the bottom of her mind: her father driving through dark night with her beside him. She had been eight, awakened by bad dreams and terrified to go back to sleep. He had taken her to the wharf to watch the fishermen prepare nets and ropes and set out to sea. Why that particular memory? she wondered. If her subconscious was trying to tell her something, she wasn't getting it. Unless it was saying she was driving around in the dark with this investigation. That she already knew.

She rubbed the heel of her hand against one burning eye and then the other. From the remote cocoon of fatigue, she thought about Floyd Kimmell. Who paid him to slaughter beef? *A guy from Kansas City. He was always smart.* From Kansas City. City fella. No, Floyd hadn't said that. Who then? Vic. City fellow. Blond hair.

She stopped at the side of the road and frowned out at the path cut by headlights. She knew of one man who fit that description. Brenner Niemen. Well, am I getting somewhere at last? She picked up the mike and got the night dispatcher. "I'm headed for Sophie's. Tell Parkhurst to get out there. And this time don't be late." Taking off again, she turned east at the crossroad.

The sky was just taking on a grayish tinge when she pulled up at Sophie's. Parkhurst had already arrived. A kitchen light was on, but the rest of the house was in darkness. Sophie's elderly white Chevy sat near the barn, and inside the barn old Buttermilk was making a commotion.

Parkhurst crunched across the gravel toward her. "What are we doing here?" He looked about as tired as she felt.

"Brenner Niemen." She told him what Floyd had let drop and her conclusion.

He raised a skeptical eyebrow and followed her to the kitchen door. She knocked. No answer. She felt uneasy.

"Don't start imagining things," he said. "Sophie could be anywhere."

"Her car's here."

"She probably used a broomstick."

"Where's Brenner?"

"Still asleep," he said. "Nobody's up this time of day except cops and Sophie."

"Where's Brenner's car?"

"Maybe Sophie's driving it."

"A bronze Mercedes?" The thought was farcical. She rotated her shoulders, trying to unkink the knots, then twisted the doorknob. It turned easily. She looked at Parkhurst and he shrugged.

Stepping inside, she squinted in the light. "Sophie?"

Somewhere a grandfather clock ticked ponderously. Three black cats blinked at them from the basket by the stove, untangled themselves, stretched with thorough satisfaction and trotted toward them, nattering about breakfast.

"Cats haven't been fed." No signs of breakfast for people either, unless they'd had cherry pie. The pie, with two pieces missing, sat in the center of the table along with two coffee mugs and two dirty plates. That didn't seem like Sophie; she'd have washed up and put away the pie.

Susan drifted to the hallway and stuck her head in the living room; it was empty and tidy. The clock ticked. Farther along off the hallway was Sophie's bedroom, bed made, room neat. "Satisfied?" Parkhurst asked.

She paused at the bottom of the stairs, one hand on the banister. "Sophie?" The silence had a creepy feeling. Switching on the light, she trudged up the stairs. The cats followed and watched, sitting patiently in doorways while she and Parkhurst glanced into each room. Everything was neat and tidy except for the dirty dishes in the kitchen.

Come on, Susan. Fatigue sozzles the brain, makes the synapses misfire. Just because they're not here doesn't mean anything is wrong. She was aware of Buttermilk still clattering in the barn as she slowly plodded down the stairs with cats swirling around her feet. Halfway down, she thought of Sophie's rifle.

"What?" he asked.

She took the rest of the steps in a quick trot, alarming the cats, who fled. In the hall closet, she searched through the raincoats, rubber boots, hats and odd items of clothing.

The rifle was gone.

"Sophie might have it," Parkhurst said, but his voice had sharpened.

"Why?"

"Maybe she went out to shoot varmints."

"Does Sophie shoot things?" People. Daniel. When had Sophie stopped being a suspect? She couldn't see Sophie strangling Lucille. Lucille was younger and stronger, but it was possible, if Lucille had been taken by surprise.

"I've never known her to," Parkhurst said.

She frowned, shook her head, wandered back through the kitchen. When Parkhurst opened the door, the cats swooped out. The sky had turned a lighter gray, with a pinkish line across the horizon. Buttermilk screamed and crashed inside the barn.

She stared at Parkhurst, then, with a quick intake of breath, ran to the barn and shoved open the door. Buttermilk, eyes wild, screamed and reared, banged front hooves against the stall.

"What the hell—" he began.

"Stay here." As she moved slowly toward the horse, she spoke softly. The old mare bared long yellow teeth, snaked out her neck and snapped with a wicked clack. Susan ducked aside. Still murmuring softly, she reached out to unlatch the door, then stood well back.

Buttermilk, snorting and stomping, bumped open the door and came out, eyes rolling with fear. Parkhurst scrambled out of her way. In an ungainly trot, she headed outside.

Susan went into the stall, throat tight with a brassy taste. Thin daylight barely penetrated the deep shadows. Sophie lay below the manger, crumpled inside the long black overcoat, her face parchment white, head resting in a sticky puddle of blood.

"Oh, Sophie," Susan whispered and knelt beside the old woman.

"Shit!" Parkhurst said, and took off running.

TWENTY

SHE YANKED OFF a glove and laid her fingertips against the old woman's throat, just under the point of the jaw. Oh Lord, oh Lord, she couldn't find a pulse; her hands were so cold she couldn't feel anything. Goddammit, Sophie, don't you dare be dead!

She blew on her fingertips, massaged them and flexed her hands, then tried again. Nothing. Shit! Wait, no wait. Oh God, please. Yes, yes. A faint thread fluttered beneath her fingers.

Letting out a long sigh, she scrambled to her feet and sprinted for the barn door. Parkhurst handed her a quilt. "Ambulance on the way," he said. The rosy flush of dawn poured light through the doorway, and as she knelt in the soiled straw, she saw evidence the horse, panicked by the smell of blood, had trampled on the old woman. How much damage had those big hooves caused? Was anything left unbroken inside that black overcoat?

"Hold on," she muttered, helping Parkhurst spread the quilt over Sophie. "They're coming." Gently, she tucked the quilt around Sophie's shoulders.

What had happened? Judging from the amount of blood under her head, Sophie obviously had a severe head injury. Had she fallen or been knocked down by the horse and struck her head? Or was it only meant to look that way?

The cats had come to watch and sat in a row in the doorway, the sun behind them creating cartoon-cat shadows.

Sophie moaned; her eyelids fluttered and she moved her hands.

"Just lie still, it'll be all right. Lie still."

Sophie opened her eyes and stared at Susan with sharp awareness. "What time is it?" she said clearly.

"A little after seven."

"Headache." Sophie fought at the quilt, trying to free her hands. "Have to get up. Feed the cats. Have to—"

"Don't try to move." Susan took the agitated hands from under the quilt to still them. "You've had an accident." Where the hell was the ambulance?

"Accident." Sophie's voice grew faint. "No... not..."

"What happened?"

"Pain... pain... hit..."

"Someone hit you?"

Sophie's eyes closed. "Brenner. I don't— Brenner?"

"Brenner hit you?" Susan asked urgently, wondering if she should be asking anything at all.

"Hurt..."

"Who hurt you, Sophie?"

The old woman's eyelids flickered open, eyes unfocused and unseeing, then closed as she moved her head, moaned. "Old sins," she mumbled, "old sins," and lapsed again into unconsciousness.

Susan looked up at Parkhurst as she felt for a pulse, dreadfully afraid the thin flutter was gone. Hearing the wail of a siren, she muttered, "About time." Parkhurst hurried out and she followed more slowly.

The ambulance roared toward the barn and a young paramedic leaped out before it fishtailed to a stop with a scatter of gravel. He raced to the rear and had the stretcher ready by the time the driver flung open his door and jumped down. Parkhurst pointed and they sped past her to the stall.

They ran knowledgeable hands over the old woman, lifted her carefully and strapped her on the stretcher.

"Is she still alive?" Susan asked as they rolled Sophie from the barn.

"So far." They slid the stretcher into the ambulance, and one paramedic climbed in beside it.

"Will she make it?" Susan asked the driver.

"I wouldn't give a lot for her chances," he said and tore off in a spatter of gravel.

No, Susan thought.

"I reported in to George," Parkhurst said.

She was a little surprised and felt a little guilty that George was already at his desk when it wasn't yet seven o'clock; dear George, no doubt doing work that should be hers.

"He'll put out a pickup on Brenner Niemen, and I told him to tell Osey to get his butt out here."

SHE HEADED FOR HOME, driving directly into the morning sun; it gave very little warmth, but its glare was blinding. She nudged the heater up another notch. Why had Brenner taken the rifle? For protection? Or to kill somebody else? If that's what he wanted, he'd had plenty of time. The phone call—assuming Sophie made it—came about one-twenty last night and—again assuming Brenner had hit her—he'd had up to six and a half hours. He could be anywhere by now.

Why had he attacked Sophie? He hadn't killed her, only dumped her in the stall to die or let the horse finish her off. Meant to look like an accident? The other two murders had been quick kills; why had he bungled on Sophie? Couldn't bring himself to off his old auntie? It wasn't a sure thing Buttermilk would finish the job, but if they had been a little slower in finding the old woman, Sophie would have been dead.

The air in the enclosed cab had grown toasty warm and thick, with a noxious stench, she suddenly realized, and sniffed cautiously. Strong enough to make her eyes water. Odors of ripe urine and horse manure saturated her clothes. Hurriedly, she rolled down the window and treated her lungs to a gulp of cold air.

At home, she left the pickup in the driveway, went straight upstairs to the bathroom and peeled off her rank clothing, then got under the shower and stood for a long time, luxuriating in the hot water beating down on her. She soaped her body, let the suds rinse off and shampooed her hair.

Leaving the bathroom in clouds of steam, she padded into the bedroom, took a pair of white wool pants from the closet and stepped into them. I've lost weight, she thought, glancing at her reflection in the mirror; the pants hung from her hipbones, and her face seemed different, thinner and harder, a little gaunt, with cheekbones more pronounced. I look older. She grimaced at her image, then put on a pale-blue silk blouse, blow-dried her hair and covered over the ravages of too little sleep with some makeup.

Her eyes were gritty and she was aware of fatigue, but she felt wired. Finally, finally, she was making progress. "You're getting there, kid. I knew you could do it," she told her reflection, then scooped up her raunchy clothes and went down to the kitchen. Under the sink, she found a plastic bag, bundled in the clothes and set it outside the door. Later she'd drop it at the cleaners.

The kitchen could use some attention: dirty dishes piled haphazardly in the sink, ashtrays heaped with cigarette butts, books and newspapers scattered over the table, dust balls on the floor and spiderwebs on the ceiling. Her mother, if she knew, would be silently disappointed.

She ran water in the teakettle, set it on the stove, then rinsed a cup and spooned in instant coffee. Waiting for the water to boil, she stood at the sink looking out the window. A pair of sparrows flew to the bird feeder, perched a moment, then flew away. She never had filled it. Sorry guys, I won't be around to feed you, I'm going home. Soon. Find Brenner, then thumb my nose at Mayor Bakover and take off.

The teakettle shrieked and she dumped water over the coffee crystals, stirred and carried the cup to the table. She munched on a piece of toast.

Brenner, with his housing development in serious financial difficulty, needed money—according to Lucille's friend

Doug McClay, a lot of money. Susan was convinced Brenner had arranged for the toxic-waste dumping and the slaughter of beef. He took money from whoever needed to get rid of waste, gave some to Vic and kept the rest, paid Floyd for freshly killed beef and sold the stuff for a profit. How much would that bring?

Enough to be worthwhile, or he wouldn't have taken the risk. He'd picked his accomplices well: Vic, vicious and amoral, only too pleased to receive money for a useless piece of his land; Floyd, with his skewed sense of being owed, overjoyed at getting back at people who had done him wrong.

Brenner. Lucille believed Brenner had killed Daniel. She had been right. Somehow, Daniel must have found out about Brenner's illegal activities.

Shaking a cigarette from the pack, she stuck it in her mouth and flicked the lighter, then stared at the tiny flame as a thought struggled through the clutter in her mind. She'd met Brenner in the small parking lot behind an office building. Sophie had snagged somebody's cat and he had released it. Ah, Susan thought, finally realizing what had made her uneasy; such a small thing and of no real importance. After Sophie stomped off, he had walked Susan across the street directly to the pickup; if he hadn't been here for nine years, as he claimed, how had he known what she was driving? He could have been following her. No. She had followed him.

She smoked the cigarette, drank the coffee and added the cup to the pile in the sink.

On her way to the police department, she stopped at the hospital and asked about Sophie. The old woman had concussion, a broken hip, broken ribs, and various abrasions and contusions; her chances were not good. Sam Rivers was still clinging to life. The doctor's tone implied his chances weren't good either.

Hazel, crooning over her spider plants with a long-spouted watering can, looked up when Susan came in. "How's Sophie?"

Susan shook her head. "But she's still alive."

"We can only hope and pray." Hazel sighed. "When is it all going to stop?"

"We're getting there," Susan said sharply.

"Hey, don't snap at me. I'm on your side, remember?"

"Sorry." Susan took a breath. "Bakover only gave me till the end of the week. But now Sophie's been hurt, I'm afraid he'll snatch back even that."

"You look like you haven't had any sleep. I'll get you some coffee." Hazel shoved the watering can in a cabinet, then poured a cup and handed it to her.

She took a sip. "Anything going on?"

"One thing," Hazel said reluctantly.

"What?"

"The hospital just phoned. Sam Rivers died right after you left."

Damn. Oh damn. She remembered the fluid movement of the bull as he lowered his head and swept Rivers up on one horn as though he weighed nothing. "Anything else?"

"Helen wants you to call."

Susan nodded vaguely. She went into her office, tossed her coat over the coatrack and sat at the desk to sort through the trickle of information that had come in about Brenner. Nothing solid so far, but they'd only just begun. The reports of lost dogs, complaints of trespassing and traffic violations, she glanced at and set aside. The one interesting item was a report from Osey, impeccably typed, of his trip to Kansas City to look into Brenner's housing development; it was on the edge of bankruptcy and Lucille Guthman had, indeed, been asking questions.

Susan wondered if Lucille had told any of the people she talked with that she was staying at the Drake Hotel and if one of them passed along the information to Brenner.

The phone at her elbow buzzed. "Captain Dayton on the line," Hazel said. "Kansas City police."

"Put him on."

"Chief Wren, I presume?"

"That is correct, but if it makes you feel any better, you can call me Susan."

He made a sound like a rusty chain pulled across wood; she assumed it was a laugh. "You have something on Lucille Guthman's murder?"

"Not yet, give us time," he said. "About that call from Ben. Asking us to check on a Joe Calvin?"

Who the hell was Joe Calvin? "Right," she said, as though she knew what he was talking about.

"Calvin is working for the Ford dealer, just like Ben thought."

Why was Parkhurst requesting information about this Calvin person?

"And," Dayton said, "there is an Emma Lou Pollock living with him."

"I see."

"A pleasure doing business with you," he paused, then added, "Susan."

So. Vic Pollock had not killed his wife and buried her somewhere; she was alive and well and living with a car salesman in Kansas City. Susan could see ol' Vic, in a fit of drunken rage, going through that wretched house and removing every trace of his runaway wife.

Joe Calvin? She *did* know that name; somewhere she'd run across it. Searching through dusty mental files, she finally remembered where she'd seen it: Lucille's office. Lucille had written an article about him for the newspaper, two months ago, saying Calvin was moving permanently to Kansas City.

IN THE LATE AFTERNOON, the wind started blowing, mildly at first, then building in violence until by five it howled fiercely and beat against the office window. Still nothing about Brenner, no sign of him, no indication where he might have gone.

She drummed impatient fingers against the desktop, shoved back the chair and prowled to the window. She wanted to be moving, doing, out there tracking down the bastard. Dammit, everything was being done that could be done. She had no idea which way the trail led and she'd accomplish nothing by tearing blindly in all directions.

Sooner or later word would come in, a hint, a scent, a possibility; from her officers, from the sheriff, from Kansas City, Florida, Brazil, somewhere. Wherever he was, she would go. She'd get him; she simply had to wait for information. She hated waiting.

The eerie shrieking of the wind scraped her nerves raw. Pulling down slats in the blind, she peered out at the growing darkness. A woman, bent almost double and towing two small children, made an erratic course along the sidewalk. The wind snatched away one child and swept him to the gutter. The woman plucked him up by the back of his jacket and staggered on.

She let the slats snap back into place and turned from the window, startled to see Parkhurst, in black pants and black sweater, regarding her with the assessing eyes of a mental-ward attendant.

"What's wrong?" she asked, more sharply than she intended, because she'd been unaware of his presence. He moved like a cat; somebody should put a bell around his neck.

"Are you okay?"

"Of course, I'm okay." She crossed to the desk, nudged the chair an inch closer with her foot, and slid into it. "How did you know Emma Lou was with Joe Calvin?"

"If two people leave at the same time, there's a possibility their leaving is connected."

"Why didn't you tell me about this possibility?"

"I might have been wrong. I hate it when I'm wrong." His tone was light but his flat gaze didn't change; the dark circles under his eyes, and the shadow of beard, gave him a sinister look. She sat up straight to resist the force of his intensity.

"If Brenner is the killer, we'll get him." Parkhurst padded to the chair in front of the desk and dropped into it.

"'If'?"

"That's what I'm worried about," he said.

"What?"

"We have no evidence."

"He fits the description of the man who set up the toxic-waste dumping with Vic Pollock. Blond, city man. He fits with Floyd Kimmell's man from Kansas City who 'was always smart.' Floyd knew him. He'll give us Brenner's name as soon as he realizes what kind of trouble he's in."

"Any number of people fit that vague description."

"How many around here can you name?"

They stared at each other, defending their positions with silence. Outside, the wind wailed and rattled the window.

"Brenner attacked Sophie," she said.

"That's not proof he killed Dan."

No, it isn't, she thought, dropping her gaze and shuffling through reports looking for her cigarettes, but it's certainly suggestive, added to toxic waste and slaughtered beef. "What did you find at Sophie's?"

"Damn-all. Except the rifle's missing. Nothing in Brenner's room to connect him with the murders, nothing to say where he might be." Parkhurst rubbed his jaw, and stubble rasped against his hand. "And nothing that proves what happened to Sophie wasn't an accident."

"She said Brenner hit her."

"No. She didn't. She only said his name. And she had a severe head injury."

Susan nodded, lit a cigarette and blew smoke at the ceiling light. Okay, but it didn't weaken her certainty that Brenner was the slime who killed Daniel.

"Don't do anything stupid," Parkhurst said.

She raised an eyebrow. "Like what?"

"Buckling on your six-guns and heading out for the O.K. Corral."

She choked on a breathful of cigarette smoke and an involuntary snort of laughter. That was exactly what she wanted to do, and given the opportunity, she wasn't sure she wouldn't. Maybe just as well she didn't know where Brenner was.

THE WIND SLAPPED against the house, shook the kitchen window and whipped through the elm tree outside. It set her teeth on edge. She stood with the refrigerator door open, peering inside and wondering if any of those containers held anything that hadn't grown green fur. The best she could come up with was some stale pumpernickel and a block of cheddar cheese. She sliced the cheese, laid it on the bread and slid the whole thing in the microwave.

The drippy, gooey sandwich tasted good, especially since she hadn't eaten in she couldn't remember how long, but one of the first things she was going to do when she got back to San Francisco was buy a loaf of sourdough bread. Still no word on Brenner when she'd left the police department with firm instructions to call if anything came in. The phone was obstinately still. The wind howled incessantly.

She poured a glass of milk and looked around the messy kitchen as she drank it. The time had come. She was too twitchy, too keyed up; cleaning would use that energy and leave her mind free. Pushing up the sleeves of her old gray sweatshirt, she stacked all the dishes in the dishwasher. It sloshed and hummed in opposition to the wind.

She emptied ashtrays, wiped down the countertops and swept the floor, then took a bucket from under the sink and filled it with hot water and detergent. On hands and knees, she scrubbed the floor.

Clutter bothered her—she did like bare surfaces—but dirt and grime she could ignore for long periods—probably in reaction to her mother's spotless housekeeping—until they reached an overwhelming point. This place had now gone past that.

She scoured tub and basin and toilet and then the bathroom floor, her ears attuned all the while for the ring of the phone. It didn't ring. The wind never ceased its roar. In the living room, she dusted, sprayed the wood surfaces with polish and rubbed until they gleamed. Wind howled down the chimney. She got out the vacuum cleaner, unwound the cord, and just as she bent to plug it in, the phone rang. Dropping the cord, she ran to the kitchen and pounced on the phone.

"This is Helen." Her voice held annoyance.

Oh damn, she'd forgotten to return Helen's call. "I apologize for not getting back to you. I really haven't had much time to think about selling—"

"I didn't call about that, although I do not know why you insist on stalling."

Soon, Susan promised silently, soon it's all yours, just as soon as Brenner is caught. Assuming he's guilty, a small voice cautioned. Yes of course, she told the voice, but I know he's guilty.

"... Brenner is out there," Helen was saying.

"Where?"

"At the farm," Helen said impatiently. "The Wren farm. Haven't you been listening?"

"Why do you think that?"

"His car was there. Bob Donato saw it. He called me this morning. Bob owns the adjacent farm, and he was on his way home from—"

"What time was the car seen?"

"Around two-thirty this morning."

Susan hung up and stared at the shiny clean floor beneath her dirty sneakers. A fever of excitement swept over her. Don't get carried away, she told herself, it's very unlikely. Why would Brenner be out there? He might be hoping Sophie's injuries were accepted as an accident and he could come back and be properly appalled at what had happened to poor old Auntie. But even if that were true, he'd surely go someplace warmer and more comfortable, where he could rig up an alibi at the same time. If he's there, he could leave at any second.

She raced up to the bedroom, put on thick socks and boots, and shrugged into her heavy gray jacket. *All right, you son of a bitch.* Grabbing her gun, she swung out the cylinder, checked the bullets and snapped it shut. *If you're out there, you're dead.* She shoved the gun in her pocket. Damned if she was going to dance around with backup. She didn't want anybody trying to stop her. In the bottom desk drawer, she found a fistful of keys. She trotted out to the pickup.

THIN CLOUDS raced across the moon. Her gloved hands gripped the wheel as she fought the wind for control, and she felt a rush of exhilaration as she sped along the deserted country road with trees whipping on both sides and brush blowing across in front of her. Half a mile from the house, she pulled onto a dirt track, badly rutted and overgrown with brush. She was taking no chances headlights would be seen.

When she climbed from the truck, the wind slammed her back against it and tore her breath away, then stroked her face and teased her hair, whispered with a seductive croon, coaxing her heart to race and her blood to sing. Shielding the flashlight beam with her fingers, she set off on the dirt track. The wind chuckled and nuzzled and urged unrestraint.

A hundred yards from the rear of the farmyard, she thumbed off the flashlight and stared fixedly at the dark outline of the two-story house. No lights. If Brenner was inside, he was freezing in the dark. The trees thrashed and wailed. She moved toward the barn, felt for the door and slid it open with a grinding rumble just far enough to step inside. At least she didn't have to worry about noise; the wind covered any sound she might make. Briefly, she flicked on the light, just long enough to see the barn was empty, no car hidden inside.

She circled the house, examining ground-floor windows and front and back doors. As nearly as she could tell in the uncertain light, no one had broken in. If he'd gotten in, he'd used a key.

The kitchen door was locked tight. After two wrong tries, she found the right key, slipped in fast and stood with her back to the wall. The howling wind was muted; moonlight and dancing trees created live shadows. The old farmhouse smelled damp and stale and long-deserted.

Her boot heels made a soft *tap, tap* as she eased into the dining room and risked using the flashlight. Empty. She tried to imagine Daniel living here as a young child, with happiness and sunshine and love. It was beyond her. All she could feel was Helen and gloom, bitterness and despair; Helen resenting the long-wanted younger brother, nursing the sickly mother and injured father, managing the farm with all the troubles of machinery breaking down and livestock destroying crops, finally killing the man responsible. Helen was right; Susan had been a pampered and petted only child, secure in the warm love of doting parents.

She edged into the living room, and her breath caught. A menacing bulk hovered in the corner. Half a second later, her mind pointed out it was nothing but a broken-down easy chair.

Bare wooden stairs creaked as she went up, hugging the wall. Large bedroom on the right, old chest with one drawer missing.

A loud crash.

She jumped, dropped the flashlight and hit the floor, pulling out her gun. The flashlight clattered and rolled with a crazy pattern of light. She squirmed to the wall, rose and waited, then darted out the door and across the hallway.

A squeak, a bang, a crash.

She tensed, both hands on the gun, and zipped through the doorway in a crouch. Outside, tree limbs beckoned and pointed and squealed against the windowpane.

Oh Jesus, if Brenner had been here, I'd have killed him. She shoved the gun in her pocket and rubbed her face with a shaky hand. What the hell is the matter with me, slinking around on half-bent knees like a vigilante?

She retrieved the flashlight and went back down the stairs on rubbery legs. Get a grip on yourself and get out of here. She left through the kitchen door and locked it behind her.

The wind rushed at her, grabbed her hair and tore at her clothes. It was worse than the Santa Ana winds in California. She felt boneless, so tired she could barely shuffle feet that seemed encased in cement, and she had a half-mile hike back to the pickup. Starting across the farmyard, she swung the light back and forth and ran it over a small shed. A small bright spot winked at her.

She stopped, slowly moved the light until it winked again. She sighed, then told herself to get a move on and trudged to the shed. One of the screws holding the plate for the padlock had caught the light. She lifted the lock. Fastened.

The wind sniffled and mourned. Far away, a coyote cried and hair prickled on the back of her neck. Bending her head against the wind, she forced unwilling leg muscles to carry her toward the dirt path.

One shiny screw?

She stopped and turned back.

Why one shiny screw? The rest were weathered and rusted.

With the light close, she bent to examine the plate screwed into the door and found small scratches from a screwdriver. Someone who didn't have a key had simply removed the hardware holding on the padlock and when he put it back had used one new screw.

Pulling off a glove, she stuck her hand in her pocket and drew out the bunch of keys; several were padlock keys.

The first one she tried slid into the lock and she snapped it free. Hinges squealed as she swung open the door.

TWENTY-ONE

WHY WOULD ANYONE want to get in here? Through the doorway the light shined on rough wooden shelves with dusty Mason jars, enamel pots, stone crocks and an ancient pressure cooker; a jumble of rusted tools on the floor, old brooms, a lumpy pile of burlap bags, a child's rocker, wooden crates; rat droppings, dust and dirt everywhere.

Kids maybe, just to see what was inside or just for the hell of it? Wind grabbed the door from her hand, banged it back against the shed and tore the top hinge loose with a shriek.

Oh hell, go home, Susan, it's only a shed with a lot of unwanted and discarded junk. *Somebody wanted in bad enough to remove the lock.* So what? Nothing to get excited about. *Then why are you so reluctant to go inside?*

She swung the light around the darkness behind her, moonlight and shadows and thrashing trees. Nobody here but you, kiddo, and with the hinge loose, even if somebody were here, he couldn't lock you inside. She stepped in.

The dust on the floorboards showed sweep marks. One of the old brooms used to obliterate tracks? She couldn't believe there'd be anything here worth stealing, and she certainly couldn't tell if anything was missing; she'd have to ask Helen.

She took another step and silky threads clung to her face. Gasping, she clawed at her face. Spiderwebs. She shivered and flung an arm back and forth to remove any others.

All right, you're inside. Satisfied now? The wind howled derisively. She played the light over the burlap bags: lumpy pile two feet high, no dirt, no dust on the top bag. Crouching, she reached out her hand and let her fingertips rest lightly on the pile.

Something dark and small and furry suddenly ran over her arm. She jerked back, catching her breath with a thin bleat. Rat! Oh Lord, *rat*. She shuddered, clamped her teeth and removed the top sack, then another and another, with the awful feeling she wasn't going to like what she found underneath. Eight bags had covered the old tarp wrapped loosely around a bulky object.

She folded back an edge of the tarp and shined the flashlight on the blond hair of Brenner Niemen. Injury to the back of the head. Hair disheveled. Face—swollen and blue with the bulging eyes and protruding tongue of a strangling victim—twisted toward the wall.

Fury raged through her. Brenner couldn't be dead. Goddammit, he was the killer.

Wind slammed the damaged door against the shed with a crash that brought her up on her toes, heart banging against her ribs. She didn't unwrap the body any further or touch anything else; the Sheriff's Department needed to be notified and Sheriff Holmes would take it from here.

She drew in a breath. Call off the search for Brenner; at least a lot of time hadn't been wasted on that. If she hadn't found his body, she'd have devoted all her attention there. The body might not have been found for some time, maybe not until the weather got warm and maybe not even then, unless somebody got close enough to notice the smell.

Oh shit. She'd been so sure. Everything pointed to Brenner. Obviously, faulty thinking on her part. Now what? She was back where she started, with no idea who had killed Daniel, and in three days the mayor would give her the boot. After a last glance around the shed, she set off on the half-mile hike to the pickup.

SHERIFF HOLMES had rigged up lights in the shed, and the harsh glare spilled through the doorway to make a bright rectangle on the gravel. Inside the shed, sheriff's deputies took photographs and crawled on the floor picking up bits of possible evidence. Parkhurst, the collar of his black leather jacket turned up, stood outside and watched, chin on his chest, arms crossed with his hands trapped in his armpits as though to prevent himself from touching anything.

Susan, leaning against the fender of the pickup, knew how he felt. She wanted to be in there doing the work and keeping a beady eye on the collection of evidence, making sure nothing was overlooked or contaminated. The residual anger at finding Brenner dead had drained away and now she was simply cold and tired and nowhere.

A dark-colored Dodge drove around the house and pulled in behind the pickup. Helen, wearing trousers and a heavy wool jacket, a brown muffler wrapped around her throat, got out and marched with her brisk stride toward the shed. Susan intercepted her.

"What's going on?" Helen demanded.

"What are you doing here?"

"I have a right to be here. I own this place."

And it's going to be yours a while longer, Susan thought, before I agree to sell. Now that Brenner's dead, you're back on the list. "How did you know anything was going on?"

In the darkness, she couldn't see Helen's eyes behind the large round glasses, but the glasses flashed her way and Helen's eyebrows twitched with amusement. "Haven't you learned yet that news travels fast? Bob Donato saw the sheriff's cars go by. What happened? Did you find Brenner?"

Susan shoved her gloved hands deep into the pockets of her jacket and hunched her shoulders against the wind; it was less fierce now, its violence diminishing with malcontented wails. "Brenner was killed."

"Here?" Helen sounded indignant.

"Maybe. Maybe killed somewhere else and the body left here."

"Why was he killed?"

Good question, Susan thought.

"Who killed him?"

Susan didn't know; she didn't know anything except that her feet were numb.

"He didn't kill Dan, then," Helen said.

That's certainly a possibility.

Helen turned her head to watch two young men maneuver a stretcher into the shed; then she looked back at Susan. "Well, missy, bit off more than you can chew?"

Susan went rigid, clamped her teeth against some brilliant response like "Up yours," and carefully arranged poised confidence on her face. Helen, paying no attention, which made Susan even angrier, had her glasses aimed at the bagged body on the stretcher being angled through the doorway. Wheels crunched on the gravel as the two men rolled it to the waiting ambulance, hoisted it inside and drove away.

Helen muttered, "Poor Sophie. She knew what kind he was, but this is still going to be hard on her."

She may never know, Susan thought. She may never regain consciousness.

Helen started for the shed and Susan put a hand on her arm. "Don't go any closer. You can't go in until they're through."

"I want to look inside. I haven't seen the inside of that shed since I locked in all those Mason jars."

"Nothing's been damaged, and probably nothing's been stolen."

"Ha! You think I care about that? It's easy to see you've never spent your summers in a kitchen full of steam. Cleaning fruit and snapping beans, filling those *jars* with tomatoes and pickles and cherries. That evil pressure cooker waiting to explode when I turned my back. The happiest day of my life was the day I put the padlock on that door." Her mouth tightened thinly against her teeth. "I simply wanted

a look at what I'm leaving behind when I sell this place."
Helen tossed the loose end of the muffler over her shoulder. "I assume we can take care of all the legalities before
you leave." Her voice held a hint of steel and the hidden eyes
seemed to send out a warning.

"What makes you think I'm leaving?"

"The mayor won't let you stay, not after this."

"I'm not leaving until I get Daniel's killer."

Helen made a short sound that might have been amusement, might have been derision. "You don't give up easy,
I'll say that for you." She strode to her car, slid in, and
backed furiously out of the driveway.

BEFUDDLED BY FATIGUE, Susan drove slowly into town,
making no attempt to engage her mind with anything more
taxing than getting herself home and into bed. Brenner's
murder would have to wait till morning. Somewhere she'd
gone wrong; she'd have to start over, sift through all the bits
of data and shuffle and rearrange until they came out right.

She thought of Sophie, so small and still in a hospital bed.
And Frannyvan came to mind, small and still in a hospital
bed. Susan had gone to see her, had sat holding Frannyvan's lifeless hand, then gone home, gotten in her own bed
and gone to sleep. In the morning, Frannyvan was dead.
During the night, she'd given up her fight. Tears welled up
and rolled down Susan's face. Was Sophie still fighting?

On Railroad Avenue she drove past the park and then,
instead of turning left for home, she turned right, continued until she came to Brookvale Hospital and pulled into the
parking lot. She had to know if Sophie was still alive.

The hospital corridors were dimly lighted and filled with
the hushed quiet of watchful waiting. Loudspeakers periodically broke through the hush calling for Dr. Janis, Dr.
Janis. Room 318. Dr. Rosenfield to ER. Code Blue, followed by a rush of white uniforms and scurrying feet.

Turning a corner, she edged past an elderly man swinging a heavy buffing machine in slow arcs across the beige floor. From the doorway, Sophie looked bad; from the bedside she looked even worse, she looked like death, skin gray except for purple bruises and red abrasions. The white bandage on her head, only slightly paler than her face, showed seepage of brownish stains. On the wall, instruments bleeped and monitors displayed jagged green lines. Breath rasped through her nostrils. Colorless liquid dripped from a bottle on a metal stand through a thin tube into a needle taped to her left hand.

Susan's mind flashed again on Frannyvan, diminished by a stroke; like Sophie, surrounded by tubes and drains; like Sophie, still and gray. She swallowed hard, blinking rapidly, then lightly touched Sophie's hand, cool and dry. "Hang on, Sophie."

Susan slipped quietly away and as she approached the nurses' station, she recognized Jack Guthman leaning on the counter talking with the nurse. When he noticed her, he straightened, came toward her and walked with her to the elevator. He didn't look a whole lot healthier than Sophie, with skin stretched tightly across his face, dark circles under his eyes and deep lines on either side of his moustache.

"Why are you here?" she asked as she pressed a button for the elevator.

He gave her a brief smile. "My mother told me to come." Then he spoke soberly. "I was having supper at home when we heard about Brenner. She worried the news would be too much for Sophie and called here to ask about her."

"Sophie's still unconscious."

The elevator doors slid noiselessly open and they stepped inside. Susan pushed another button and the doors closed just as noiselessly.

"Doctors wouldn't tell her anything, so she sent me to find out how Sophie was. Why my mother thought I'd have more success than she did, I don't know."

"Mothers are like that."

When the elevator door opened, they walked through the brightly lit lobby and outside to the parking lot. Jack stuck his hands in his pants pockets and asked diffidently, "Brenner—do you know . . . ?"

"Not yet." She felt beaten down, run into the ground, and it was taking all she had to stay on her feet long enough to get to the pickup and then home. She hadn't anything left to parry questions with or to ask any of her own.

"It's all so strange," he murmured. "Not even real. Dan walks across an empty pasture and gets shot. Lucille has an argument with Dad and gets strangled. Sophie bakes a cherry pie and gets hit on the head. Brenner talks with a reporter and ends up dead on Dan's farm. I just can't—"

A thought battered at the edges of her fatigue and then was gone. "Reporter," she said sharply. "Who?"

He gave her a puzzled look. "Doug McClay."

"When?"

"Yesterday evening." Jack took his hand from his pocket and rolled plastic pellets across his palm.

"How do you know?"

"Brenner called to ask about Lucille, if there was anything new, and mentioned McClay was coming to see him."

"At Sophie's?"

"I don't think he said. I assumed so."

Doug McClay, she repeated to herself to make an impression on her tired mind. When they reached the pickup, Jack said good night and angled across the parking lot to his own car.

It took her two tries before she got the key in the ignition; then she backed from the parking slot, turned onto Railroad Avenue and drove through the quiet, deserted streets; most houses dark, but here and there a light burned inside. Watches of the night, she thought, whatever that might be. Actually, it was only a little after midnight, probably not late enough for watches.

Tell Sheriff Holmes McClay had an appointment with Brenner the evening he was killed. McClay. Involved with the murders? Couldn't be. No motive. Had she looked carefully enough? Maybe the motive was there and she missed it. Her mind, too tired and lumpish to care, refused to examine the possibility; it simply kept insisting Brenner was the killer. He killed Daniel, he killed Lucille.

Taking one hand from the wheel, she rubbed her forehead; she felt dense, stupid. Something was nagging at the edge of her mind, something important, something Helen had said, and she couldn't remember what it was.

At Elm Street she made a right, went four blocks, pulled into the driveway and thumbed the opener. The garage door rattled up and the interior light came on. As she rolled inside, a flicker in the rearview mirror caught her eyes and she twisted to look through the back window. Driveway empty, no movement on the dark street; probably a tree limb swaying in the wind.

The overhead light went off and after cutting headlights and motor, she sat in the dark hearing the little ticks and clicks of cooling metal and waiting for enough energy to get out of the truck. Taking a breath, she opened the door and slid out, then turned to disentangle the shoulder-bag strap from the gear shift.

A split second too late, she was aware of movement, a presence behind her. She pivoted, tried to turn toward the attack. White pain exploded through her mind, shot through with iridescent lights.

Not alert—too tired—if hadn't been—should have—

Colored lights dazzled across the growing darkness; then the lights faded and the darkness closed in.

TWENTY-TWO

RATS. Large gray rats. Red eyes. Swarmed from the black tunnels behind her. They were gaining. Would trample her, get Doug McClay before she could reach him. Run. Faster.

Her heart pounded. Loud. Bang. Bang. Her head—the pounding hurt her head. She stirred, heard a moan, struggled up through the dream. Hazy thoughts floated on the pain in her mind. She had stopped at the hospital to see Sophie, she'd driven home, into the garage. Why does the garage smell like a horse barn?

She moved her head, felt scratchy matting under her cheek and groped at it with her fingers. Straw. Ah, straw. She was quite pleased with herself for working that out, then wondered uneasily why the garage was covered with straw.

Something happened—something—

She remembered turning to reach for her shoulder bag and then...and then.... Someone had come up behind her.

Her eyelids flew open on total blackness. Panic gripped her. *Blind. I can't see. I'm blind.* Pushing hard with her hands, she managed a half-sitting position and dizziness rolled over her. She heard a snort, then puffing and blowing and a bang against wood.

In a stall. With a horse. That I can't see. No, calm down. Not totally dark. Not quite. She could just make out the large bulk of the animal, slightly paler in the darkness, the sway-backed shape and bony head.

Buttermilk. Sophie's barn. The old mare snorted and huffed and shifted her rump, banging her head against the doors. Both doors were closed, and Buttermilk didn't like it. Latches would be on the outside. Strong, sturdy latches: no way to open the doors, no way to get out.

Bringing her knees up under her made a slithery sound across the straw. Buttermilk's heels shot out and crashed against the side of the stall, just missing Susan's head.

She drew a shaky breath. Buttermilk might be old but she could still do a lot of damage with those big hooves. Bracing herself against the wall, she worked herself upright.

"It's all right," she said in a soothing murmur. The mare neighed and kicked. A heel caught Susan's shoulder and knocked her flat.

So much for soothing words; they only agitated the mare more. Better to say nothing. Keep quiet. She lay without moving for long seconds, then edged along the side of the stall, wanting to get out of reach of those rear hooves.

Buttermilk shifted with ungainly speed, and like pistons her back feet drove out and landed in Susan's stomach. She fell back against the wall and slid down it, unable to breathe.

Finally, breath whistled through her throat like wind in a tunnel. She huddled close enough against the wood to leave an imprint. This box was big enough for the mare but not much else, and no place to get out of the way. Buttermilk was frightened of this horrid, mewling creature crawling around in the straw.

If Susan didn't move, didn't make a sound, she might survive until someone found her. Someone would have to find her, someone—a neighbor—someone was taking care of the mare and feeding Sophie's cats; sooner or later that person would show up.

Gingerly, she touched the lump on the back of her head; pain buzzed through her mind. She must have made a noise because Buttermilk lashed out; a hoof struck just above Susan's knee. Warm blood trickled over her leg. She pressed the edge of her jacket against it.

Good thing the old mare wasn't shod, or the cut would have been much worse and those wicked feet would trample her to death. Might anyway. No telling when the neighbor would show up. Maybe too late.

She had no handkerchief or muffler to tie around the cut, and she was afraid to try anything like ripping the lining from her jacket for fear the noise would send Buttermilk into another frenzy.

Bleeding to death would probably suit her attacker just as well as being trampled. I'm too cold to bleed to death; freeze maybe. She shivered, clenched her jaw to keep her teeth from chattering; even that might set the mare off.

Why had she been attacked? Obviously, to dump her here and let Buttermilk finish her, but she didn't know why anybody wanted her dead. Or who. She wished she had a cigarette. No, never smoke in a barn. Too dangerous. She felt perilously close to hysterical laughter.

Somebody thought she knew something, thought she was getting too near, had to get rid of her. Goddammit, what is it? What makes me dangerous, what do I know?

Nothing. I know nothing. I don't know who killed Daniel. I don't know who killed Lucille and Brenner. I don't know who is trying to kill me. That made her madder than anything; if she was going to die, she wanted to know who was doing the killing. He—she—whoever—had taken her weapon. Couldn't afford to leave it in case Buttermilk didn't do her in. Probably intended to return it after she was a corpse.

Her head ached with a dull throb that formed a shield and wouldn't let cohesive thoughts through; her shoulder hurt, her stomach hurt, her knee hurt, her eyes burned. She let her eyelids droop.

Helen had said something important. Standing outside the shed where Brenner's body was. Something about Mason jars. *Why* can't I remember? Concussion. Concussion can cause— Can! That was it, canning tomatoes. No, fruit. Canning fruit, canning cherries—

Buttermilk screamed and stomped. Susan's head jerked.

Her eyes flew open. She was one gigantic ache from head to foot, cold and so stiff she wondered if she could even move her legs. The injured knee seemed permanently bent, and when she forced it to straighten, the movement caused the cut to start bleeding again.

Buttermilk snorted and clattered against the doors, now edged with a thin strip of gray light, angling her head to peer through the cracks.

Susan heard the large barn door rattle open. Her breath caught, a pulse hammered in her ears. A neighbor coming to feed the mare? Or the bastard who bashed her head coming to make sure she was dead?

Buttermilk waggled her rump and kicked out. Susan scrambled to the opposite corner, and the mare snaked her head around with a vicious clack of long teeth. She screamed and tossed her head, ears flattened, eyes showing rims of white.

The stall door latches slid back with a squeak of metal and the doors opened. Weak light filtered in. Buttermilk clomped out, snatching a bite as she went past at whoever had opened the door.

Susan, back against the wall, inched toward the doors and clasped her hands tightly together above her head. Someone in dark clothing leaned forward to shine a flashlight into the stall.

She brought her hands down hard, aiming for the back of the neck. The person dodged aside and Susan's hands landed on a shoulder. Numbing pain raced up her arms and the jar set off sparks in her head. A hand closed around one wrist.

She jerked free, tried to rush past and found herself caught with arms like a vise around her shoulders, pinning her wrists against her stomach. Breathing hard, she kicked back with a booted foot, banged her head against his nose.

"Jesus Christ. Take it easy."

She pulled away and spun around to face him, planting her feet and pulling in air. "You."

Parkhurst pressed exploring fingers against his nose. "You were expecting someone else?"

"Depends. Did you come to kill me?"

"No. I've been looking for you half the night. The sheriff tried to call and couldn't get you." He bent to pick up the flashlight. "What happened? You all right?"

"Couldn't be better." She raked hair away from her face.

"Your leg—"

She looked at the black stains of blood on her jeans. "Just a cut. What did Sheriff Holmes want?"

"To let you know Floyd Kimmell finally admitted Brenner hired him to slaughter cattle. Holmes picked up Vic Pollock and expects him to come through with Brenner's name as the man who set up the toxic-waste business. We'd better get you to a doctor. Can you walk?"

"Never mind that. I know who killed Daniel. Come on."

Parkhurst tipped his head and eyed her suspiciously. "Who?"

"Come on." She limped toward the barn door, dizzy and nauseated; her vision wasn't too clear. Smacking her head against Parkhurst's nose hadn't done her head any good. Buttermilk glared balefully from a corner of the barn.

"Susan—"

"An error, a little slip. Cherry pie. Should have caught it immediately. If I'd been alert, I wouldn't have spent the night in a barn."

She paused in the doorway looking out at the weak predawn light; quiet; crisp fresh air; somewhere a rooster crowed, birds stirred in the eaves, and along the outline of the hills a thin line of pinkish hue was barely visible.

"Susan—"

"Like sleet," she told him angrily. "Just like sleet. Why did it take so long to figure that one?" She stepped outside.

Parkhurst, beside her, said, "You're not making any sense."

She shook her head to clear her vision and try to arrange thoughts in some coherent order. "Last night Helen talked about canning fruit, cherries, and then—"

A rifle shot shattered the stillness.

Parkhurst clutched his shoulder with a grunt of pain and a muttered curse, fell back against the barn door and began to slowly slide down it. She wedged her shoulder under his uninjured arm, and with her arms encircling his waist, half supported and half propelled him back inside.

Slumping under his weight, she subsided to her knees and he went down with her; then he leaned back, propping himself against the wall. Buttermilk snorted resentment at these aliens returning to invade her territory, and ambled into her stall.

Susan unsnapped the leather strip and yanked the .38 from the holster on his hip, then crouched by the open door. The flashlight he'd dropped lay in a fan of light. She blinked rapidly in an attempt to clear her vision and searched through the murky light for movement. Her eyes teared from the cold air; she had no idea where the shot had come from. Through the trees, she made out Parkhurst's Bronco parked near the kitchen door.

She looked at Parkhurst. He hadn't moved. The bullet had caught him on the right side of the chest, about four inches above the nipple; a small hole and not much bleeding, at least on the outside. No telling how much on the inside. A lung might have been nicked. He needed medical attention immediately.

"Knew you were the kind...only went to the best... places," he said, his voice low and breathy, with a soft undercrackle that scared the shit out of her. It could mean blood pouring into his lung.

Her mind flashed back to that squalid apartment and the eleven-year-old kid with a gun, the sound of the shot, astonishment and then the awful awareness of drowning in her own blood.

"I hate to make you move, but I want a look at your back."

Kneeling at his side, she pulled him forward and winced at his obvious pain. His breathing stopped, then rushed on laboriously and his forehead dropped heavily onto her shoulder. She suppressed a sigh of relief—no exit wound three times larger than the entrance wound pumping his blood out on the barn floor. The bullet must have ricocheted before it got to him. She eased him back against the wall.

"Who...?" The single word was only a soft overtone as he exhaled.

"Jack." She edged nearer the doorway and squinted out, trying to judge the likelihood of reaching the Bronco with the radio inside: Still not much light, trees for cover, but she wouldn't put money on her chances. She had Parkhurst's .38, but that left him without a weapon. Was there a better chance of getting inside the house and reaching the telephone? Even if she could creep around to the side or reach the front, she'd have to break a window to get in. Jack would hear and that would be the end of her. And Parkhurst.

Where the hell *was* Jack? Waiting for her to do something idiotic like trying for the house? How long would he wait? Not forever, and what did he have in mind when he got tired of waiting? He must have a plan, he couldn't simply skulk around out there until they all died of old age.

Movement caught her eye, and she watched as the kitchen door opened and Jack came out carrying an armload of what looked like sheets or towels, cloth of some kind. Sheets?

Icy chills crawled along her nerves. Dry old wood, hay and straw; the barn would go up like a torch.

He still had the rifle, holding it level in one hand. A moment would be needed to get it in position to fire. She stretched out prone, .38 gripped in both hands. All she needed was one clear shot.

Goddammit, he'd been in the house. While she'd been dithering around she could have streaked for the Bronco and radioed for help. Did he yank the phone? Probably.

She shifted her position, trying to get a better angle, and raised the gun. Trees were in the way; she couldn't get a shot.

Jack zigzagged to the Bronco, opened the door and got in behind the wheel. In a moment or two he got out again. Just enough time to sabotage the radio. For some seconds he was out of sight; then she saw him. He was carrying a gas can. She had to get herself and Parkhurst out of here.

Jack, in the dim light, darted from a tree, to the Bronco, to the house, careful not to give her a clear shot at him. He sprinted toward the barn. She fired, missed wide as he slid around the side.

There was a long stillness broken only by the hammering of her heart and Parkhurst's harsh breathing. Then something splashed against the barn wall.

She squirmed backward away from the door and got to her feet. "Parkhurst," she whispered. He grunted. Somehow he'd have to be carried out.

She spotted harness hanging in one stall and ran to investigate. Awkward hands fumbled through halters, lead straps, a complicated set of straps and buckles for hitching to wagons. The smell of gasoline floated in the air. Finally, she found a bridle with reins intact, grabbed it and slung it over her shoulder.

In the next stall, near stacked bales of hay, was a barrel of oats. She scooped several handfuls into a pan and forced herself to move slowly toward Buttermilk. The mare threw back her head and swung her rump back and forth. The odor of smoke was scaring her.

"Just calm down," Susan murmured, half to herself, half to the horse. Fire sputtered faintly as it bit into dry wood. "Calm down. It's all right." She shook the pan.

Buttermilk's ears pricked forward and she eyed Susan warily, huffing softly and stomping her forefeet, torn between greed and fear.

Greed won out. She made little whickers of anticipation, allowed Susan to enter the stall and pour oats in the manger. Velvety lips nibbled daintily. Susan eased the bridle up the bony nose. Buttermilk flattened her ears, tipped her head to bite. Susan squeezed her nose. "Behave yourself," she crooned. "We'll all burn."

Nostrils flared; the upper lip peeled back. Susan tightened her grip and forced the bit between long teeth, and at the same time slid the bridle over the ears, then buckled the cheek strap and knotted the reins over the muscular neck.

Burning wood crackled. Buttermilk started, tossed her head. Even in the dimness, Susan could see a haze of smoke. Tiny flames flickered along the edge where wall joined floor.

Her eyes stung. She coughed, darted into the adjacent stall. Tugging and shoving, she maneuvered a bale of hay toward Parkhurst. His breathing was more labored, his skin pallid and his facial muscles tight with pain.

With a whoosh, the stacked bales burst into flame. Roaring clouds of orange billowed up and licked at the hayloft. Smoke choked her. Her eyes watered. Buttermilk screamed. Parkhurst was seized by a racking cough.

She ran for the mare, clutched the bridle near the bit and yanked. Buttermilk, eyes white-rimmed with fear, planted her feet and refused to budge. Flames raced up the sides of the stall. Susan shouted at her, smacked her cheekbone with an open palm. The straw under her hooves smoldered, then flared. The mare lurched from the stall. Susan led her to Parkhurst and Buttermilk stood, mouthing the bit and dripping foam.

In the flickering firelight, beads of sweat glistened on his sallow face. His attention was wandering.

"Listen," she said sharply to bring him back. "Get on the horse."

"No. Asinine. Go." The effort it caused him to say the three words left him breathless.

"Do it!" She knelt beside him, put his uninjured arm around her shoulder and struggled to help him to his feet. He managed to get up on the bale and tried to put a leg over the broad back.

"No," he said. "You—"

"Shut up!" Roughly, she jerked up his foot and shoved his leg over the mare, boosted on his rear to get him astride.

Buttermilk flicked her ears and rippled the muscles along her shoulder. Flames roared through the hayloft with the noise of a freight train. A burning timber fell with a crash. Smoke poured around them.

She twisted Buttermilk's mane through Parkhurst's fingers. "Stay awake for the next few minutes. And hang on."

She scrambled up behind him, put her arms around him and gripped the reins and the mane in both hands.

Was Jack waiting?

One side of the loft fell with a thundering crack. Fire shot up all around them. The heat was intense. Any moment the roof would come down.

She clapped her heels against Buttermilk's flanks. The mare clomped reluctantly to the open doorway, then stopped.

"Go!" Susan dug in her heels. Buttermilk snorted, tossed her head, pranced sideways and backed into the roaring fire.

Susan yelled. The mare jumped forward and burst through the door in a bone-jarring trot. Her hooves clattered on the gravel. Susan urged her faster. Buttermilk stopped. "Move, you stupid nag!" She kicked hard.

A rifle shot whistled past her ear and grazed the horse's rump. With a scream of panic, Buttermilk broke into a gallop. The rifle cracked again as they lumbered across an empty field. Parkhurst bounced and swayed. Her arms ached with the effort to keep him from falling.

Buttermilk stumbled across a shallow ditch and headed up a hill. Above the roar and crackle of the fire, Susan heard the sounds of a car engine. Some seconds later, headlights made erratic sweeps through the gray light as Jack's car jounced over the uneven ground behind them.

Their only hope was the woods, and she kicked the old mare faster down the slope. Parkhurst started to slip. She took one hand from the reins and fastened it on his belt. What was this doing to his injuries?

Buttermilk, lathered in sweat, was tiring and blowing hard as she pounded toward the trees. She slowed of her own accord when Susan tried to guide her through trees and around wild tangles of brush. Susan's arms trembled with strain. She couldn't hold onto Parkhurst much longer.

The gray dawn light didn't penetrate the thick trees, and Jack couldn't yet be right on their tail. She spotted an odd-shaped boulder; flat on top, one side slanting sharply in. A fallen tree lay across it, creating a makeshift cave.

Stopping the mare, she slid off, then did no more than break Parkhurst's fall as he tumbled. From the look of him, he was nearly unconscious: eyes glazed, face ashen. She staggered under his weight, pushed and prodded him into the space between the rock and the tree trunk.

"Don't move. I'll get help."

He pressed cold fingers against her hand. "Be careful."

She nodded, shoved tumbleweeds around the opening and across the fallen tree to hide him. Jack had to be lured far away from this spot and then disposed of. She scrambled back on the mare.

As quickly as possible, she wound through the trees, with no idea where Jack was. He had to track them on foot and he might be uncertain which direction they'd taken. She saw no sign of him and heard no sounds of movement through the brush.

Did she have to wave flags and send up flares to get his attention? A rifle shot cracked around her. Buttermilk lunged to a gallop. Susan ducked and dodged to avoid raking branches and glanced over her shoulder. The mare swerved against a tree trunk, smacked Susan's knee and scraped her off.

She sprawled in dead leaves and broken branches, rolled to her stomach and wriggled into the low brush. Sprigs snagged her jacket and scratched her face. In the center she found a hollow area, trampled flat for a bed by some small animal. There was barely enough room for her to sit hunched over bent knees. Long thorns pricked her skin through the jacket.

With her forehead resting on her knees, she drew in deep breaths. She heard thrashing sounds, jerked her head up and froze like a wild animal aware of a predator. She tried to see through the thorny bush and could only make out small patches of pale light. Somewhere Buttermilk snorted and then Jack grunted with satisfaction. The riderless mare told him Susan had to be nearby. The thrashing sounds continued; she couldn't tell how far away he was, only the direction he seemed to be moving.

She waited. The lacy frost on the branches melted into crystal beads that rolled down the sprigs and dropped with tiny pit-pats. Her back ached, her muscles cramped. She inched out through thorns just far enough to see. Dark clouds seemed to rest on the treetops; here and there long rays of the rising sun filtered through the dark masses, slanted across the shallow hills and highlighted large boulders. The entire landscape was in dull colors of winter, shades of brown and beige and gray. Trails of smoke drifted like fog.

Her eyes caught movement and she barely glimpsed Jack, brown pants and tweed jacket in harmony with the background. She pulled the .38 from her pocket. It was time to stop being the hunted and start being the hunter.

She scuttled across the clearing and crouched behind a tree. Birds twittered in the branches. With the longer range and greater accuracy of the rifle, he had a definite advantage. He'd want to keep a safe distance and shoot at the first opportunity. With only a handgun, she needed to get within twenty-five yards to be certain of success; closer would be better. More daylight made her more easily visible but would help her avoid nests of crackly leaves, twigs that could snap or rocks that might roll and have her flailing instinctively for balance.

Carefully, she worked through low brush and the patches of frozen snow hidden in the densest areas, in the direction he'd gone.

After what seemed like hours and might have been thirty minutes, she heard him ahead, crashing through the underbrush and breathing hard from the effort. Her lungs craved deep breaths also, but she didn't dare give in, even under cover of his noise.

She stopped behind the trunk of a huge cottonwood tree to wait, get her breathing under control. She felt lightheaded. Cold breezes brushed her face. On a limb above, a squirrel, incensed at her trespass, scolded her with furious chatter, trembled with indignation and then with a final flick of his tail scampered off.

Everything was quiet; no sounds. Alarmed, she risked a look around the tree. Forty yards away, she spotted Jack, tweed jacket blending in with the brush. She raised the gun, fired and knew she'd missed. He was too far away.

He dropped without a sound and crawled into the brush. "It's all gone wrong," he yelled, his voice thick with an anguish that burbled in his throat like blood. "Nobody was supposed to get hurt. He said it would be easy."

She didn't respond, but watched the bushes thrashing and jiggling and wondered if he was distracted enough to allow her to cross an open area. She'd be vulnerable for only about two seconds. Taking a breath, she darted out. A bullet whacked into the tree behind her. She slithered into brush and waited, face in the dirt.

"I'm sorry," he called. "I have to. You knew—when I said 'cherry pie.'"

She crawled along a small twisting path, probably an animal track, inside the tangle of growth. The air was heavy with the odors of earth, damp vegetation, rotting wood and tree sap. Over the rustling and crackling of her progress, she heard the sound of running water; a stream somewhere nearby. She fought her way to the edges of the brush and came on another open space. Just beyond was a ravine, a narrow groove that started out shallow, then dropped sharply and curved in a half-circle. If she could get to it, it might take her around behind him.

She started to inch out; her sleeve caught a twig and snapped it with a sharp crack. Dammit! In a half-crouch, she scuttled to the cleft, and a bullet thwacked into the dirt at the rim. Fighting for breath, she moved into the deep part of the ravine on shaky legs.

"He killed Lucille," Jack yelled. "He swore he didn't, but I know he did. She knew."

If she'd had it in her, Susan might have felt some sympathy for Jack. He was a young man struggling in the shadow of a powerful father. He'd qualified for a profession of his own and should have achieved success and recognition, but he'd fallen under the sway of someone stronger and unprincipled. They had murdered Daniel and now he'd shot Parkhurst and meant to kill her. She felt no sympathy; all she wanted was to put a bullet through him.

Long before it gained her the advantage she needed, the ravine began to shallow out, the bottom rising easily to meet the lip covered with overhanging brush. She'd dropped into a neat little trap and all he had to do was pick her off when she poked out her head. Was he waiting at this end? Or at the other end, where she'd been careless enough to snap a twig?

The sun was higher in the sky and each passing moment gave him more daylight. She found a rock the size of a baseball and threw it as hard and as far as she could back down the ravine. It thunked into the frozen dirt.

The rifle cracked, deafeningly close.

Oh Christ, he was right above her. She went up, fast, over the lip and caught a glimpse of him, braced against a tree with the rifle pointed away from her. With incredible speed, the barrel swung toward her and he fired.

She plunged into brush, moving low and quick, with no thought for the branches snatching her clothing and scratching her face. When she broke through into the open, her foot landed on a rock. It rolled, and her ankle twisted. She fell hard and tumbled down a stream bank. The .38 was torn from her hand. She heard it plop into the stream. She came to a stop at the edge of the water, scrambled to her feet and pressed her back into the wall of the bank. She waited for Jack to appear. Nothing happened. Far above, a hawk, wings outstretched, floated on an air current, circled and then disappeared.

She sidled along the bank and her boots squished through partially frozen mud. The stream had chunks of ice floating in the grayish-white water. At a narrow section, she tried to leap across, splashed in the water and smashed painfully into the bank on the far side.

Scrabbling at the stunted growth, she managed to pull herself up the bank. She found a boulder surrounded by brush to hide in. Her heart hammered away at her ribs and the gulps of cold air hurt her lungs. She wasn't very well hidden and the light might now be good enough for Jack to notice the damage she'd made crawling in.

The edge of the woods was near; through the trees she could see an open field, and Buttermilk, head down, nibbling at dead grasses. She felt a small ray of hope. When all else fails, turn tail and run. The only little problem was getting to the mare before Jack shot her. With great effort, she wriggled out of the brush and plodded through the sparse trees.

Her legs were leaden, her head light, and she was so beaten with exhaustion, she wanted to sink to her knees and wait for a bullet in the back. Her only consolation was that she'd at least led him a long distance from Parkhurst. With any luck, the smoke would be noticed and help would come before Jack could find him.

She heard a splash as Jack tried to clear the stream, then sounds of him climbing up the bank, and felt a rush of anger. She was sick and tired of being chased and shot at. She snatched a fallen tree limb, sturdy, three feet long, two inches thick with a forked end, and ran toward the stream.

When Jack came over the rim of the bank, he held the rifle, barrel pointed up, in front of him. She swung the limb with an explosion of all the fury and hatred and fear within her. The forked end tore into his ear, raked across his forehead, smashed against the barrel and wrenched it from his hands. He gave a startled cry of pain, and she snarled with satisfaction.

The rifle skittered across dead leaves and landed somewhere to her left. She swung the limb again, but the vicious arc was too wide and he had time to jump back. He turned and dodged through trees, headed for the empty field.

She spent precious seconds locating the rifle, hung it by the webbed sling across her back, then ran heavy-footed toward Buttermilk. The mare lifted her head, snorted and sidled away, but Susan grabbed the reins and smacked the bony forehead. She swung astride and dug in her heels. Buttermilk set off in a heavy gallop, pounding hooves throwing up mud and grass. Cold wind tore at Susan's face.

Jack looked back over his shoulder, rubbed blood from his face and stumbled, then recovered and ran at an angle.

"Faster," Susan yelled. Buttermilk, affected by her frenzy, lumbered straight at him. He zigzagged, but Susan kept the mare on his heels and gained ground with each stride. When she was almost on top of him, the mare tried to swerve, but Susan yanked her back and, unable to stop, Buttermilk crashed into him and knocked him down. She trampled his hand as she ran on.

Susan slid off, hit the ground with jarring impact and brought the rifle around. Jack, face bloody, sat with his knees bent, cradling his injured hand against his chest.

"You killed Daniel." She felt quite calm as she pointed the barrel at his head.

"No."

"You killed him." Her finger curled around the trigger.

"I didn't."

"You bastard! You shot him." Her finger tightened.

"Brenner shot him," Jack said in a tired, distant voice.

She watched his eyes and saw in them the knowledge that she was going to kill him. A split instant before the rifle fired, she shifted the barrel and the shot went wide.

TWENTY-THREE

"So YOU FOUND who killed your man." Sophie, propped up in the hospital bed, still looked white and frail, but the bandages, at a jaunty angle on her head, gave her the air of an aged rake. "An eye for an eye."

The winter sun shone through the window, and outside the sky was a soft blue with masses of cottony clouds. Susan shifted slightly to avoid the glare; it should have been gray out there to match her mood. The street below was quiet with Sunday morning emptiness. The heavy scent of the blood-red roses on the bedside table made her slightly sick.

"Now what?" Sophie's pale-blue eyes gazed into Susan's darker-blue ones with the calm intent of poking through the murky corners of Susan's soul, and Susan was reminded again of Frannyvan, that indomitable woman who'd had such an impact on her life.

One more thing to do; then I can go home. She'd accomplished her goal—found the answer to Daniel's death—and the burning rage that had carried her had no further purpose. She felt flat and empty. Anger was a very single-minded emotion. It spread throughout the body, gripping every nerve with a killing passion, and the mind focused on only those things directly concerned with the rage and its resolution. No thought was spared for fear or pain or responsibility or consequences. With the purpose gone, the anger dissipating, there seemed nothing left; even home held no appeal.

"Are you going to tell me or not?" Sophie said. "Trussed up in this bed like a plucked chicken, I don't know what-all's going on. Easy for you to smile, young lady, but I'm not used to finding out secondhand. They were stealing, were they? Jack and Brenner, my own husband's brother's son."

"Stealing bull semen, and selling it on the black market. Jack needed money to continue his experiments with plastic hay and Brenner wanted to save his housing development."

"What's going to happen to it now, Jack's research?"

"I don't know," Susan said. "With Jack facing a murder charge, it's unlikely he'll see his plastic hay, which he invested so much in, develop as a commercial product. Unless he decides to turn the research over to someone else."

"How was it Dan came to be shot?"

"He saw Jack give Brenner a canister and saw Brenner put it in his car. It puzzled him. I don't think he realized the implications, but it worried him enough that he meant to discuss it with Parkhurst. He never got the chance."

"Did Jack shoot him?"

Susan hesitated. "No," she said gently. "Brenner shot him." She paused. "With your rifle."

"My own nephew," Sophie muttered. "Well, come on, come on. Are you going to make me pull it out of you? How come Otto didn't miss it?"

"Jack replaced the cannisters they stole with cannisters containing straws filled simply with egg yolk." Only Slater, Guthman's fussy foreman, had noticed anything amiss— equipment not returned to its exact place—Slater and the man who had called Guthman to complain his cows weren't pregnant.

"Weak, Jack might be. Otto was always too strong and Jack could never measure up. But nobody could ever say he wasn't smart. I suppose you're gonna tell me Brenner killed Lucille, too."

"I'm afraid so. They had an argument late one night. Nat, the boy who works for Otto, saw them. I think Lucille accused Brenner of killing Daniel. She went to Kansas City to dig into Brenner's affairs and see if she couldn't find something to prove his guilt."

"Lucille, poor thing, I always felt sorry for her." With a shaky hand, Sophie poured water from a carafe into a glass. Susan started to help but Sophie shook her head.

"Did she know about Jack?" Sophie took a sip of water and frowned at the glass. "That would've almost killed her. Adored him, she did."

"She was desperately afraid Jack had killed Daniel. She was present when Parkhurst found...him." Even now, Susan couldn't bring herself to say "Daniel's body." "There was heavy sleet that night, the road was icy with it, she found some of the plastic pellets Jack was always carrying around in his pockets. In the dark, on the icy road, they looked just like sleet." At least, Susan assumed that's what the words meant on the scrap of paper she'd found in the hotel room.

She remembered Lucille in the corridor outside the autopsy room, asking questions of Parkhurst, on the night she'd seen Daniel's body. Lucille had stuck her hand in her pocket and immediately pulled it out again. The pellets had probably been in her pocket, and later she'd put them in the small box in her desk drawer. In searching Lucille's bedroom, Susan had seen the pellets, but they'd meant nothing to her then.

"She never told anybody," Sophie said.

"I think she convinced herself Brenner shot Daniel and planted the pellets to implicate Jack. She wanted proof that Brenner was the killer before she said anything."

"It got too much for him, did it? Jack? That why he killed my Brenner?" There was a shine of moisture in Sophie's eyes, and she turned her head to stare out the window.

Susan felt sympathy. Sophie was fiercely pretending her nephew's death didn't affect her. "Yes. He started falling apart after Daniel was shot. He wasn't cut out to be a killer.

Then Lucille disappeared and he really came unglued. When I talked with him the afternoon Mrs. Guthman reported her missing, Brenner was waiting for him in the barn.''

''Jack knew that?''

Susan nodded. ''He'd refused to steal any more bull semen, and Brenner had everything set up with a buyer for that very night. Brenner was there to exert pressure, but he couldn't afford to be seen. When I bumbled into the barn, he unlatched the door of Fafner's stall.''

''How'd you know Jack killed Brenner?''

Susan smiled ruefully. ''I was slow on that.'' And almost got myself and Parkhurst killed. ''Jack mentioned you had baked a cherry pie. It wasn't until later it occurred to me Jack couldn't have known unless he'd been to your place.''

''That all of it?''

''Except what happened the night you were attacked.''

''Don't remember much.'' Sophie pulled at the sheets. ''The trunk was open, Brenner's car; he was inside. All crumpled up.'' She paused and scowled. ''All I can remember.''

Then Jack hit her, Susan thought, and left her to die in Buttermilk's stall. ''You talked about old sins.''

''Nonsense. I never have any truck with sins.'' She clamped her mouth into a straight line.

''What old sins?''

The old woman took a breath and let it out with a deep sigh; the faded blue eyes dulled with sadness. ''When you've lived as long as I have, you know about too many old sins. There was Arthur Wren hampering Helen like he did. And Helen killing Billy Kimmell so many years ago and causing Floyd to grow up all funny and feeling he was owed something and stealing steers. Otto, so concerned with his bulls, he didn't have time for his family.''

''Was it you who called that night and told me where Floyd was slaughtering a steer?''

Sophie nodded, then closed her eyes. "Brenner. I always felt in my bones he set the fire killed his folks. Maybe that's what I was thinking." She opened her eyes and glared at Susan. "Or maybe I was thinking about my own sins. I might own up to one or two."

"Like helping Lucille a few years ago?"

"Never you mind."

"You gave her money."

Sophie took a sip of water.

"For what?"

"Doesn't matter."

"For an abortion?"

"If you knew, why'd you ask?" Sophie said belligerently, then sighed and set the glass back on the table. "It was the right thing to do, but still and all it worried me. I was afraid somehow, sometime, the punishment would come."

"Brenner was the father?"

Sophie nodded. "I tried so hard to have one of my own and there was Lucille and—" She broke off, sniffed and then loudly cleared her throat. "You never answered my question."

"Question?"

"Question was, Now what are you gonna do?"

"Now I can go home."

"If you want to," Sophie said slyly.

"It's over."

"No, child, it's never over till you stop breathing. There's your job. You gonna just walk away from the job? And the old Wren place. You gonna let Helen sell it?"

"Yes." It was Daniel's dream and Daniel was gone; his dream was finished. She hoped Helen would finally realize some of hers.

"And there's Ben Parkhurst. You saved his life. That's not over—just getting started, I'd say. You mark my words, child, there's a lot more to come there."

Susan smiled. "I'm glad you're feeling better. You sound almost like your old self."

"Ha. Takes more than a whack on the head and a few broken bones to kill me. I got work to do."

Like stealing cats, Susan assumed, and rose to leave. Sophie refused to say good-bye; she only smiled a canny smile.

NOW I CAN GRIEVE, Susan thought as she walked from the hospital. The only thing still to do. I can weep. I can cry. I can wail.

I loved you, Daniel.

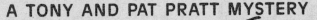

You have the right to remain silent

NOBODY'S TALKING

Down the mean streets of Manhattan's Alphabet City, Marian Larch discovers that even a cop's tough emotional hide can be riddled by the area's violent, twisted crime. Another murder is added to her caseload, and it's a beauty: four corpses—well-dressed, white-collar, unidentified men—handcuffed together and shot through the right eye.

It's a sensational killing meant as a warning to remain silent about something big. And just what the secret is remains to be seen.

A SERGEANT MARIAN LARCH MYSTERY

BARBARA PAUL

First Time In Paperback

"This is a dandy—gritty, fast-paced, believable, humorous…"—UPI

Available in November at your favorite retail stores.

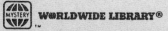

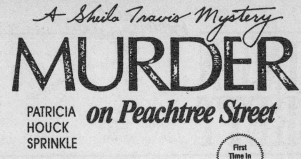
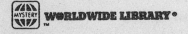

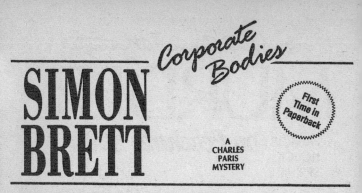

SIMON BRETT

Corporate Bodies

A
CHARLES
PARIS
MYSTERY

First
Time in
Paperback

By the author of *Mrs. Pargeter's Package*

Surviving thirty years of an actor's fluctuating fortunes, Charles Paris had played many roles. But until now, a starring role as a forklift driver in a corporate video had yet to grace his résumé. Costumed in coveralls, he read his lines with finesse and his performance for Delmoleen foods was flawless. But the finale was murder.

A young woman is crushed to death with the forklift while the crew is at lunch. Industrial accident . . . or murder? Paris suspects a cover-up. The whole company atmosphere is troubling: the happy Delmoleen family seems riddled with mockery, jealousy, lust, envy. And secrets that may make this performance Charles's last.

"The most engaging new murder-solver in recent years has been Simon Brett's Charles Paris."
                                                                      —Los Angeles Times

Available in October at your favorite retail stores.

To reserve your copy for September shipping, please send your name, address, zip or postal code, along with a check or money order for $3.99 (please do not send cash), plus 75¢ postage and handling ($1.00 in Canada) for each book ordered, payable to Worldwide Mystery, to:

In the U.S.

Worldwide Mystery
3010 Walden Avenue
P.O. Box 1325
Buffalo, NY 14269-1325

In Canada

Worldwide Mystery
P.O. Box 609
Fort Erie, Ontario
L2A 5X3

Please specify book title with your order.
Canadian residents add applicable federal and provincial taxes.   BODIES

WORLDWIDE LIBRARY®